Louise Miller
Mysteries

BOOK ONE

Breeding Trouble

KAREN CULLEN, DVM

Library and Archives Canada Cataloguing in Publication.
Cullen, Karen. Louise Miller Mysteries: Breeding Trouble.

This manuscript is a work of fiction. Characters, places, and events are a result of the author's imagination. Any similarities to people living, or dead, is co-incidental.

ISBN paperback: 9781778151903
ISBN EBook: 9781778151910

Published by: IV Lines Publishing

Cover Design: Britt Wilson - Indie Publishing Group
Formatting: Chrissy Hobbs - Indie Publishing Group

*For all the compassionate veterinary teams doing
their part to make the world a happier and healthier
place for all living beings… animal and human.*

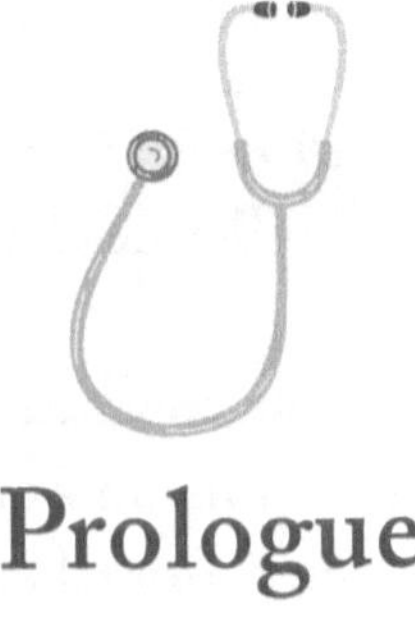

Prologue

BRIGHT LIGHTS, CONTRASTED against the dark sky, burned like fire into her eyes. Tall, shadowy figures rushed around her, touching her forehead, their fingers like cold blades against her skin. So many voices mixed with shrieking whistles. She tried to call to the shadows, to ask who they were and what was happening. Her voice failed her. Was one of them speaking to her? The words were jumbled. Her brain told her arm to move, to wave to the strange figure, but her hand simply lay by her side, unresponsive.

A familiar voice broke through the muffled chorus. "Save my sister."

Maryanne, is that you? What's happening? My head—it's so heavy. I can't move my arm. Where are you? I can't see you.

Then another familiar voice echoed through the night—screaming and wailing like nothing she'd heard before. No… she had heard something like that before—on TV. The sound of a person in shock, inconsolable, after the death of a loved one. *Did someone die?*

Thick, sticky liquid dripped from her brow to her chin. Was it raining? The grass under her left hand was coarse and dry. It wasn't raining.

With her right hand, she touched her forehead, wincing against the stinging sensation the movement created. A warm, rusty-smelling liquid trickled from her fingers. The metallic scent of blood, mixed with the nauseating gasoline fumes, made her heave. One of the shadows rolled her over. *Where I am?*

She'd been driving Zack home after a graduation party. The yellow traffic light popped on, and Louise had slowed to a stop. They had been laughing and talking about their future. They were planning to attend the same college so they could stay together. The glare of headlights came from nowhere, speeding towards them. She had no time to react, to get out of the way. The noise—it was so loud. Then pain.

The static red light was replaced by a flashing orange and blue kaleidoscope dancing above the intense white beams.

That woman was still screaming. Sobbing.

Louise tried to sit up, but the hand that had rolled her over lay heavy on her shoulder. A soft voice assured her everything would be okay then the volume intensified. "This one is conscious. Get the gurney over here."

Zack, where are you? The lights dimmed as she slipped into unconsciousness.

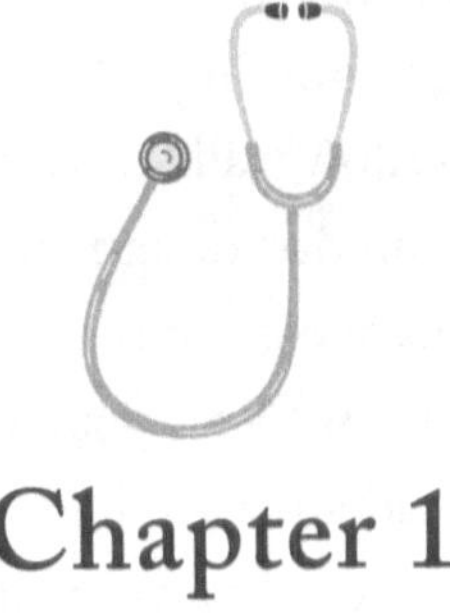

Chapter 1

THE HALLWAYS WERE deserted. *Where is everyone? Probably already in class.* Louise Miller was about to miss another class but couldn't help it. The location of the class had been changed. Again. *What is it now? Five different classrooms in the past two weeks?* She hated change and now she was lost again. Panic, frustration, anger. All those negative emotions she was constantly battling were starting to overtake her. If she missed one more class there was a real possibility that she would not graduate.

What a waste of six years of her life. All the studying. All the money. She didn't have enough money for another year of tuition. And rent. And food. Where was she going to get money for food? No food means no chocolate. Could she go on without chocolate? *Why don't they think of these things before making changes?*

Louise looked down at the university's app on her smart phone. There it was. The notice about the classroom change. Room 223 in the McNally Building. Tuesday at 10 a.m. She had the right day and time, and she could tell from the decorating that she was in the right building. The McNally Building was known for its mustard yellow walls and lime green doors with big windows. A horror of interior design that she'd normally comment on if there was anyone around to comment to. The doors displayed the usual wear and tear. Scuffs near the bottom. Evidence of hundreds of students with hands full of books pushing the doors open with their feet. Stains around the knobs. Evidence of hundreds of book-free greasy hands. And the smell. That overpowering aroma of disinfectant used to mask the fact that the original, worn tiles hadn't been replaced in decades.

"I'm sure I have the right building." Louise shoved her phone into her back pocket. "So, where's room 223? Come to think of it, where are the numbers?" She stomped down the hall, searching every door. No numbers. She paused, threw back her head, and let out a guttural sound akin to the growl of a dog. "Well, that's just great."

She kept moving, looking through the window into each classroom, hoping to recognize someone. She didn't. Not even her best friend Daphne sitting in her usual seat on the far left of the row. Two things she could count on about Daphne. She was never late and, being left-handed, she always wanted to sit on the far left of a row. She should have been in class already, but no Daphne. In fact, no anybody Louise knew. She froze. Was she in the right building? Did another building on campus have the same horrible color scheme?

Her head spinning, Louise leaned a shoulder against the wall. In the past she would have given up, tossed her books to the floor and headed home, but she wasn't that person anymore. Daphne wasn't only her best friend, she was the person who led Louise to Christ. She knew better than to let frustration get to her. And if she forgot, Daphne was always there to remind her. Taking a deep breath, Louise pushed away from the wall and turned around to head back down the hallway. She jumped when she saw Daphne, her blonde, fair-complexioned friend, standing in front of her.

Louise squinted, looked over her shoulder, then back at Daphne. "Where have you been? I've been looking all over for you."

"Is something upsetting you, Louise? You've been doing a great job of keeping your anger under control. Don't let it get the better of you," Daphne said. "The Bible says to forgive. You forgave Eric. Remember?"

"Eric didn't need forgiving." Louise adjusted the strap on her backpack so it sat more comfortably on her shoulders. "He was just a kid in need of help so we helped him."

Fifty yards behind Daphne, a young man dashed around the corner. Louise skirted around her friend and ran after him. When she rounded the corner, the man had run into a large clearing. The floor of the McNally building transformed into a grassy field as the walls faded into clear blue sky. The sun was bright and she squinted against it. The man ran in the direction of the sun. Not far ahead of him the field ended at a steep cliff.

Louise's heart pounded in her chest. "Stop, Eric. You'll get hurt."

The man didn't stop. Had he heard her? Suddenly, he disappeared over the cliff. Louise screamed. Dropping her backpack to the ground, she scrambled to the edge of the cliff, lowered herself to her stomach, and peered over.

"Eric!" Her scream echoed off the rock face of the cliff, followed by silence. *Wait.* Flipping onto her back, she sat up and stared down the hallway of the McNally building. Why was there a cliff in the building? And what was Eric doing there? She didn't even know him yet. Eric wasn't supposed to be in this dream.

The second she had that thought, she found herself in a large, dark lobby with people rushing around in a flurry. Everyone heading this way and that, all seeming to know where they were and where they were going. Only Louise didn't know where she was. Or did she? She scanned the space and blinked. Yes. She did know. This was the registration office. Why was the registration office just a desk in the middle of a lobby? Louise shrugged and headed over to the desk. After giving the lady behind the desk her name, she asked for the location of her class. Without saying a word, the woman handed her a piece of paper listing the courses Louise had been taking.

Louise scanned the list. Someone from the dean's office had written the word *pass* or *fail* beside each one. She found the name of the class she was looking for at the bottom and a lump rose in her throat. She was too late. She must have missed the class, because next to it was the word *fail.* Her heart sank. It was over. All those days spent mucking through dirty barns and learning the fine art of continuous sutures had been for naught. Her dream of saving lives and solving medical mysteries was over. Resisting the urge to crumple her body into a ball on the floor and sob, Louise instead crumpled up the paper and tossed it onto the floor. She had failed veterinary college because she didn't make it to music class.

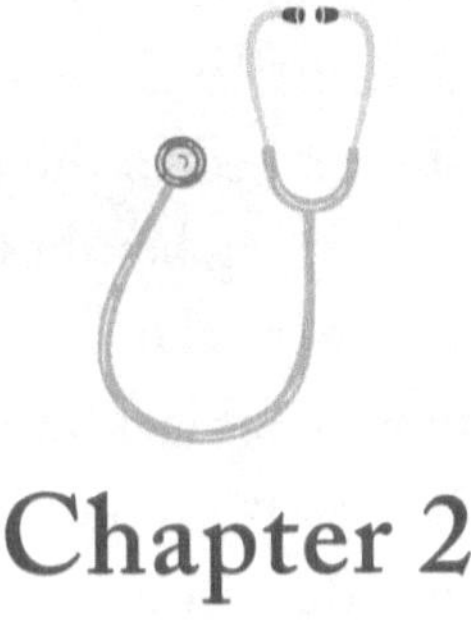

Chapter 2

D R. LOUISE MILLER rolled over and hit the snooze button when the local weather report interrupted her disappointment in flunking out of vet school. She couldn't believe she'd had that same dream again but was glad that it was only a dream. *Imagine flunking vet school because I didn't make it to music class.* She would definitely not be a veterinarian today if being musically inclined was a requirement. Shaking the odd dream from her mind, Louise rolled over, hoping to catch another ten minutes of sleep before the radio came on again.

She was no more successful at finding that ten minutes of sleep than she'd been at finding that elusive music class. No wonder. She had a lot on her mind. Their new associate was starting today. Her best friend, Dr. Daphne Carling, who was also her business partner, would be going on maternity leave soon so they had hired a locum veterinarian to give Louise a break.

Louise jumped out of bed followed by Oscar, her four-year-old, short haired, brown tabby cat. Like most cats, he was anxious to get his breakfast, so he followed Louise into the bathroom and waited patiently while she showered. He stayed at her heels as she walked to the closet, ending up too close to her left leg and tripping her. Louise did a double hop on her right foot to regain her balance. "Careful, buddy. Can't show up to work today with a black-eye. It wouldn't be good to scare the new associate away on day one."

She opened the closet door and stared at her wardrobe for a couple of minutes. After yanking a couple of pairs of pants off their hangers, she tried them on. Neither fit comfortably.

"You know, Oscar, it might be time to go shopping for new clothes. What do you think?" He regarded her with what some people might think was a scowl, but it was simply Oscar's normal look. That look had been one of the things that made her fall for him the first time she saw him in the arms of a client who had brought the poor little stray into the clinic after he'd been hit by a car.

"I must be getting taller, because my pants are getting tighter." She tossed the cotton pants aside in favour of a pair of grey scrub pants, complemented by a matching scrub top.

Once Louise had thrown her dark hair into a ponytail, Oscar raced for the stairs, as he did most mornings. "You don't miss a beat, do you Oscar? Yup. It's time for food."

At any other time of the day he would do what many cats loved to do—he'd attempt to zig zag through Louise's legs while she was walking down the stairs. Always a fun challenge for Oscar, and for Louise, trying to get to the bottom without breaking her neck, but this was breakfast time, not a time for feline shenanigans. Obviously, his mission was to get to the bowl as fast as possible and he was not happy if his person didn't do the same. When she reached the kitchen, Louise was met with a loud meow. She hadn't been fast enough. She smiled at her furry companion as she opened a can of his favorite tuna-flavoured food. Her face contorted in response to the smell.

"How can you eat this stuff?" Bending down to place the food bowl on the plastic mat on the floor, she heard the familiar vibration of her phone. "Can't be good, getting a message this early." She filled Oscar's water bowl before scanning the message from her friend, Alex Hines, a detective with the Bathurst Region Police Department. The two of them had been friends since meeting during a social gathering in university.

Break in at the vet clinic in Amherst overnight. We need to talk later. I can stop by the clinic. Is Eric working today?

Louise's pulse quickened. This was the second clinic break-in in less than a month. Two weeks prior, Dr. Cheryl Smith's clinic was burglarized. Cheryl, owner of the Georgetown Veterinary Clinic, was not just a colleague, but also a friend of Louise and Daphne's. And why was Alex asking about Eric?

Louise grabbed her work bag and headed for the door. "No time to make breakfast for myself." Placing her hands under Oscar's belly, she raised him up from his food bowl and kissed the top of his head. He responded by wiggling as he did every morning when she lifted him before his bowl was empty. "I'll grab something on the way." She wanted to get to the office early because changes always made her a bit anxious, and today would be the start of a few big changes.

As she traipsed down the front stairs and headed for her car, thoughts of their young technician Eric invaded her mind. Louise frowned as she tugged the keys from her jacket pocket and hit the remote button to unlock the doors. "Why was he in my dream? And what prompted Alex to ask about him in his text?"

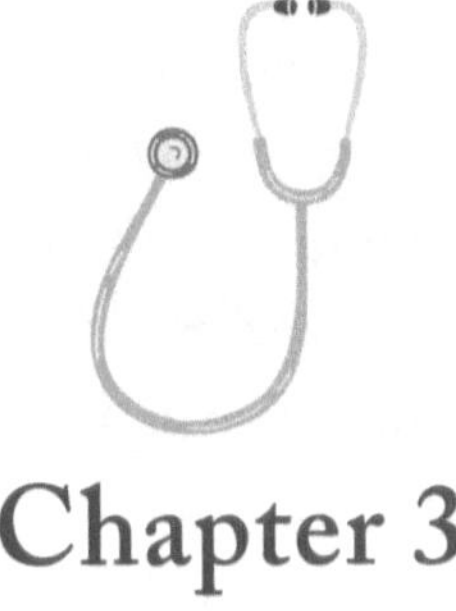

Chapter 3

THE PARKING LOT was full when Louise arrived at the clinic in the small town of Coverdale, Ontario. On days like this she was glad they had designed the clinic with staff parking and an entrance in the back where they could sneak in unseen by the clients. While Louise and Daphne appreciated their clients, and even thought of many of them as friends, it was nice to get settled in before being asked about ongoing cases.

Rita, the office manager, was not as easy to avoid. She had clearly been watching out her office window on the upper level for Louise to arrive, because the moment Louise stepped through the back door of the clinic Rita was upon her. Louise hadn't had a chance to take off her coat or set down her bag before Rita said,

"Dr. Kurt is here already. His appointment wasn't until nine, but he was here at eight. Seems kind of desperate."

Rita seems kind of annoyed. Louse smiled at the middle-aged woman she had met when Rita was a registered veterinary technician, commonly referred to as a vet tech, and Louise a vet student at a clinic in the next town. Rita had enough experience in veterinary medicine to know that anything could happen during the day to throw the whole schedule off. She was understanding if the something was a sick or injured animal, an ill co-worker, or a distressed client, but she had very little patience for people who were late—or even early it seemed—for an appointment.

"That's fine, Rita. Perhaps he got the time wrong."

Rita sniffed. "I'm glad you're finally here. I don't have time to entertain the new vet."

Louise forced another smile. She knew Rita well enough to know that she was blowing wind and would, more than likely, be very welcoming to Dr. Bob Kurt once they began working together. "Thanks, Rita, I'll take it from here. Is Daphne in yet?"

"She's in the doctors' office." Rita spun on her heel and started down the hall. Before Louise could reply, the office manager had disappeared.

The Black Creek Animal Hospital was a two-storey brick building built in the mid-nineteenth century by the community's first medical doctor. The building had undergone many renovations over the years. It had gone from being the town doctor's home to a lawyer's office and eventually a sandwich shop before taking on its current role as an animal hospital.

Before going to her office, Louise headed to the treatment area. Even if it had only been a silly dream, she felt the need to check on Eric.

Pushing the door to the treatment area open, Louise was met with the familiar smell of a tomcat. Kennels had been set up at the far end of the room for sick patients and those scheduled for surgery. In a large open area, a mobile pen housed a large Labrador retriever who was barking at a smaller dog. Heidi, their senior vet tech, was taking a blood sample from the object of the lab's barks, with help from Jenny, another of their three vet techs, who held the small dog still on one of the two stainless steel exam tables.

"Morning ladies." Louise scanned the room to see how many patients had been admitted. "How's the morning treating you? Smells like we have a cat neuter booked for this morning."

"Gee, Louise." Heidi placed the needle into the top of a vacutainer tube. "How did you know?" Heidi, twenty-seven years old with blonde hair and a slim build, had started working with Louise and Daphne soon after they started the practice. She was young, but mature for her age and eager to be part of a start-up clinic.

"My many years of training and experience." Louise laughed. "Is Eric in yet?"

"Not yet. He isn't scheduled till later. What's up?"

"Oh nothing." Louise strolled over to the mobile pen where the lab was still barking. "What's this big fella in for?"

"That's Meals. He's been vomiting. The Thompsons dropped him off on their way to work." Jenny restrained the little dog, a six-month-old Jack Russell terrier named Sadie who had been admitted for an ovariohysterectomy, commonly called a spay. Jenny, a twenty-six-year-old brunette with an average build, was a friend of Heidi's from college. When she graduated a year after Heidi, her friend recommended her to Louise and Daphne who were having difficulty at the time finding a new tech.

Louise patted the top of the lab's head. "Has Daphne had a look at him yet?"

"Not yet," Heidi answered. She applied a small bandage to the spot where she had inserted the needle into the little dog's leg. "The new vet showed early, so she's been talking to him. He seems okay."

Jenny lifted the dog off the table and returned her to a kennel. "Yes, he does." The lab stopped barking and sniffed Louise's palm. "He seems pretty excited to be here."

Heidi washed her hands at the sink between the tables. "I didn't realize you'd met him before."

"I've seen him a few times. Nothing too earth shattering. He was here last week." Louise scratched Meals under the chin. Meals started to drool.

"He was? I guess I wasn't around that day."

"Sure you were. You helped me clean him up."

Heidi spun around, her hands dripping water on the porcelain tile floor. "Excuse me?"

"He was all wet and smelly when he came in. Must have rolled in something in the yard."

"Dr. Kurt was rolling in the yard?" Heidi grinned as she reached for a couple of paper towels from the dispenser and handed one to Louise.

"What? No." Louise chuckled as she wiped the doggy drool off her hand. "Not Dr. Kurt. This guy. Meals. But speaking of Dr. Kurt, I'd better head up to the office and meet him, because you're right. *Him*, I haven't met before."

After leaving the treatment area, Louise's mind returned to Eric and her odd dream. She was tempted to call his cell phone to make sure he was okay, but that would be foolish. Shaking her head, she headed to her office.

She found Daphne and Bob chatting in the doctors' office, as Rita had suggested. Louise repressed a smile. *Seems it is Daphne, not Rita, who's been keeping the new doctor busy. Or entertained, as Rita put it.*

When Louise entered the room, Daphne opened her mouth as though she was about to introduce Louise. Before Daphne had a chance, their new associate stood up to shake Louise's hand. "Hello, you must be Dr. Miller. It's very nice to finally meet you."

"And you must be Dr. Kurt." Louise took their new hires hand and met his gaze. What was that in his eyes? Fear? Over-confidence? Guilt? *Why would he look guilty? I must be over-tired.* The man was a stranger. She'd have plenty of time to figure him out while Daphne was on leave. She withdrew her hand. Her palm was wet.

"It's nice to meet you too. I'm Louise to everyone here. We're not a very formal bunch."

"Louise it is. And I'm Bob." He turned to Daphne. "Daphne was filling me in on a few of your clinic routines. I'm looking forward to becoming part of the team, even if temporarily."

Louise wiped her hand on her pants when Bob turned away. "Great," Louise said as she glanced at Daphne unsure of what to think of their new hire.

Louise hadn't had the opportunity to meet Bob prior to this meeting, because she was away at a conference when Daphne interviewed him. Daphne had taken an immediate like to the man and was impressed by his resume, in spite of the fact that he had only graduated two years prior. He'd worked at a busy clinic in the city after graduation, and his resume included glowing reference letters from his previous employers and from two of his college professors.

As they exchanged pleasantries, Louise studied the latest addition to their team. Bob looked familiar, but she couldn't place him. Had she seen him at a conference? She'd have to ask him about that later. She agreed with Rita, he did seem anxious to please, which made her suspicious.

Did they have any reason to worry about Dr. Bob Kurt?

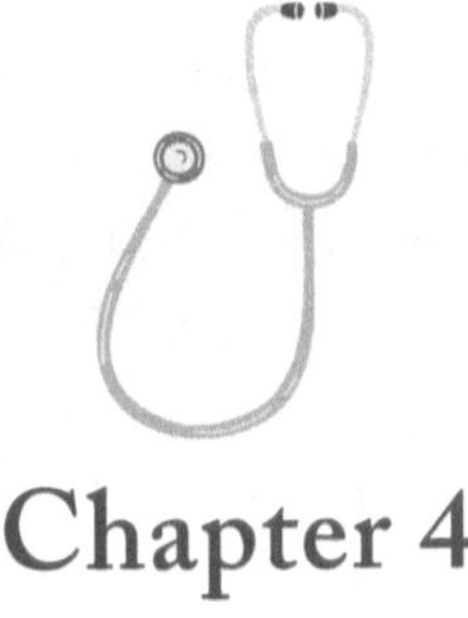

Chapter 4

R EVIEWING THE MORNING schedule, Louise saw that they were going to be as busy as she had expected when she saw the full parking lot earlier in the day. In addition to the cat neuter, not one, but three, dog spays were on the list. The tinge of anxiety that always crept in when a dog spay was scheduled on her surgery day worked its way through her.

Now silently dreading her morning, Louise made her way down to the treatment area to do a pre-operative examination on her surgery patients. As she was turning the corner into the pharmacy area she was met by Heidi who was rushing into the treatment area with a cat in her arms. Drops of blood had splattered on the floor and the towel wrapped around the cat's left foreleg was bloody.

"George Rogers." Heidi pushed the treatment room door open with her back and hurried in. Louise followed. "Mrs. Rogers found him this morning in the wine cellar. He'd been missing for half an hour before they thought to look there for him."

Heidi placed George, a six-year-old brown tabby cat, onto one of the exam tables. Louise held him for her as she removed the towel from around his leg. Jenny stood ready with the emergency kit and bandaging materials. A two-inch laceration marred the lower part of George's limb.

"That's a clean cut, and fresh," Louise said. "We should be able to suture it up no problem. The bleeding has slowed down. Any idea how this happened?"

"Mrs. Rogers thinks he followed her into the cellar this morning and knocked over a bottle on a shelf after she left." Heidi handed over George's file. "When Mrs. Rogers found him, he was sitting on the floor beside a pile of broken glass and spilled wine, bleeding and licking his leg."

Heidi poured antibacterial soap onto a two-by-two gauze square and gently swabbed the skin around the wound.

Jenny gave George an injection of pain medication.

"Not sure he needs that." Heidi cupped the cat's head in her hand and looked him in the eye. "I think he's a bit tipsy."

"You little boozer," Louise patted George on his back. "You're lucky you didn't cut your tongue when you were licking up the wine." She strode to the stainless-steel sink between the exam tables to wash her hands. "We'll get George sutured up before starting the other surgeries. I'm happy to put those dog spays off for an hour. I can't believe they booked three of them on one morning."

Bob walked into the treatment area. "Not a fan of dog spays?" he asked.

"You caught me." Louise reached for a paper towel. "Nope. Not a fan at all. I'm fine with any other surgery, but dog spays? Definitely not. Too many hard-to-get-to blood vessels surrounded by all that fat in the ligaments. I can't really explain it."

"You're not the first vet I've met who doesn't like them. They're not as routine as people think they are."

"Definitely not," Louise pressed the pedal to open the garbage can and dropped the crumpled towel into it. Was Rita right about Bob? *He does seem to be trying way too hard to please.* Oh well. He was in a new clinic. She would probably be nervous too, in his position.

Bob walked past her and placed his coffee mug on the counter. "I'd be happy to do those spays for you. Being my first day, I don't have any patients to see or files to write up."

Any reservations Louise had about the new vet left her mind. "Well, that's an offer I can't refuse." The muscles that had knotted across her shoulders when she saw the schedule relaxed. "I'll get George here fixed up then the techs and the surgeries are all yours."

"I'd be happy to do this for you too."

"Oh, no worries here. I enjoy this type of surgery. Really, any surgery other than dog spays. Stick around though so we can chat a bit."

While the two vets were talking, Jenny extended George's right foreleg. Heidi swabbed the skin with rubbing alcohol then inserted an intravenous catheter, securing it in place with surgical tape.

Jenny lifted George and transported him into the adjoining surgery room. Heidi retrieved a new needle and syringe. "Do you want him on iso?"

Louise tapped her chin with her finger. "No. I think I

can get it done with Propofol alone. No need to put him on gas." She donned a disposable surgical mask and handed one to Bob.

Heidi retrieved a bottle of white liquid from the refrigerator, drew three cc's into a syringe, and headed into the surgery room.

Using surgical soap, Louise scrubbed her hands and dried them on a sterile towel before heading into the surgery suite. Bob followed her. Heidi had clearly administered the fast-acting anaesthetic, as George slept soundly on the table.

After putting on a pair of surgical gloves, Louise lifted George's leg to show the wound to Bob. "He's a lucky boy. The glass narrowly missed his cephalic vein."

"Oh, yeah. That was close."

Louise let go of the leg. "Have you been to Coverdale before?"

Bob hesitated. "Um, no. Not until I met with Daphne last week. And I haven't been back since. Not before, um, yesterday. I found a small apartment, in a rooming house actually, on the other side of town. Not huge, but it'll do for now."

Louise made a mental note of the *for now* comment. They had told Bob when they offered him the position that it was full time while Daphne was on maternity leave, but that they wouldn't be able to keep him on full-time on her return. They were hoping they might be able to offer him a part-time position if they were busy enough, and if he was a good fit for the team.

After suturing up George's wound, Louise headed to her office. With Bob taking over the rest of the morning's surgeries, she was free to catch up on her much-neglected paperwork.

While she was working her way through the pile on her desk, she came across a newspaper from a couple of weeks prior. She was terrible for creating these paper piles and the staff loved to give her a hard time about it.

As she was tossing the two-week old issue into the trash, a photo caught her eye. The piece was a story on a break-in at a pharmacy in town. One of the faces in the photo was familiar. Their new associate Bob stood in the crowd. *Odd.* She took a closer look. Clearly it was him. Same short wavy brown hair, slim build with a prominent chin, and thin-rimmed glasses. He even wore the same plaid shirt. *Guess this is where I saw him before, but didn't he say that he hadn't been to this area prior to last week?*

Daphne had done a thorough job of confirming Bob's references and even his veterinary license, since it wasn't unheard of for someone to claim they were licensed with the College of Veterinarians of Ontario, or CVO, when in fact they weren't. Since an unlicensed veterinarian found to be diagnosing patients and prescribing medications could lead to a number of problems for the clinic, they were diligent about checking credentials. Hoping to set her mind at ease, Louise powered up her laptop and brought up the CVO website. She typed Bob's last name into the veterinary search area.

"Yep, there he is." With a quick glance at the door, she exited the site, not wanting anyone to wonder why she was investigating the new hire.

She returned to clearing off her desk and tried to forget about the photo in the paper, but it kept nagging at her. Louise was experienced at using the internet to investigate the background and social life of potential employees. Being a person who enjoyed puns, she laughed at the idea that she was vetting the vet while she typed, "Bob Kurt DVM Ontario" into her internet search engine.

She hit the enter key and scanned the search results for anything that might raise alarms. Nothing stood out. He was listed as an 'associate' at a couple of the clinics he had worked at. That was nothing new—they were all listed on his resumé. Two sites for dog kennels came up, but that wasn't anything unusual either. Many breeders and kennels posted the name of a veterinarian they recommended on their websites.

Not finding anything concerning under Bob's name, she did a search for more on the pharmacy robbery. She couldn't imagine that the man they had just hired would be involved in a robbery, but it didn't hurt to dig a little deeper. She found the article from the paper on her desk right away. The only other article had been posted a few days later. The police had caught the teenagers they suspected were responsible for the break-in. Louise let out a breath. Her new associate had a fairly boring internet presence.

Guess I didn't hear him right. She tried to concentrate on the rest of the mess on her desk. It didn't work. Giving in to her suspicious nature, Louise strode to the beige metal filing cabinet along one wall of the office and retrieved Bob's resumé from their employee files. She scanned the list of clinics he had worked at and could see from the check marks she'd made that Daphne had called them all. Hearing footsteps on the stairs, Louise slid the folder into the cabinet drawer and returned to her desk. She'd have a look at it again later.

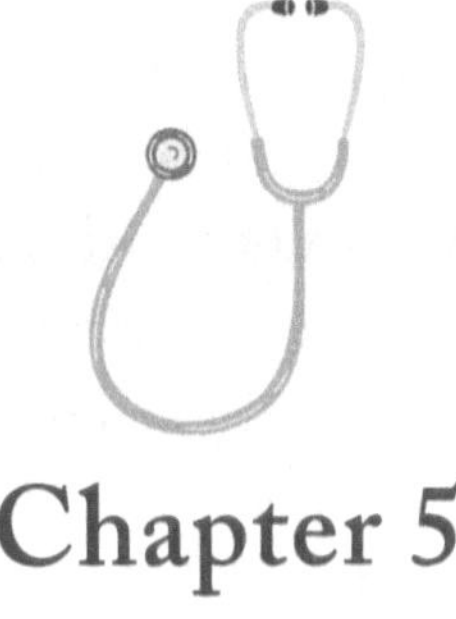

Chapter 5

IT WAS STILL early in the morning. The lights in the house were out, but the street lights cast enough light through the window for her to see around the bedroom. Two single beds and a four-drawer dresser in one corner that she shared with her sister filled the small room. In another corner, a small table and chair had been set up for them to do homework. Pansy always kept the curtains open to let the light from the street lamps in. She never liked sleeping in total darkness, but their foster dad wouldn't allow a night light.

"A waste of electricity," he yelled at her when she asked for one. "Anyway, only babies need night lights. Are you a baby"?

Telling him that her friend in school had one didn't help.

If anything, it made him angrier. He forbade the girls to talk about their home life outside of the house. If they did, and he found out about it, they would lose one of their few toys. If he was really angry, they might even lose dinner.

In the dim light from outside, Pansy slipped out of bed, careful not to wake her younger sister. Li'l sis, as she called her, was too young to understand the need to be quiet early in the morning. The rule stated that they weren't allowed out of their room until breakfast was ready, which ensured that they didn't wake the adults before the adults were ready to get up. Some days, Pansy would stay in bed as late as possible so as not to cause any fuss, and would sometimes even sneak food into their room the night before so that, if their foster-mom and dad slept late, she and Li'l sis wouldn't get too hungry.

In the early days of living here, Li'l sis started crying from hunger one morning. Their step-dad stormed into the room, his angry, hulking presence a warning in itself. He didn't hit the girls, but the threat of violence—and the fact that he was in a horrible mood the rest of the day—was enough to terrorize them into not making that mistake again.

This morning was different, though. Tomorrow was her birthday, and Pansy was flooded with memories of the past that kept her awake. Her real mom used to make a big fuss over her on her birthday. There'd be cake and presents and friends. And a new dress. The day before her birthday her mother would take her shopping for a special dress to wear at her birthday party. Then she'd wear it again on school picture day.

Pansy padded across the cold wooden floor to the window. She longed to see a car carrying her father pull up. The foster-parents at this house had laughed at her the first time she shared with them the hope that her father would return some day for her and Li'l sis. That was the last time she had shared any of her dreams, hopes, or thoughts with them or anyone else.

She was too young to understand why her dad didn't come for them. A year had gone by now since her mom took her shopping for a special birthday dress. The last three birthdays she could remember were not as happy as the earlier ones. And last year something had happened that she never really understood.

Chapter 6

ONCE THE MORNING surgeries and appointments were completed, Louise, Daphne, and Bob headed to a local family restaurant called Sweets for lunch. After they had discussed the vet colleges they'd gone to, their professors, and some of the crazy things that had happened during their college years, Louise was tempted to share a story about a prank that she and Daphne had played on one of their classmates. They had put notes in his mailbox, trying to convince him that he had a secret admirer, but later learned that they had frightened him because he thought he might have a stalker.

Louise reached for her coffee mug, deciding not to share the story. It wasn't really appropriate to share on a first meeting. More importantly, she didn't want to let on to Bob that Daphne was fond of practical jokes, as her associate might already have something in mind for their new associate.

"Daphne, do you remember Aida Negal and her cats?"

"Salt, Pepper, and Shaker? How could I forget them?"

"Seriously?" Bob rolled his eyes.

Louise frowned. Making fun of their clients' name choices was unprofessional and didn't sit well with her. "Yes, them. Aida was one of our first clients, Bob. She found the three kittens in an alley one night. They couldn't have been more than three weeks old."

Daphne clapped her hands. "They were so cute, and vulnerable. Aida nursed them back to health. Reminds me of the other litter that was found in a ditch a few months ago."

"Oh yeah. They were brought in by some teenagers who found them. We were lucky to find them all homes."

"That's for sure. It's not easy to place six kittens, no matter how cute they are."

"One of them had cerebellar hypoplasia, but we were still able to." Louise glanced at Bob. He was tapping his fingers on the table and gazing into the distance. Hmm. Did he not like cute stories, or did he have other things on his mind? Louise grasped the mug with both hands. Maybe he wasn't a cat person. Not all vets were. He might be great with dogs.

Bob returned his attention to his colleagues. "Is she still a client?"

"Yep." *Are you pretending to be interested in the story because you noticed my displeasure with your eye roll?*

As Louise shared what she thought was a cute story about a kitten with the neurologic condition, Bob repeatedly smiled and nodded as though trying to give the impression that he was listening, but when he slid his left arm under the table and glanced down, clearly checking the time, Louise inhaled deeply. *Are we boring him, or does he have somewhere else he needs to be?*

Trying to put aside her normal suspicious nature, Louise decided to give their new colleague a chance to share his own experiences. "So, Bob, have you had any memorable patients you'd like to tell us about?"

Bob snapped his head up to look at Louise. "Yeah. Sure. I used to see a klepto cat in Edmunston. He was always stealing items from the neighbors' porches and taking them home to his owner. A sweet lady. I think she was an artist. He was a funny cat."

Louise leaned back as the server set her sandwich and fries in front of her. The smell of bacon wafted from the plate and she took a deep breath.

"What would he steal?" Daphne squirted some ketchup onto a clean area of her plate.

"Oh. Pretty much anything he could carry." Bob turned his arm to check his watch again. "One day he dragged a bag of golf balls home."

"Lucky for his owner. I guess. If she golfs." Daphne laughed at her own joke.

While Daphne and Bob chatted about the kleptomaniac cat, Louise studied the man, her brow furrowed. *I don't remember seeing Edmunston on his resumé.*

Bob's eyes met hers and he swallowed hard. *He looks like he just got caught with his hand in the cookie jar.*

Bob cleared his throat. "So, George, eh? That cat's something else. He put on quite the show after he woke up from the anaesthetic."

"Yes." Daphne snagged a French fry from Louise's plate and dipped it in her ketchup. "He's always been a big goofball. He showed up at the Rogers' house one day during a rainstorm. One of their kids had left the door open, and George walked right in. They found him sitting in the kitchen, dripping all over the floor. The kids wanted to keep him, of course, but Mr. Rogers said no way. Once the rain stopped, they were to put him outside. That was two years ago and they still haven't put him outside." Daphne laughed at the memory, but Louise only smiled, still intent on the new vet.

Bob shifted on his chair. "You'll be on leave for four months, right, Daphne? If you don't mind my asking, why only four months?"

Daphne dipped her grilled cheese sandwich into her ketchup. "As a business owner, I'm not eligible for government-funded maternity leave, so my husband Joe is going to take an eight-month paternity leave when I return to work."

"That's great." Bob speared a forkful of Caesar salad, the aroma of garlic drifting from his plate. "What type of work does Joe do?"

Louise pursed her lips. Why did he seem so intent on shifting the conversation away from his past employment?

"He's an accountant in some government office." Daphne pulled down on her upper lip with her index finger and stared at the ceiling. "You'd think I would know which one, but I can never remember." She paused to wave at a toddler at the next table. "Isn't he cute? Anyway, yes, I'll be sticking around for another week. We thought we'd have you start before I left to give you time to get used to our routines and the staff."

"I enjoyed working with Heidi this morning. She's very attentive to the patients."

"Yes, she's definitely one of the best. Don't know what we'd do without her." Daphne grabbed her dessert—butterscotch pie with whip cream topping, a lunch meeting must-have—and slid the small plate onto her empty large one.

Bob's phone vibrated. He tugged it out of his pocket, glanced at the screen, and jumped up. "I'm sorry. I hate to be rude, but I really need to take this call if that's okay."

"Sure." Louise waved a hand through the air. After Bob scurried out of the restaurant, she set down her fork. "That was odd."

Daphne nodded. "What could possibly be that important, do you think?" Daphne tipped her head to drain the last drops of her tea before setting the cup on the saucer.

"No idea. Did I mention that Alex sent a text earlier?"

Daphne slapped both hands to her cheeks in mock surprise. "No, you didn't. That's big news." She lowered her hands. "Oh wait. Doesn't he call or text you every day? If he only called once a day, *that* would be big news."

"Ha ha. Funny lady. But, speaking of big news, sadly, he had some. Seems that there was another break in at a vet clinic last night. This time in Amherst."

"Wow. That's unnerving. It was just last week that Cheryl's clinic was broken into. Imagine the poor kennel staff who arrived to find the back door open."

"I can't. Thankfully she had the sense not to go into the building. She remained in her car and called 911."

On the far side of the restaurant, an elderly couple stood and waved towards Daphne and Louise. Daphne nodded a greeting and waved back. "I should give Cheryl a call to see if there's been any progress on the investigation."

"And to let her know that we're here for her."

"Yes, that too."

Dr. Cheryl Smith, who owned the veterinary clinic in neighboring Georgetown, often hung out with Louise and Daphne at local veterinary meetings. The two clinics helped each other out at times if one was short on supplies, or swamped with emergencies.

"I suppose they never caught the people responsible."

Louise glanced around the spacious dining room. The lunch rush had ended, and theirs was one of only four tables left occupied. "Not as far as I know. They didn't get much. Just the jar of catnip toys on the front counter."

Daphne shock her head, "Why?"

"Maybe they thought it would work on them? Luckily they weren't able to get into the locked drug cupboard. Cheryl upgraded to the same high security unit we have after you told her about it last month."

"The vets in Amherst must be stressing out. I don't know them, but I think I'll call them and offer to help in any way we can."

"Good plan." Louise checked her watch and glanced towards the restaurant exit. "Do you think he's coming back?"

Daphne shrugged. "Maybe another tea?"

After ordering more tea for Daphne, and coffee for herself, Louise filled Daphne in on the dream she'd had that morning. "Do you think God talks to people through dreams?"

"I suppose He might. God communicates with us in many ways."

"True, but I can't shake the worry I've been feeling for Eric since I woke up. I hope he's not getting himself into trouble again. Since the robbery at Cheryl's clinic, and the one at the pharmacy, Alex has been voicing concerns about having Eric at the clinic. He's been happy to help Eric out in the past, but he's apprehensive about him being so close to controlled drugs. And now another clinic has been targeted. What if Alex is on to something? What if Eric is involved somehow?"

"I'm sure it was only a dream. Eric knows better than to get mixed up with his old crowd. We all have dreams some- times that come from old memories. Sometimes they can feel so real it's freaky, but that doesn't mean they're actually real."

"It was crazy how lifelike it seemed. Even the smell of the musty hallways and look of the cracked tiles in the McNally building."

"Oh, don't remind me. We should make a donation to the college and specify that the funds should go towards new tiling."

"Not a bad idea." Louise laughed. "And a new paint job. Eric went through so much, and he's come such a long way. I guess the thought of him getting himself into trouble again really rattles me."

"I know Eric appreciates all you and Alex did for him after the robbery and his arrest. He's told me a few times how grate- ful he is. Besides, Eric never took drugs. Or sold them."

"No, he didn't. But some of his old friends did. Anyway, he'll be in this afternoon, so I can ask him how things are going." Louise checked her watch again. "He's probably there now. Actually, we should be getting back to the clinic. I didn't realize how late it was getting. I think this is one of the longest lunch breaks we've ever had."

"You're right. Lunch is usually half a sandwich on the fly."

"We should hire a new associate more often." Louise placed Daphne's dessert plate onto her own and pushed them to the edge of the table. "We'd get to take long breaks like this more often."

Before Daphne could respond, Bob returned to the table.

"Four months of full-time work followed by part-time on your return, Daphne, should work fine. I'm involved in a few other projects right now, so that timing is good for me."

Louise didn't miss the fact that he failed to apologise for the length of time he'd been away from the table. *Guess he's hoping we didn't notice.* "What type of projects, Bob, if you don't mind my asking?" Nothing in her Internet search had revealed anything else he might be involved in.

"I don't mind." Bob picked up his fork. While their plates were clean, half a salad still covered his. "I've been working with the National Kennel Club the past year, providing the vet checks before some of the shows. I really enjoy working with the dogs and their trainers, and I've gotten to know quite a few of the breeders."

Louise and Daphne exchanged a smile. While some breeders were very good clients, many could be a real challenge to work with.

Bob tossed the salad around on the plate with his fork, but didn't eat any of it. "Very few clinics have breeding programs, but it's a growing field in veterinary medicine. Have either of you given it any thought?"

"No." Louise caught the server's attention and showed her credit card to signal that they were ready for their bill. She had no desire to get into the breeding business.

"I've read a little about artificial insemination in dogs." Daphne said. "I honestly don't know if I see the point, but I suppose there must be one. I first heard about it from a company selling vaginoscopes at the Orlando conference last year."

Louise blinked. How did she not know that her partner was interested in this? Perhaps she shouldn't have answered so quickly. On the other hand, how interested could Daphne be if she hadn't mentioned it in a year? Or had she?

While Louise and Daphne were equal partners in the practice, Louise was definitely the more opinionated, stronger voice. Daphne tended to be less reactive and more thoughtful in her approach to things. *Oh well, what's the danger in getting a little information?*

After handing the clinic credit card to their server, she focused on Bob as he separated the components of his salad onto different areas of the plate. Her antenna had already been up, but his strange behavior at lunch had increased her concern. Was the man hiding something? They were trusting this person with their patients, their staff, their clients, and their clinic. Louise hoped that they wouldn't regret it.

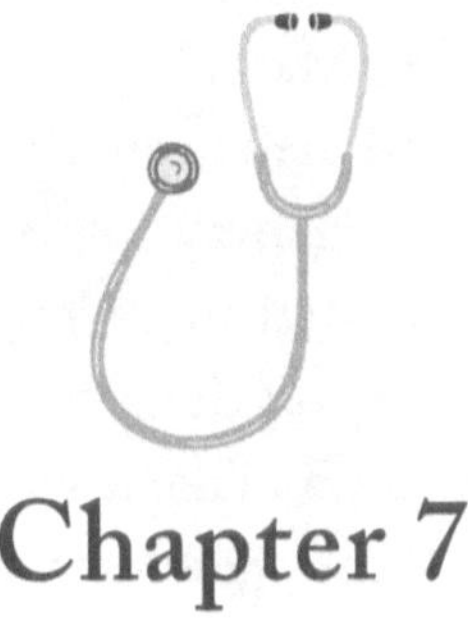

Chapter 7

S HORTLY AFTER LOUISE and her colleagues returned to the clinic, they encountered Mary, one of the clinic's two receptionists, in the treatment room.

Mary handed two files to Louise. "'Bout time you all dragged yourselves back to work." Mary glanced at the clock on the wall and shook her head. "And good thing you brought the new vet back with you."

"What did you think we were going to do with him?" Louise lifted her lab coat from its regular hook and slipped it on.

"I can't say, but I was starting to wonder. We already had a full schedule this afternoon, then an itchy spaniel and a limping German shepherd walked in."

"By themselves? That's impressive. We should give a special discount to patients who come in on their own. What do you think, Daphne?"

Daphne grabbed her stethoscope from the treatment room table. "Sounds good to me. Might be a bit tricky getting a full history from them, though."

"True. Anything else, Mary?"

"Oh, just your typical 'he's been off his food and vomiting for a week, and we're going away tomorrow so we need to be seen today' call on a busy afternoon. You remember the Simpsons? It was them. They're on their way in. With the three of you here, I figured we could make it work."

Louise shrugged. "If they get here while we still have three techs on, no worries."

"Sorry, that's where my brilliant plan falls apart. Eric's not here yet. He should have been here half hour ago." Mary held up both hands. "I'm sure he'll be here soon" She tilted her head. "Is something wrong?"

Louise shot Daphne a look while retrieving her stethoscope from the hook over the treatment table. "No. You're probably right. He'll be here soon. In the meantime, we should get to work."

"Okay. I'll let him know you're looking for him when he gets here." Mary returned to the front office.

Louise flipped through the files, then handed one to Daphne. "I'll take the itchy spaniel if you take the limping shepherd."

"Sure." Daphne took the file with one hand, and pushed the treatment room door open with the other.

Louise started to follow. The swinging door missed her by an inch when she paused. Was something wrong? It wasn't like Eric to be late. Given the nightmare she'd had the night before, she was starting to get a very bad feeling.

Entering the waiting area, Louise had no problem identifying her next patient. The golden-coloured dog sat on the floor, digging at his side with his right hind leg. Multiple areas on his torso were missing fur.

Louise smiled at the dog's owner, an older gentleman with a toothless grin and stubble beard, as she bent down to examine the dog. "Hello, John. How are you today?"

"Not too bad, Doctor, but poor Cocoa's been digging at 'imself for a few days now. It was so bad last night, none of us got much sleep."

Louise ran her hands through Cocoa's coat then scratched his back with several quick strokes. "I think he may have fleas John."

"Fleas? Oh no. They can be difficult to get rid of. Had a dog years ago we had to bath lots and spray stuff all over the house."

"No worries. Fleas are fairly easy to get rid of these days. And to prevent. But first I need to confirm that's what this is."

"I don't remember them being itchy with fleas. The other dogs, I mean."

"When a dog is this itchy, it's because they have an allergy to the flea bites, which is pretty uncomfortable for them. I need to get a bit of water. I'll be right back."

"You're going to tell if it's fleas with water?"

"A bit of a trick. You'll see." Louise headed to the treatment area, retrieved a spray bottle filled with water, and started for the front office, passing through an exam room.

As she was passing by a window, a movement caught her eye and she stopped. Eric. Staring at the phone he held in one hand, he reached for the front door handle with his other hand. Louise expected him to acknowledge Mary with a goofy sounding hello as he did every day. Despite their twenty-five-year difference in age, Eric and Mary had become close after Eric started working at the Black Creek Animal Hospital. Mary had taken the young man—who was fulfilling a court-ordered community service sentence—under her wing. Their relationship grew to one of mutual respect, with a large amount of good-natured teasing.

Mary lowered her glasses to the brim of her nose. "And just where have you been, young man?"

Eric continued to stare at his phone as he walked right by her, headed for the treatment area.

"Hey, Eric. Hello?"

Eric stopped in front of Mary's desk. When he lifted his head, Louise drew in a quick breath. His eyes were tired, and he hadn't shaved.

"What's up with you?" Hands on her hips, Mary drilled him. "You're never late, and now you don't say hi?"

"I'm sorry. I was … I was talking to a … friend. Sorry."

Mary narrowed her eyes. "Everything okay?"

"Oh sure. But you're right. I'm late. Talk later?" Eric shoved the phone into his back pocket and hurried to the treatment area.

"Sure," Mary said to a now absent Eric. "We'll talk later."

Once Eric was gone, Louise approached the front desk. "That was unlike him."

"Sure was. Hey, what are doing? Spying on people now?"

"No." Louise shifted her weight from one foot to the other. "I had to grab a bottle of water," she held up the spray bottle, "and was returning to John and Cocoa when I saw Eric come in."

"Letting it warm up while hiding around the corner, were you?"

"Ha ha. I wasn't hiding. I just didn't make it out of the room in time to say hi. Anyway, I have a patient to see."

"Would you like me to put them in an exam room?" Shirley, the younger of the two receptionists, rose to escort the pair.

"No, that's fine, Shirley. Thanks. John has arthritis. He's comfortable where he is. This won't take long."

Louise returned to John and Cocoa. She scratched Cocoa again then moved the small dog aside. She sprayed water on the spot where the dog had been sitting when she scratched him and waited a couple of minutes.

"Ah ha! Just as I suspected. See this John?" She pointed to several red dots on the floor.

John put on his glasses and bent over. "What's that?"

"That's flea dirt. Flea poop, actually. Fleas feed on the dog's blood. When the flea dirt is moistened, it turns red."

"Neat trick. It's like vet forensics."

Being a fan of forensic and CSI shows, Louise grinned. "I guess it is. I'll have Jenny get you set up with medication to get rid of the fleas, prevent more fleas, and to make Cocoa more comfortable."

"Thank you, Doctor."

That taken care of, Louise strode to the treatment area. She needed to have a chat with Eric.

When Louise got to the treatment area, Eric wasn't there. After sending Jenny to collect the needed supplies for Cocoa, Louise helped Heidi get radiographs on the large lab she had seen earlier in the day. They were in the X-ray room lifting Meals down from the table when Eric entered the room. He dropped his lunch bag on the nearest counter and rushed over to give them a hand with the struggling 110-pound dog.

"Great timing, Eric, but we could have used your help getting this guy up on the table. Where have you been?" Louise crossed the room to retrieve the portable X-ray viewer.

"Sorry about that." Eric rested a hand on Meals' head, not meeting her gaze. "I'm a bit behind today. I'm really sorry."

Louise bit the inside of her lip. Eric did sound genuinely sorry. He hadn't been late prior to this, and she often was, so who was she to judge? *I'm letting a silly dream affect my judgement. Still don't know why Alex asked about him, but Eric has never given me reason to doubt him.*

Louise patted Eric's shoulder. "Don't worry about it. You're here now, and it's a good thing. From the look of these rads, we're going to need to get an ultrasound on Meals."

Louise enjoyed teaching, and knowing that Eric had an interest in diagnostic imaging, she pointed to the radiographs on the tablet. "See right here? There's poor contrast in the cranial abdomen, just below Meal's stomach. His stomach is distended with fluid. He may have a foreign body obstruction or ileus from pancreatitis. He's always getting into things, this guy."

Heidi laughed as she returned Meals to his enclosure. "Typical lab."

"That he is." Louise handed the tablet to Heidi. "The ultrasound will tell us whether it's an obstruction or pancreatitis. I don't want to take a dog with pancreatitis to surgery. We should get it done ASAP in case he needs surgery. I'll need you to transfer the rads to his file."

"Can do, but I'll get set up for the ultrasound first." Heidi collected a few hand towels, a container of ultrasound gel and a bottle of isopropyl alcohol.

"Thanks." Louise pressed the intercom button on the wall. No response from the reception desk. "Hmm. I need them to call Mrs. Thompson." She tried again. Still no response. "Guess they're both on the phone."

Louise headed to the front office. When she reached the spot in the hallway where she'd listened in on Eric and Mary's conversation earlier, she caught her name and skidded to a stop. Were Mary and Shirley talking about her? She shouldn't be eaves-dropping on her staff—again—but what were they gossiping about?

"He's a real cutie." Mary sighed. "I don't get it why they're still only friends."

"Maybe they're not. I'm sure Louise doesn't tell us every-thing."

"I don't know. If Alex was my *friend*," Mary said, "he wouldn't still be single, that's for sure."

Not wanting to hear more, Louise dropped a pen to let Mary and Shirley know that someone was nearby before she entered the front office. She didn't like it, but it wasn't unusual for people to gossip about their employers. As long as it was friendly and light-hearted, she was content with knowing that her staff got along well with each other.

"I hope you're not gossiping again, Mary," Louise placed the pen in her pocket.

"Me? Never,"

"Never is a strong word. You know the rules about gossip-ing during work hours."

"And after work?"

"What you do on your own time is none of my business, but I'd hope you wouldn't be gossiping about co-workers at any time."

"I wouldn't have to gossip if you'd spill the beans about you and Alex."

"You exasperate me." Louise laughed. She enjoyed the back and forth banter with Mary.

"Then my work here is done!" Mary brushed her hands together, a smug look on her face.

"Not quite. I need you to give Mrs. Thompson a call about Meals. Could you get her on the phone please and let me know when you have her? I'll be at my desk."

"Sure thing, boss lady."

"You're the best, Mary. What would we do without you?"

"I often wonder that myself."

Chapter 8

UPON RETURNING TO the office, Louise found Bob sitting at Daphne's desk with a white binder and a coffee. One foot tapped the floor and he drummed his fingers on the desk as he flipped pages with his other hand. Was he nervous or were the two coffees he'd drunk at lunch hitting him?

"Hey Bob, how are you getting along? I guess there hasn't been too much for you to do since we got back from lunch." Louise cleared a spot on her desk for Meal's file.

"I've been trying to keep busy familiarizing myself with the clinic. I found this binder in a drawer down in the pharmacy. It's titled Clinic Procedures. I thought it might be helpful to give it a read."

Louise frowned. "Really? Can I see that?" She couldn't remember such a binder. Bob closed it and handed it to her. "That's funny. I think we put this together when we first opened the clinic. Don't think I've seen it since. I'm not even sure what's in there."

"When I'm finished reading it, I'll let you know." Bob winked at her.

"Thanks. Appreciate it. Maybe we've been doing things wrong all this time." She laughed at her own joke. "We'll be doing an ultrasound on Meals in a bit. Once I get a chance to speak with Mrs. Thompson. You're welcome to join us."

"Sure, I'd be happy to help."

"Eric will hold him for us. Meals is a very cooperative patient, so I'm sure he'll happily lie on his side for an ultrasound belly massage."

The intercom buzzed. "I have Mrs. Thompson on the line for you."

"Thanks, Mary, put her through."

Louise explained her findings thus far to Mrs. Thompson as well as the benefit of doing an ultrasound exam. After Mrs. Thompson agreed to the test, Louise told her she'd call with the results within the hour.

Louise picked up Meals' file. Her eye caught the newspaper with the story about the pharmacy robbery in the trash can. Using an old file folder from her desk, she concealed the paper. She couldn't know if Bob had seen it. She didn't know why she cared if he did, but something compelled her to hide it from him in case he hadn't. "Have you had any ultrasound training, Bob?"

"Nothing formal. I've done a few pregnancy checks, but that's about it."

"Well, come on then. I'd like to take advantage of any chance we have to teach you how to do a basic scan in emergencies."

"Sure. Sounds good."

When they got to the small room Louise had set up for performing ultrasounds, Eric and Jenny already had the fur on Meal's belly shaved off, and had him lying on the exam table. The ultrasound machine sat on a wheeled cart to the left of the exam table. Louise squeezed some of the special ultrasound gel onto Meals' abdomen. When she placed the probe on his belly, an image appeared on the screen.

Louise pointed and Bob leaned closer. "I'm pretty sure it's a foreign body. Meals eats everything he sees. Underwear and action figures are two of his favorites."

"Old Doc Johnson used to say that if a lab comes into the clinic vomiting, take him straight to surgery. Don't waste time and money on all those fancy tests."

Louise stopped moving the ultrasound probe. "I don't consider an ultrasound a waste of time or money. I'd rather confirm it's a foreign body and know that it's not a case of pancreatitis before I put a patient through surgery."

"Oh, I agree with you completely." Bob backed up. As he did, his foot got caught on the wrong side of the table leg and he stumbled. Grabbing onto the back of Louise's chair, he was able to keep himself from falling. "Oops. Sorry. Yes. Doc Johnson. He was old school, that's for sure. He was resistant to any change."

Louise ignored the intrusion to her personal space. *Nice save, man, but who's Doc Johnson? I don't remember any Dr. Johnson on your resumé. You're talking about this guy like you're close, but you didn't use him as a reference? On the other hand, if he's really is that old school, maybe he isn't someone you'd want to use as a reference.*

"Take AI," Bob straightened his tie. "Doc Johnson would have thought the whole idea of AI in dogs was insane. He would have..." He stopped and cleared his throat. "Heidi seemed keen on the AI idea."

The image on the screen became still, then vanished as Louise lifted the probe from Meals' skin. She spun her chair around to look at Bob but caught sight of Eric and clamped her mouth shut. Returning the probe to the patient, she concentrated on finding what was troubling him. She'd talk to Bob later about discussing his ideas with her or Daphne before talking to the staff about them.

Bob offered his hand to Eric. "I guess we haven't been formally introduced yet. You must be Eric. I'm Dr. Kurt, but call me Bob."

Both hands occupied holding Meals, Eric offered his elbow. "Good to meet you."

"Right, sorry." Bob shook Eric's elbow.

Louise thought Eric's voice sounded weaker than normal. *Maybe he's not getting enough sleep. Hanging out late with friends? Maybe Bob will be a good influence on him.*

Bob moved over to Eric's side of the table and slapped Eric on the shoulder. So, you're the only guy working here eh?"

"Until now. I guess. No big deal."

"All that girl talk. Must drive you crazy sometimes eh? Come on. Be honest."

Louise glanced in Bob's direction. *On the other hand, maybe not such a good influence. Where is this going?*

"It's not so bad. We all get along fine. Jenny's a big hockey fan. Heidi's into baseball. It's not all soap operas and hoola hoops."

Louise returned her attention to the ultrasound monitor. *Good for you, Eric. Don't accept those sexist comments.*

"My coworkers are my friends. Why would being the only guy be an issue?"

"Sorry. I was only joking. Maybe you can show me a place in town a guy can get a drink and watch the game sometime."

"Sure. Maybe later. After my shift."

"Sounds good." Bob returned to Louise's side of the table. "Do we have a diagnosis yet?"

"We do." Louise pointed to the gray image on the screen. "There's the problem. An obstruction at the distal duodenum." Grabbing a soft cloth from the end of the exam table, she wiped the gel from the probe before placing it in its holder. "Bob, would you mind turning the lights on?"

Louise wiped the gel from her hands with a towel. Bob had told Heidi about their lunch time conversation. Was he going to share his ideas about a breeding program with Eric as well? What else might he be up too? Was he going to be a bad influence on Eric? Eric's past was proof that he was easily influenced, and Bob seemed eager to be buddy-buddy with him. "Eric, once we get Meals down and back to his kennel can you set up for surgery, please?"

I'll be in my office biting my tongue.

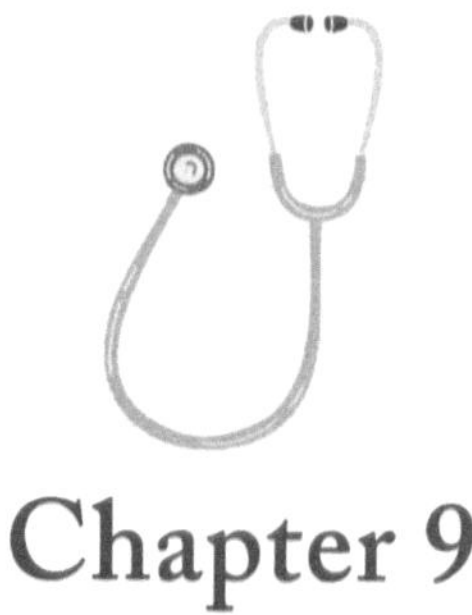

Chapter 9

LOUISE WAS HAPPY to get out of the clinic on time that night. She planned to meet Alex at the movie theater where the next installment of their favorite science fiction franchise was playing. They hadn't missed an installment of Galaxy Invaders since their friendship blossomed while they were in university.

She had been participating in a community clean-up project with the campus group Students for Christ when she slipped and fell into a puddle. Despite the pain shooting through her backside, she found herself laughing at her clumsiness. Someone else was laughing. She raised her chin to see who it was, and her gaze connected with a brown-eyed stranger's. Stubble the same shade as his wavy brown hair dotted his chin. A tingling sensation swept across her neck and face.

She grasped the hand he offered. He pulled her out of the puddle then introduced himself. Alex Haines, a biology major focusing on criminology and forensics. They'd been friends since, but over the past few months that friendship was changing, for her, anyway. She found herself thinking about Alex more often and had little interest when friends at church wanted to fix her up.

It was dark when she arrived at the movie theater, but she readily spotted Alex's car under one of the light poles and pulled in beside him.

When she opened the door to the theater, she was met with the satisfying aroma of freshly popped popcorn. She inhaled deeply and smiled.

"Is that smile for me?" Alex, his hair slightly mussed, handed Louise a large bag of popcorn.

She accepted the treat. "It is now."

The tension of the day evaporated when Alex's six-foot, sturdy frame enveloped her in a hug. "I needed that."

"What's up?" He gave her another hug.

"Nothing worth mentioning right now. Do you have the tickets?"

Alex removed his phone from his pocket and showed her the display. "Bought them online earlier. No waiting in line. More time to buy popcorn."

"You are a genius. Did you get lots of napkins?" Louise licked a little butter off her fingers.

"Of course." He pulled out a huge wad from his other pocket.

"You're such a nerd." She looped her arm around his as

they headed to theater five. They found their seats as the advertisements were ending.

After the movie, they headed to the small, 1950's themed restaurant next to the theater. The place was crowded with young and old fans of the space aged movie. Some were dressed in costume to honor their favorite character.

Alex pointed to the far corner. "There's a table over there." He gently nudged his way through the crowd. Louise followed. Her smaller stature made negotiating her way through the excited patrons more difficult, as they didn't tend to move out of her way as they did for Alex.

When she finally made it, she flopped onto the wood bench. "I feel like I've piloted a spaceship through an asteroid field."

Alex handed her the one-page menu. "And a fine job you did."

"Thanks." She set the menu aside. "I'll have my usual."

"A chocolate shake and fries."

"You got it."

"I can't resist the smell of their burgers. They taste pretty good too."

Alex placed their order at the counter before returning with two glasses of water. "So, what did you think of the movie?"

Louise rearranged the bottle of ketchup and salt and pepper shakers on the table. "It was fairly good, but I did have a few concerns."

"Oh yeah? Like what?"

"They said that they found proof of life on Mars."

"Pretty standard sci-fi stuff."

"And that it evolved from the same basic building blocks that humans did."

"Still pretty standard stuff."

"Because the aliens had the same number of chromosomes on their genes that humans do? Really?"

Alex shook his head. "I don't follow."

"Genes are *in* chromosomes. Chromosomes aren't *on genes*. Aliens or not."

"You do remember that this is science fiction, right? The key word being fiction."

Louise threw her hands up and scanned the young crowd. "But people actually believe all this stuff."

Alex nodded. "You're right. It is surprising what people will believe. No concrete proof needed. Hear it from enough sources, and it must be true. And yet the world is full of mysteries."

"That it is. We even had a few of our own today." Louise bit her tongue. She'd intended to avoid the topic of Alex's earlier text.

"Those mysteries don't involve Eric, do they?"

Louise swallowed hard. "No. Of course not. Eric is Eric. Look, our food is ready." Louise jumped up and retrieved their order. "Our new associate, on the other hand. I'm not sure what to make of him." Louise set Alex's plate in front of him before sliding onto the bench. "That greasy mess on your plate looks good." *Please don't ask any more questions about Eric.*

After saying grace, Alex took a large bite of his hamburger. "It is good. What's wrong with him?"

Louise winched at the sight of ketchup running over Alex's lower lip. "That's disgusting."

Alex wiped his face with a paper napkin. "Sorry. What's wrong with the new guy? What's his name again?"

"Bob Kurt. I'm not sure if anything is actually wrong, but I'm getting this strange feeling, like something is a little off. He talked to Daphne and me about artificial insemination and dog breeding at lunch."

Alex returned his burger to the plate. "Talk about disgusting. That's quite the lunch topic."

"And what do police detectives talk about at lunch?"

"Good point. Carry on."

Louise coated her fries with ketchup and salt. "I found out later that he had been speaking to Heidi about it too. It's like he's trying to push it on us."

"Go easy on that stuff." Alex eased the salt shaker from Louise's hand. "Would it be beneficial to the clinic?"

"Maybe, I don't really know. Honestly, I don't know much about the dog breeding world."

"You should go to a dog show. I hear there's one at the Bathurst Center this week."

"I suppose it wouldn't hurt. Daphne and I are both off this Saturday. I could see if she wants to go." Louise slurped the last of her milkshake. "That wasn't the only mystery. We had another one."

"Oh yeah? A real mystery? Or a crime scene imagination mystery. Get it? CSI. Crime Scene Imagination."

Louise flicked her straw towards Alex. A few drops of her milkshake hit him on the forehead. "Ha. Ha. Funny man."

Alex wiped the thick liquid from his brow. "You really gotta stop watching all those forensics shows."

"What if someone lied on a resumé? Or left something out?"

Alex furrowed his brow. "Such as? Did he forget to mention a criminal record? I thought you verified Bob was licensed."

Louise leaned to the left to avoid being knocked on the shoulder by a group of young people making their way to the next table. "We did. Only today, when we were talking, he mentioned a clinic in Edmunston that wasn't on his resumé."

"Maybe he worked there as a student?"

"No. I'm pretty sure he was a vet already. I couldn't get it out of my mind, so before meeting you, I looked the number up and called them."

Alex picked at the abandoned fries on Louise's plate. "What did they say?"

She pushed her plate closer to him. "Not much. It was pretty clear that the person who answered the phone didn't like Bob. That in itself doesn't necessarily mean much—not everyone gets along. But I asked about this Dr. Johnson guy that Bob mentioned. Bob talked about him like he was some hero type."

"And?"

"Dr. Johnston used to own the Edmunston clinic. They wouldn't tell me anything about him. I found him on the CVO website though. He surrendered his license last year after being accused of falsifying rabies certificates for some rescue group."

"And Bob looks up to this guy?"

"See what I mean? How could he look up to someone who would cheat the system like that? Rabies is a serious disease. Lying about the vaccination status of dogs is dangerous."

Alex retrieved a few bills from his wallet and tossed them on the table. "Maybe Bob didn't know about it?"

"It wasn't hard for me to find out about it, so how could Bob not know? Anyway, I asked the woman on the phone to have the clinic owner call me."

A college-aged woman inserted a coin in the old jukebox at the other end of the diner. When Buddy Holly's, "That'll Be the Day" rang out through the diner, Alex did a dance in his seat. "That's awesome. I didn't think that old thing worked."

"I heard the new management had it repaired. He was before my time, but I loved Buddy Holly's music when I was a teenager." Louise glanced out the window and spotted a client. She waved. "So, what are you working on these days, big shot detective man?"

"You know my work is top secret."

Louise nodded. "Of course it is. Until the morning paper comes out."

"True. Actually, a number of teens have been rushed to the hospital the past few weeks. They got a hold of some drugs from a kid who dropped out of the local high school last year."

"How could you know that?" Louise asked. "I thought drug users were pretty tight-lipped about where they get their drugs."

"They usually are, but these kids aren't regular users. They were so freaked out by the whole experience that they told us who sold them the drugs, and we were able to pick him up. We searched his house and found a large supply in his room."

Louise shook her head. "His room?"

"Yup. His bedroom. In his parents' house. They said they had no idea what he was up too. Claimed he's being set up, but he has a record."

"Are they criminals too?" Louise asked.

"Not that we know of. If they are, they haven't been caught. Anyway, he had cocaine in liquid form. I knew it was out there, but didn't think I'd ever see it in this area. A few months ago a couple of guys returning from a trip to Brazil were detained and questioned at the Toronto airport. A border patrol officer found two small perfume bottles."

"Not perfume?"

"Not perfume."

Louise shivered. "That's scary stuff."

"We've set up a task force." Alex grabbed a napkin and wiped a splotch of ketchup off the table. "The pharmacy robbery, two clinics broken into, and now liquid cocaine at the high school. We've been keeping an eye on a couple of fellas who are new to town."

"Any idea who they are?"

Alex tossed the crumpled napkin onto his plate. "No. Promise me you'll make sure your doors are locked at night. At the clinic and at home."

The milkshake and fries shifted in her stomach. Alex hadn't pressed her on Eric. For that she was thankful, but all this talk about robberies and drugs concerned her. Should she tell him that Eric had been late for work?

No. That was probably just a coincidence.

Chapter 10

SATURDAY MORNING LOUISE woke up to find Oscar sitting on her chest, staring into her eyes. She stared back before cupping his head in her hands and rubbing his ears.

She glanced at the spot on her night table where she used to keep an alarm clock before she started using her phone to wake herself up. "What time is it? It can't be time to get up yet." She attempted to retrieve her phone from the night table. "You know, Oscar, it's not easy turning over with a fifteen-pound cat on my chest." She repositioned Oscar to the unused kitty blanket at the foot of the bed.

"Shoot. It's after six o'clock already. Daphne's expecting me to pick her up at seven. Nice job, pussy cat. Every other

Saturday I have off you wake me at five. Today you choose to sleep in. Hmm. I may have to dock your treat allowance this week."

Oscar jumped off the bed and scampered downstairs. *He doesn't seem concerned.* She dutifully followed, fed him, and then got ready to meet Daphne.

When she arrived at the two-story yellow house that Daphne shared with her husband, Joe, and their two-year-old daughter Ella, Daphne was sitting on the porch reading. As Louise drove up the unpaved country driveway, she rolled down her window and breathed in the fresh country air. Unable to resist, she stopped her car fifty yards from the house and lost herself for a moment in the tranquility of the countryside. The wide-open fields of green. The vegetable garden Daphne had planted in the front of the house, and the red barn on the far side of the paddocks that housed Daphne's horse, Jo-el. Then she gagged.

Daphne opened the passenger door and climbed in. "Good morning."

"What is that smell? Cow manure?"

"Ah yes. Isn't it great?" Daphne inhaled deeply. "The smell of the country."

"It's … unpleasant."

"It's … necessary. The farmers were up early this morning spreading fertilizer."

"True. We do need food."

"And it's not nearly as bad as some of the smells we encounter in the clinic every day."

"True again."

After turning the car around and driving back onto the road, Louise rolled up the windows, switched on the air conditioner, and pushed the recycle-air button. "That's better. What's Joe up to today?"

"I think he's working. He has several projects to finish up before taking his paternity leave. His mother, Alice, is coming over later to watch Ella. I thought it would be good for them to spend some time together before the baby arrives. Alice is going to stay with us for a few weeks once I go back to work to make sure that Joe can handle things okay."

Louise stopped at the four-way stop intersection. "Is Joe worried about being alone with two young children?"

"Not at all. It's more his mother. I think she's using it as an excuse for a prolonged visit. Are you worried about invisible cars?"

"Excuse me?"

"You're supposed to stop at a four-way, not park for a while."

"Sorry, I haven't had my morning coffee yet." Louise turned left onto the road that would take them to Amherst, the small city that housed the Bathurst Center.

When they arrived at the Center, a two-story modern building designed to host a variety of events from hockey games to large scale conventions, Louise stopped to take a parking ticket from the automatic dispenser. "Look at all the cars. It'll take longer to find a spot than it took us to get here."

Daphne pointed to an opening three cars over. "There's one right there."

Louise sighed. "I suppose it'll do. A little walk might be a good thing. I guess these dog shows are pretty popular."

As soon as Louise parked the car, Daphne retrieved her sling bag from the floor near her feet and hopped out.

Louise slammed the door and rushed to catch up with her friend. "What's the hurry?"

Without looking back, Daphne said, "Oh, I thought I'd give you a little privacy to get all the grumbling about poor parking out of your system."

Louise tapped Daphne's shoulder with her fist. "Ha ha. Funny lady." Daphne might be kidding, but there was some truth to her words. Louise was aware of her tendency to complain about life's little inconveniences and prayed about it often.

Louise purchased their tickets and accepted a map of the complex. When they passed through the main doorway, the aroma of hot dogs mixed with sweaty gym socks greeted them. Down a large hall to the left, a series of doors led to locker rooms, according to the signs on the doors. Straight ahead, a hockey rink was visible beyond a large window. Daphne headed in that direction.

Louise, unseen by Daphne, pointed to the right. "I think we're this way. There's an arrow under that dog show sign. It must be down this corridor."

"Aren't they cute?" Daphne peered through the window at a group of young children playing hockey. "Joe is already talking about getting Ella and this little one," Daphne patted her belly, "into hockey."

"That baby will be skating before he or she walks. Come on. Let's get going."

They reached a set of doors at the end of the corridor. Louise opened one and waved Daphne through. "This must be the right place."

"What's that? I can't hear you over all the barking."

Louise followed her friend through the doorway. "Look at

all the dogs. This place is huge. I thought it would be a small arena with a few show dogs."

"I believe you were wrong. Let's see what they're selling."

Multiple vendors had set up booths inside the entrance. They were selling a variety of products including specialty dog foods, grooming services, and doggy outfits for every occasion. Louise and Daphne made an attempt to look at some of the grooming items, but the crowds were unyielding.

Louise gestured for her friend to follow her. "Let's leave the shopping for now. Might be fewer people later."

In the center of the arena, rows of small kennels had been set up on tables. Larger kennels lined the floor. Dog owners snaked their way between the side arenas and the kennel area.

Louise spotted a group of border collies. "I wonder if they'll be doing agility today? I'd love to see that."

"Isn't this more of a dog show, not a sporting event?"

"I don't know, but they could be held at the same time. There's enough room in here."

"True. It would be fun to watch agility trials. But how can we figure out what's happening? Hmm. Maybe we should take a look in that program they gave you?"

"You are truly a genius." Louise glanced at the schedule. "We're in luck. An agility trial starts in an hour. That should give us plenty of time to look around."

They started their tour down the aisle that housed a number of the smaller breed dogs. Louise spotted a shih tzu with a litter of puppies. "Aren't they sweet? I wonder if they're sedated? They're pretty quiet for their age."

"I can assure you that the dogs are not sedated."

Louise spun around. A portly gentleman who looked to

be about fifty years old stood behind her. His white beard and round spectacles reminded Louise of her favorite uncle.

The man tapped his clipboard with a pen. "Sedating a dog is strictly against National Kennel Club regulations."

Louise lowered her head. "I'm sorry. I was just kidding around. I'm sure these dogs are used to being in this type of environment."

"Yes," the man said. "But if you stick around long enough you'll see they're not always this quiet. This litter arrived an hour ago and they're still tired from traveling. I think it's all the squirrel watching while in the car. Even at a young age, some dogs are squirrel crazy." The man produced a large grin and extended his hand to Louise. "I'm Cliff Mariner. I'm a judge with the National Kennel Club. Is this your first time at a show?"

Louise felt an immediate fondness for this gentleman. He did remind her of her uncle, both in looks and in personality. "Yes. We thought we'd come by and see why parking is such a challenge today."

Daphne rolled her eyes at Louise before shaking Cliff's hand. "Hi, it's nice to meet you. I'm Daphne Carling." She pointed to Louise. "And this is my friend Louise Miller. We're veterinarians. We're considering introducing a breeding program into our clinic and thought that coming to the show today may teach us a few things about the world of dog breeding."

"Nice to meet you both," Cliff said. "I'd be happy to show you around and fill you in on our club and the world of breeding, as you put it."

"That would be lovely, wouldn't it, Louise?"

"It really would be. How long have you been a judge?"

"I've been working with the NKC since it started up

about fifteen years ago. I started out as a volunteer. I didn't know what I was getting into at first, but I love being around the dogs."

Cliff motioned for the two women to step aside as an English Mastiff was escorted back to her kennel. "She's a lovely dog, but she's a drooler, that one."

Louise offered the back of her hand to the big dog. She sniffed Louise's fingers, then licked them. When the dog was gone, Louise examined the wet spot on her hand. "You're not kidding about the drool. Guess I should have known better. And brought a towel."

Daphne handed Louise a baby wipe. "We parents of toddlers are always prepared."

Louise accepted the wipe. "What did you mean when you said you didn't know what you were getting into?"

Cliff shook his head. "Silly stuff. The man who was in charge of the volunteers at the time, Tim Gates, told me the position was janitorial. I thought I'd be mopping the hallways and maybe cleaning the bathrooms. Turns out I was cleaning up after the dogs in the ring. It's very humbling cleaning up after dogs with hundreds of onlookers."

Daphne covered her mouth with her hand and giggled. "Oh my."

"Once I retired, I worked at getting my qualifications to become a judge. I've been judging shows for a few years now. I work occasionally at the administration offices too."

Louise eyed the clock on the far wall and started for the border collies. She didn't want to miss the agility trials.

Daphne held onto Louise's sleeve and gave her a knowing look. "What would you like to show us first Cliff?"

Cliff directed his gaze left, then right, before motioning

to his guests to follow him down the aisle on his right. "Let's start with the show ring."

Louise's shoulders slumped as she followed Daphne and Cliff to the procession of well-groomed poodles and terriers in the show ring. She unfolded the schedule in her hand and, careful not to bump into anyone in the crowd, snuck a peak. *Yes.* There were a couple more agility runs scheduled today. They should have plenty of time to watch one of them before they had to leave.

Cliff stopped at a row of seats set up outside the ring. He approached the woman sitting by a sign that read "coordinator" and handed her the show ribbons he had been carrying. When he returned to Louise and Daphne, he led them to an area behind the row of judges, giving them a clear view of the contestants. "This first arena is more of what people expect when coming to a dog show. Here the individual dogs are compared to their breed standard. Are you familiar with the point system involved in championships?"

Before Louise could answer, a tall slim man in an expensive suit strode toward them, his gaze focused on Cliff.

"There you are. I haven't got all day to chase you around."

Cliff stepped closer to the man. "Hi, Tim. I'm sorry if you couldn't find me. I've been here on the floor all morning."

"Just make sure everything is ready to go later. No mistakes this time." The man stomped off.

Louise followed the angry man with her eyes. "Who was that?"

"Tim Gates. My boss."

Daphne edged closer to a table with dog kennels. "The same Tim Gates?"

"Yes. He's president of the NKC now. I forgot the certificates for the winners at the last show, which embarrassed him. He won't let me forget it."

Louise shook her head. "That was a lot of anger."

"Yes. He's an angry man—I've never understood why. He did remind me of something, though."

Daphne was petting a Yorkshire terrier through the bars of a kennel. "What's that?"

Cliff laughed. "That I forgot the certificates for tomorrow's trial. I'll have to sneak into his office later to get them."

Louise laughed. "You don't seem the sneaking-in type."

Cliff waved his hand in the air. "It's easy. The lock to the main entrance has been broken for ages. Tim doesn't want to spend the money to fix it."

Daphne stopped petting the terrier when the dog's owner returned and glared at her.

"Hmm. I hope I can trust the two of you not to break into the NKC offices now that I've shared that little secret with you."

Louise shook her head. "I can't imagine why I'd ever have the need to do that."

The three shared a laugh as they continued on their way to the canteen. The happy mood was again disrupted when a middle-aged woman with a determined look on her face approached them and wagged a finger under Cliff's nose.

"I expect more from you today. You gave my Scarlet a low score yesterday. Why did you do that?"

"I'm sorry, Miss…"

"Never mind any excuses. My dogs are top of the line. Champions bred from champions. And don't you forget it. They have the DNA certification to prove it. I'll have to report you to your superiors if this keeps up." The woman stomped off towards the other side of the arena.

A man standing near the door under an Emergency Exit sign caught Louise's eye, and she nudged Daphne in the ribs. "Is that Bob over there?"

Daphne peered over, squinting. "It does look like him. I wonder who his friends are?"

Bob stood with his arms crossed as two men in baseball caps spoke to him. The taller man shoved Bob, who stepped back and raised his hands defensively.

Louise started to walk in Bob's direction. "Whatever's going on over there, I don't think those guys are his friends."

Daphne followed. "I think you're right."

Cliff trotted along at Louise's heels as she and Daphne made their way to the exit, slowed by the crowd. When they reached their destination, Bob and the other two men were gone. Hoping she wouldn't set off an alarm, Louise cracked the door open. She breathed a sigh of relief. No alarm. Peering into the parking lot, she spotted Bob's assailants getting into a van. She made a mental note of the first part of the license plate. ADS. The rest was covered with dirt.

When Louise glanced over her shoulder to let Daphne know that the bullies were driving away, her companions had already moved on. She pushed her way through the throngs of people to catch up to them, then silently followed Daphne and Cliff, catching only parts of their conversation. Daphne asked Cliff about the woman's DNA certification comment, and Cliff explained what she meant. Louise's mind was still on Bob and the men from the van. Who were those guys? Was Bob in some type of trouble? Would he bring that trouble to the clinic?

Louise's attention returned to her companions when she

walked into the back of Daphne, who had stopped abruptly. "What's wrong?"

Daphne's face was flushed. She pulled the brochure out of Louise's hand and fanned herself. "I think I'm in labor."

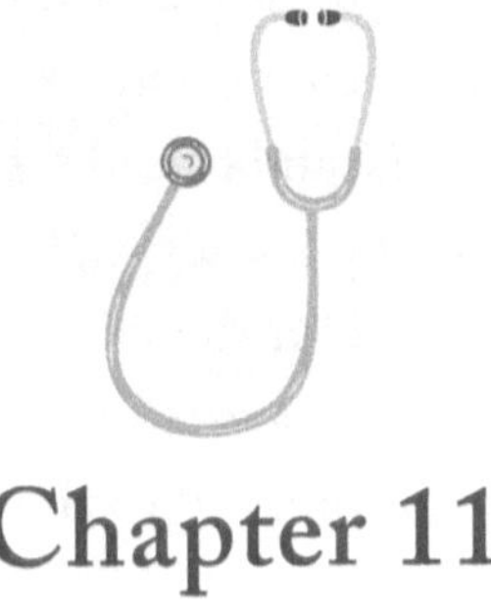

Chapter 11

MONDAY MORNING THE Black Creek Animal Hospital was buzzing with activity. The early arrival of Daphne's second child, a boy she and Joe named Benjamin, meant that the schedule for the next two weeks would have to be adjusted to accommodate Daphne's sudden absence.

Upon her arrival at the clinic that morning, Louise walked into the front office and stopped short. "What is that?" Leaning against the filing cabinets behind Mary was a four-foot-high teddy bear wearing a sailor suit.

Mary left her desk to lift the bear to a standing position. "A little something for baby Ben."

Louise playfully slapped her forehead. "A *little* something?

I don't think Daphne's house is big enough for it. They'll have to put it in one of the horse stalls."

"Ben will love it. I know Ella still loves the one I got for her."

"I'm sure he will." Louise held up a sheet of paper. "I printed out the doctors' schedule for this week. Would you mind rebooking all of Daphne's appointments? Bob can take over her surgery days. Is he here yet?"

Mary took the schedule and placed it by her computer monitor. "Yes. I saw him heading upstairs right before you came in."

"Great." Louise started for the second floor. She wanted to talk to Bob about what she saw at the dog show on Saturday, but before she made it to the foot of the stairs, Heidi met her in the hallway.

She tapped her left palm with her right index finger. "Good. You're here. We had three surgeries booked for Daphne this morning, but now she's not here. You're fully booked with appointments. Should we call the owners and have them reschedule? Only one is elective. One is a cystotomy. Remember the dog that blocked last week? I don't think we can put that one off. And then there's—"

Louise placed her hand on Heidi's shoulder. "Whoa. Calm down. We have another vet, remember? I was about to go up and chat with him."

Heidi relaxed her shoulders. "You're right. I'll start getting things set up. Can you ask Bob to let me know which surgery he'd like to start with?"

"Consider it done."

As Heidi turned towards the treatment room, she narrowly missed a collision with Jenny who was rushing into the hallway.

Jenny skidded to a stop. "We just got a call from Mr.

Brown. Blue was attacked by a bigger dog when out for his walk this morning. They're on their way in—about fifteen minutes out. I only got bits and pieces of the story. A big dog came out of nowhere and attacked him."

"We better get set up for their arrival." Louise raced into the treatment room behind Jenny. "How are they getting here? Neither of them drive anymore."

"Mr. Brown said a man at the park is driving them."

"Okay, good."

Jenny retrieved the emergency cart from the far corner and parked it near the treatment table. The cart was stocked with items they might need easy access to in an emergency such as syringes, needles, blood pressure monitors, and a suction unit for blood or air in the thorax. It was also stocked with emergency drugs that may be needed if the patient went into cardiac arrest or had fluid in its lungs.

Their new high-school co-op student, Mel, had been cleaning the kennels. Jenny pointed to the shelf above the sink cabinet. "Mel, grab that package of gauze from the shelf over there."

Heidi showed Mel where the bandaging materials were kept. "Blue's just a small Jack right?"

"Yup. Big dog little dog."

Louise removed the packaging from a bag of IV fluids. "Let's get set up for IV and radiographs."

Heidi answered from the X-ray room. "Way ahead of you."

Melanie deposited the gauze squares in front of Jenny. "What's big dog little dog?"

Jenny produced a calculator from her pocket. She calculated the shock dose of fluids for a dog Blue's size. "When a larger dog attacks a small dog, they'll grab them by the back of the neck or right on the back. They sink their teeth in and shake the little dog. It can be pretty devastating. Besides the puncture wounds, the shaking can cause internal injuries."

Mel's skin paled. She leaned on the counter. "That's awful."

Louise retrieved a stool and motioned for Mel to sit. "Are you okay? If you're feeling light headed or sick, don't be embarrassed to sit for a few minutes. We don't need anyone fainting on us. One emergency at a time."

Mel sat. "Thanks."

Jenny shuffled through the medication drawer. "Has anyone seen the Lidocaine?"

Heidi had finished inputting Blue's data in the X-ray computer and was now drawing medication from a brown glass bottle into a syringe. "Yes, sorry. I grabbed it when you had your back turned." She dropped two small syringes labeled "Lidocaine - Brown" on to the emergency cart.

As Jenny and Heidi completed their preparations, Mary arrived with Blue. He lay quietly in her arms, wrapped in a towel. "He doesn't seem to be bleeding."

Louise checked his gum color and listened to his heart and lungs with her stethoscope. "That's a plus, Mary, but I'm concerned about internal injuries."

Mary placed Blue on the examination table. Jenny checked his vital signs, noting her findings on Blue's chart. Heidi placed an IV catheter and connected it to a bag of Lactated Ringers to support his circulatory system and allow quick access of any medications that might be needed.

Satisfied that Blue was stable, Louise made her way to the exam room to speak with Mr. and Mrs. Brown.

When Louise entered the room, Mrs. Brown rose from her seat and clasped her hands together. "Dr. Miller, how is he? It happened so fast. That big dog came out of nowhere and grabbed him."

Louise wrapped her arm around Mrs. Brown's shoulders. "We've stabilized him. We'll need to take X-rays to look for fluid in his chest or abdomen and to make sure there are no broken bones." Louise removed her arm and motioned for Mrs. Brown to sit down. "Are you okay with us going ahead with that? I hate talking finances at a time like this, but I'll need to have Rita come in and go over a quote with you."

Mr. Brown dabbed his eyes with a handkerchief. "Doc, do what you have to do. You've taken care of Blue since he was a puppy. We know you'll do what's best for him."

"That I will," Louise assured them. She was very fond of the Browns and Blue. *God, please be with them, and Blue.*

After letting Heidi know that it was okay to proceed with radiographs, Louise started up the stairs to her office. Realizing that she hadn't made it to the second floor yet that morning, she returned to the clinic's back door to retrieve her bag and no-longer-hot coffee. After bending over to pick up the bag, she turned towards the stairs. She gasped and jumped back, coffee sloshing through the small hole in the top of the cup. "Rita, what are you doing sneaking around?"

Rita, who had been descending the stairs, joined Louise at the base. "I'm not sneaking around. Mary buzzed up and said you needed me to go over a quote with Mr. and Mrs. Brown. I was on my down to do that, and to find Eric. He's supposed to be here by now, but no one's seen him yet this morning. I'll see if he's helping with Blue before I go in with the Browns."

Louise shook her head and slung her bag over her shoulder. "You can try Rita, but I was just in there. I didn't see Eric."

"You didn't see me either a minute ago."

"That's true. My mind was on something else. But you know, it is dark in this corner. Maybe we need better lighting."

"Maybe you need better glasses?"

"I don't wear glasses."

Rita smirked. "Maybe you should?"

Louise frowned. "Maybe you should go find Eric?"

Rita left Louise standing near the back door. Where was Eric now? Late again? The back door opened. Expecting to see their young technician walking through the door, she sighed with relief. Her relief was short-lived when Alex appeared.

Louise returned her bag to the floor. "What are you doing here? Is something wrong?"

Alex picked up her bag. "Are you just getting in?"

She stared at him, her forehead wrinkled. "No. We had an emergency. What's up?"

He shifted the weight of the bag in his hand. "We need to talk. In private. Can we go to your office?"

"Bob's up there." Louise glanced over her shoulder. "We can talk here. Everybody's busy."

"You were telling me yesterday about a man you and Daphne met at the dog show Saturday."

"Yes, Cliff. Mariner, I think his last name was. Really nice fella. What about him?"

Alex rubbed his chin and inhaled. "He was found dead this morning in the NKC headquarters."

Louise sank onto the step behind her. Dogs barked in the kennel room. "Dead? Really? That's so sad. Was it a heart attack?"

Alex sat beside her and lowered his voice. "No. He was murdered. It might have been a robbery gone bad. We're still investigating."

Louise eyes widened. Her mouth felt dry and she sipped the cold coffee. "That's horrible. He was such a sweet man. Who would do such a thing?"

Alex glanced up the stairs and down the hall. "That's why I'm here. We have a couple of suspects. The owner of the building gave us the video from the outside security cameras. Mr. Mariner could be seen entering the building a little after nine pm. A couple of other men went into the building that night around the same time, but we don't have a clear view of their faces."

Louise dabbed her eyes. "How can I help?"

Alex leaned closer and lowered his voice. "Two other people appeared on the video tape around the same time."

Louise gazed at Alex. She sniffled. "And?"

"One of those two people was Eric. The other is one of his old buddies."

Louise's heart rate increased. Her hands shook. "What would Eric be doing there?"

"That's what I need to know. Is he here?"

Louise shook her head. "No."

"Where is he?"

The grip Louise had on the coffee cup loosened. Coffee dripped onto her shoe. "I don't know."

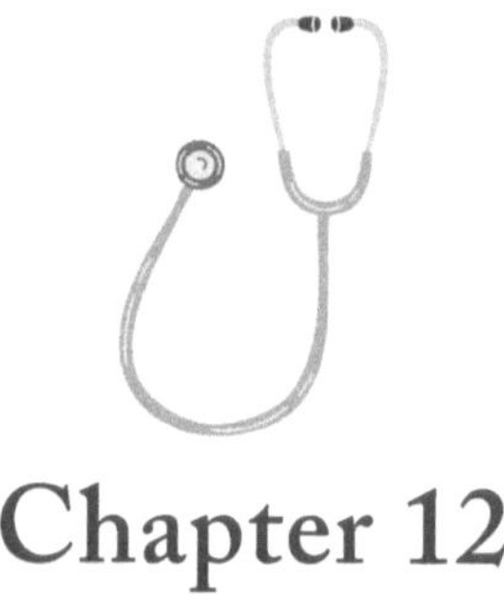

Chapter 12

"PANS. WAKE UP." Her father's voice roused Pansy from a deep sleep. "Mommy's not well. I need to take her to the hospital."

Seven-year-old Pansy forced her feet over the side of the bed. She rubbed her eyes. "What's wrong, Daddy?"

"Listen to me, Pansy. Mommy's had a bit of an episode. Auntie Quinn is coming over to sit with you and your sister."

"But today is my birthday. Will Mommy be home in time for my party?"

"Shoot," Pansy's dad muttered under his breath. "I don't know. Listen. You get up and get your little sister ready, okay?"

Sirens wailed outside.

Her father lifted her out of bed. He opened her dresser drawer and picked out a top and shorts for her. "Aunt Quinn will be here soon. You know the rule—no going into the kitchen when no adults are in the house."

When Pansy's little sister was a year old, her mother had taken the baby to an afternoon doctor's appointment and left six-year-old Pansy alone in the house. Pansy had stayed home from school that day because she had woken with a fever. Her mother didn't want to disturb her nap, so she decided to leave Pansy alone, sleeping in her bed.

Shortly after her mother left, Pansy woke up. Her fever was gone and, not having had breakfast, she was hungry. She decided to make herself some toast by placing a piece of bread on the stove top. Fortunately, a neighbor had heard the smoke alarm and was able to get the small fire under control. No one called the fire department or the police, since they didn't want to get Pansy's mother into trouble. Later that day, Pansy's parents showed her photos of what fire does to human skin, hoping to deter her from using the oven when she was alone. It worked. She never again went into the kitchen unless someone else was in there.

Pansy did as her father asked. After getting dressed, she woke her sister and got her ready for the day. A short time later her Aunt Quinn arrived with her cousin Blair. Pansy didn't enjoy being around Blair, as she was fond of picking on her younger cousins.

Pansy had spent that morning worrying about why her mother had to go off in an ambulance, but after lunch her mind turned to her party. Her friends were to arrive at two o'clock and stay until four. The plan was to order pizza at three, followed by cake and ice cream. Being shy in school,

Pansy only had a handful of friends, but she didn't care. They were good friends, and she always had a lot of fun with them. At two o'clock her friends started to arrive. Some of the parents looked a little shocked to see Aunt Quinn answering the door instead of Pansy's mother, but they didn't ask where Pansy's mother was. Maybe they were afraid of upsetting the birthday girl.

Pansy remembered that birthday well. Not because of the presents or games, or because of the pizza or the cake. What she always remembered when she thought of that day was what her Aunt Quinn did to ruin her party.

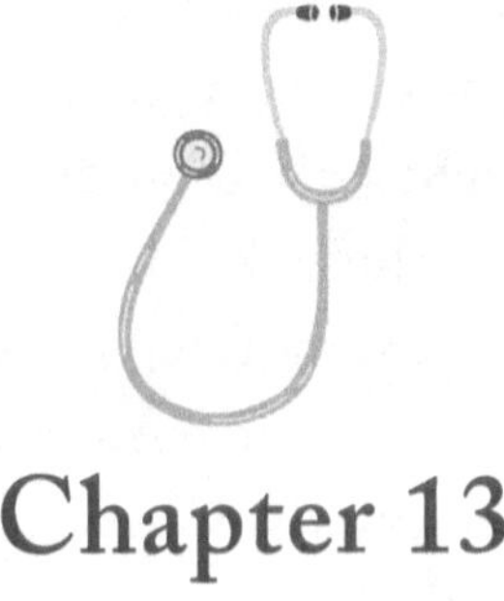

Chapter 13

LOUISE MINDLESSLY FANNED the stack of papers in her hand while she glanced out the window of the room that they were converting into a lab for the breeding program. She frowned. Another day of dark clouds and unyielding rain. The weather matched her mood. She was overjoyed by the birth of Ben, but the good news had been overshadowed by the death of a new acquaintance, not to mention their missing employee. Every morning for nearly two weeks Louise had driven by Eric's apartment building hoping to see his car in the parking lot. It was foolish. If he was okay, he'd call. If not, he wouldn't likely return to his apartment.

She wanted to help find him, but Alex discouraged her involvement. He evaded her questions, only assured her they were doing everything they could to find the young man. *Sure you are. Because you think he's involved in a murder.*

In the meantime, Louise was trying to keep busy. She'd been reluctant to welcome a breeding program into the clinic, but after consulting with Daphne, they felt that introducing a new service might be a good distraction for the staff. They hadn't thought it through. Their goal had been to take everyone's mind off a missing Eric, but with a new service, a missing staff member was more obvious and added to everyone's stress. It had been exactly twelve days since Alex told her about the death of Cliff Mariner, and in that time, no one at the clinic had heard from Eric.

Louise returned her attention to the small stack of receipts in her hand. One was for four small liquid nitrogen tanks. Another for fifty artificial insemination kits for dogs. There were various receipts for other supplies and several for semen samples.

"Mary told me I'd find you in here."

Louise dropped the papers onto the counter and turned around. It wasn't her imagination. "What are you doing here?" She held out her arms. "Do you have my new little godson with you? I could use a Ben hug."

Daphne hugged Louise. "Sorry, you'll have to do with a Daphne hug today. Ben's at home with Joe."

"Oh well. I guess that'll do for now. Are you sticking around for a while?"

Daphne pulled a bar-chair out from the counter and sat down. "Yes, I am. I'm back to work."

Louise gave her a playful slap on the shoulder. "Sure you

are. After all, you've had a *whole* two weeks off already. That's plenty of time to recover from having a baby."

"For me it is. After Ella was born, I was restless being at home for so long. I love being a mom, but I also love being a vet. I can do both. Besides, Joe is a natural stay-at-home dad. He loves it."

"This doesn't have anything to do with all the craziness that's been going on, does it?"

Daphne tilted her head. "Of course it does. Any news on Eric?"

Louise picked up the papers she'd set down earlier, rolled them into a cylinder, and tapped the counter. "None. I'm so worried about him."

Daphne nodded. "We all are."

"I don't believe he's involved with what happened to Cliff, but..."

"I don't believe it either. They must have other suspects. Has Alex said anything?"

"No. He's pretty tight lipped."

Daphne sighed. "I guess we'll have to leave it to the police. Alex will find Eric."

"I hope so."

Daphne scanned the room. Louise followed her gaze. The liquid nitrogen tanks were lined up on the floor. One was already in use. A small fridge had been installed in the far corner. Daphne retrieved a small box from the counter and examined the contents. "I see things are rapidly progressing here." She removed a package of vials from the box and placed it on the counter.

"They are." Louise handed Daphne the receipts. "I was just looking at these. We've used a lot of supplies already, and we're only a week into the program. Mary tells me that Bob has had appointments every day with people wanting to breed their dogs."

"I'm sure he had several contacts he would have gotten in touch with as soon as we gave him the green light to set up."

"True. I still wonder why we need AI in dogs at all." Louise circled the room, peering into the boxes and tanks. "Why not let nature takes its course? Lots of dogs in shelters need a home. They don't need to be purebred to be great pets. And all these new fancy-named mixed breeds people are shelling big money out for? Drives me crazy. They pay thousands for a mixed-breed dog, then grumble when we want to charge for our services to keep the poor dog healthy."

Daphne smiled. "Go on any rants lately?"

Louise laughed. "Sorry. Pet peeve territory."

"I understand what you're saying, but remember, we aren't talking about backyard breeders or puppy mills, we're talking about established breeders who want our help producing healthy puppies."

"Some breeds have so many defects it turns my stomach."

"True, but as we've discussed, this is an opportunity to educate new breeders about genetic diseases and how to screen for them. Every industry has its good and bad, so why not help those who are striving for quality over quantity?"

"I hate it when you get all logical on me."

Daphne opened another box and removed the stuffing, followed by a package of yellow plastic tubes. "What are these for?"

Louise eyed the package. "No idea. Heidi has been helping Bob get the lab set up. My only involvement has been to name this area the AI room."

Daphne placed the package back into its cardboard container. "Glad to see you are on top of things." She laughed then rose to her feet. "Let's go over to the office. The chairs in there are far more comfortable."

Before following Daphne across the hall, Louise snuck a peak out the window at the parking lot, hoping to see Eric's car. It wasn't there. She ambled across the hall to the doctors' office and poured herself a coffee before slumping into her chair.

Daphne turned on her computer. "Remember what Cliff had been telling us about DNA testing? We should look into that. Maybe we can offer the service here. I wonder what lab the NKC sends their samples too?"

Louise left her desk to stick her head out into the hall. Rita's office door was closed. Louise closed the door to their office and dragged her chair closer to Daphne's desk. "Speaking of the NKC, I was thinking of paying their offices a visit."

"Are they open again?"

Louise bit her lower lip. "No."

Daphne lifted her shoulders. "Then why go there?"

"In case the police missed something. I just want to look around."

Daphne slapped her hand to her head. "You want to look around a crime scene? You're not serious. Wouldn't that be dangerous? And possibly illegal? How would you get in?"

Louise held a finger to her lips. "Shh." She leaned in closer and lowered her voice. "Remember what Cliff said about the broken lock?"

Daphne's eyes widened. "You *are* serious? No. This is crazy. You can't go over there."

"Well, I am. And I'd appreciate it if you kept this to yourself. I don't need Alex interfering."

Daphne jumped up. "You're not going alone. I'm going too."

Louise motioned for Daphne to return to her seat. "Sit down. I'm not going now. And no, you're not coming along. It's too dangerous."

"You just said it wasn't dangerous."

"No I didn't. I simply ignored your comment about it being dangerous. Of course it's dangerous, but I have to find out what happened to Eric."

"Either I join you, or I tell Alex. You're choice."

Louise sighed. "Fine, but you stay in the car. We'll keep our phones on. You can let me know if anyone is approaching the building."

A loud crashing noise came from the hallway. When Louise opened the door, Bob was bent over a box, retrieving its contents from the floor and returning them to the box.

Louise stared at him. Had he overheard her conversation with Daphne? Is that why he dropped the box? "What happened here?"

Bob didn't meet her eyes. "Nothing. Clumsy me. Walking too fast." He shook his head and offered her a smile that looked forced. "Tripped over my own foot. I'd better get this stuff put away."

Louise furrowed her brow. "Sure. As long as everything's okay."

"It is. It is." Bob scurried into the new AI room. The door slammed behind him.

Louise closed the office door and scrunched her face. "I hope this new program isn't a mistake. We've been so busy that I haven't had a chance to really talk to Bob about it."

"Did you ask him about the incident at the dog show?"

Louise looked confused. "What incident?"

"Remember, the two fellas who were pushing him around?"

Louise had been removing her jacket from the hook on the door. She stopped, arm in air, and glanced at Daphne. "I'd completely forgotten about that with the baby and then Cliff and Eric." Lifting down the jacket, she reached into the pocket. "I've had so much on my mind." She produced a piece of paper. "Look, I even wrote down the license plate number of the vehicle they were driving. Part of it, anyway. ADS. I can't believe I forgot about that. Let's ask him about it now." Louise grabbed the door handle.

"Except that it's been two weeks and nothing has happened. Right?"

Louise returned the paper to the pocket and threw the jacket onto the back of her chair. "You're right. It was probably nothing." She grabbed a pad of paper and a pen from her desk before sitting next to Daphne's desk. "Let's work out the plan for tonight before my next appointment gets here."

Chapter 14

LOUISE HAD TOLD Daphne that she would pick her up at her home at 10 p.m. At 9:58 she stopped her car at the foot of Daphne and Joe's driveway. She removed her black toque and combed her hair with her fingers. What was she doing? Could they even get into the building that housed the NKC office? Would security or even the police be keeping an eye on the entrance? Alex had told her that there was video surveillance. Was it active? It had been two weeks since Cliff Mariner had been murdered, but it was still an active crime scene. Would the murderer, or murderers, return?

Louise returned the toque to her head. Taking Daphne into a potentially dangerous situation was not a good idea.

This was a task she'd need to take care of without her best friend. She grabbed her phone from the passenger seat and sent Daphne a message. "Changed my mind. See you tomorrow." It wasn't really a lie—she had changed her mind about taking Daphne with her. Visiting the crime scene was still in her plans.

Dressed in a black jacket and black pants to match her toque and gloves, Louise shifted the transmission to drive. After checking her mirrors for oncoming traffic, she pulled into the lane and drove past Daphne's home. The NKC office was on Main Street in downtown Riverview, a small city west of Amherst. It would take her twenty minutes to get there, giving her time to rethink her plan. She wouldn't have Daphne in the car acting as a look out, so she'd need to take extra care to keep out of sight when entering and exiting the building. If she saw a security guard, she'd abandon the plan and go home.

Traffic was light on the highway. Louise passed a couple of transport trucks and a police cruiser. When she saw the cruiser, her heart rate increased. She inhaled deeply and held her breath for a couple of seconds. Her heart rate returned to normal. The police officer didn't know what she was up to, but still she was relieved when the cruiser passed her and headed into the express lanes. Hers was the next exit. She switched on the right turn indicator and eased the car over to the off-ramp. The office building was visible from the highway. At fourteen stories, it was the tallest building in Riverview. The name of the building owner, Collins, was displayed below the roof line.

Appreciating the well-lit streets, Louise pulled into a spot in front of the Collins building. After shifting the car into park, she scanned the area. The street was deserted—a benefit of this being a business district. During the week, the same area would be flooded with cars and pedestrians.

Stopping short of opening the car door, she remembered the video camera. The toque wouldn't hide her face. Pressing her head against the head rest, she sighed. *Not even out of the car, and I've already blown it.* She was about to push the Start Engine button when she caught sight of a dark blue ball cap on the floor in front of the passenger seat. She smiled at the irony. It was Alex's hat. If he knew what she was up to he'd have a meltdown, but now he was, in a way, helping her. She retrieved the hat and put it on after throwing the toque into the back seat.

"Okay, Louise. You've come this far. Time to find some evidence to clear Eric. God bless him and protect him, wherever he is. And please protect me too. I can't believe I'm doing this, but…" As she exited the car, she glanced one direction then the other. The street was still quiet.

The outer walls of the building were made of gray concrete blocks. With no eye-level windows, the interior was not visible from the street. A stroke of luck for someone breaking in. A single glass door stood between Louise and the lobby.

She grasped the handle with her left hand and turned it counter-clockwise. It moved an inch. *Yes.* Only an inch. *Poo.* She leaned on the door. A click. The tension on the handle lightened and she was able to negotiate it to the open position. Louise inhaled deeply and gave the door a tug. It opened. The lock was still in disrepair as Cliff had told them. Louise smiled at the memory. At the time he had teased them about not using the information to break in. She had laughed, but now she was indeed breaking in. *I didn't promise you I wouldn't break in, Cliff. I simply expressed my doubt that I'd ever have the need to. I was wrong.*

She glanced at the floor and shook her head. *You didn't deserve what happened to you.* The muscles in her shoulders tightened as she entered the lobby. How could anyone hurt a nice person like Cliff? Her hands closed into fists. There was already so much violence and crime in the world, and now it was invading her small community. *Stop. Getting mad doesn't help. You need a clear head.*

Louise didn't detect any sign of a security guard or police presence when she entered the lobby. *Maybe the police don't know the lock is broken? If the NKC rents, why would Tim Gates be in charge of fixing it?* She shook her head. *Not important right now.* She entered the elevator and pushed the button for the fifth floor.

When the doors opened on the designated floor, Louise hesitated. How many offices were on this floor? The NKC office was closed, but what about the other offices? She gripped the edge of the door to keep it from closing and peered into the hallway. No movement. No noise. As far as she could tell, she was alone.

On the wall across from her, a directory listed the businesses that were housed on the fifth floor, with arrows indicating in which direction a visitor should turn. Louise scanned the list. The NKC office was to the left. She headed that way and found the door, easy to spot near the end of the hallway. The yellow police tape with 'Crime Scene. Do Not Enter' was still stretched across the entrance. The crime unit had likely already dusted the door knob for prints, but she kept her gloves on in case they examined it again. Grasping the knob, she turned it. She was in luck. The door wasn't locked.

She inhaled deeply. Had she gotten lucky that the door to the office she needed to get into was unlocked, or was it possible that God was helping her? She glanced heavenward and mouthed the words *thank you*.

Not wanting to turn on the lights, Louise closed the door and retrieved a flashlight from her satchel. The room was small, but nicely decorated. A large mahogany desk sat to her right. To the left, mahogany book shelves covered the walls on either side of a window. An expensive Arabian rug partially covered the hardwood floors. Louise had seen similar rugs in one of the high-end furniture stores in Amherst that she had gone into after buying her house. She'd left without making any purchases, as the rugs—and everything else in the store—were beyond her budget. The pictures on the office walls appeared to be original oil paintings, not prints like Louise had in her office.

Behind the desk sat three four-drawer filing cabinets. Louise stepped around the desk, intending to check their contents. She lowered her flashlight and caught a glimpse of a white line on the floor. She followed the line of chalk as it curved, then led to a narrow, tubular shape. The flashlight slipped from her hand. It was the outline of a body. Cliff's body. Standing in the dark, she shivered. She was standing in the very spot where Cliff had been murdered.

A few deep breaths later, Louise composed herself and located the flashlight with her foot. She bent down to pick it up. The light was directed towards the filing cabinets, drawing her eyes to the corner of a piece of paper sticking out beneath one of the cabinets. Placing her index finger on it, she pulled it out. Water had damaged part of it and some of the contents had been blacked out with a marker. Louise could make out partial words only: ipment and razi. *What does that mean?* At the bottom she could make out: $100. It was an invoice. There was a red smudge on one corner. *Is that blood?*

Keys rattled in the hallway. Louise froze and held her breath to settle her drumming heart. She needed to hide. She scurried under the desk and, after scrunching the document, shoved it in her pocket. She braced herself for the inevitable—the swinging open of the door and someone finding her hiding beneath the desk. Would it be a security guard? The police? The murderers?

Louise pulled her knees close to her chest and concentrated on being quiet.

Chapter 15

"WHAT HAPPENED TO you last night? Where were you?"

Louise, who had been setting up the coffee maker, spun around. Daphne stood in the doorway to their office, arms crossed. Louise swallowed hard. "Didn't you get my text?"

Daphne headed to her desk. She removed her jacket and placed it over her chair, then eyed Louise as she sat down. "The…'I changed my mind' text? Yes. I got it. I didn't believe it, so I tried to call you. You didn't answer."

Louise studied the ceiling. "I was driving."

"You have hands free, Bluetooth, call display, et cetera. I think you could have answered. You went to the NKC office without me, didn't you?"

Louise flopped onto her desk chair. "Yes. I couldn't take you with me. What if something had happened?"

"What if something had happened to you and no one knew you were there?"

"Well. It didn't. It was close, but I was fine."

"What do you mean *close*?"

"I almost got caught. A security guard was doing his rounds. I heard him in the hall and hid. No worries. He didn't even come into the office, so I was able to get out undetected. I'll be more careful next time."

Daphne rose to her feet. "What do you mean *next time*?"

The intercom buzzed, and Louise tapped the speaker button. Some kind of commotion in the background made it difficult to hear Mary clearly. "You might want to come to the front office. We have a bit of a situation here."

Louise glanced sideways at Daphne and shrugged. "We'd better see what's up." Thankful for the reprieve, she raced out of the office.

Daphne followed. "This conversation isn't over."

Louise and Daphne hurried to the main floor of the clinic. When they turned the corner into the front office, a fiery-eyed woman in a white polyester sports jacket with matching white pants stood at the front counter. She looked as though she'd stolen a costume from the TV show *Miami Vice*. The snowbird wannabe was sticking a pale, wrinkled index finger into Shirley's face. Shirley, a sweet person who always strived to offer their clients the best service possible, stared at the woman, eyes wide and hands shaking. Mary, who normally had no patience for bad behavior, sat at the desk, her mouth agape.

The woman leaned closer to Shirley. "You had better just know lady that you clearly don't know who you are speaking to. If I want to go past those doors I will do so whenever I wish. How dare you tell me I'm not allowed?"

The woman looked familiar, but Louise wasn't sure where she'd seen her. She marched into the waiting room. "I don't know who you are either. What is going on here?" In the past Louise's natural response to someone treating her staff in such a manner would have been to ask the person to leave the clinic. However, she was learning patience and diplomacy when dealing with difficult people, because it was impossible to avoid such characters when running a business.

The woman, her face as red as the bright red nail polish that matched her bright red lipstick, glared at Louise with squinted eyes, her lips pursed. "I'm Nancy Wells. I'm here to see Dr. Kurt about my dog Scarlet. This person here tells me that I cannot go back to see him."

Ah. The memory flooded back. Louise glanced at Daphne. Did she recognize the woman? She could see from Daphne's expression that she did. It was the woman from the dog show who had accosted Cliff Mariner.

Louise moved closer to Shirley. "First off…" Louise sent an 'I look out for my staff' smile to Shirley, "*this person* has a name. Shirley, and it's her job to keep people from going into the back of the clinic without supervision. It's a matter of security and privacy for everyone involved. If you need to see Dr. Kurt, I'm sure that Shirley or Mary would be happy to schedule you an appointment."

Nancy Wells shoved her hands onto her hips. "I don't have time for that. This is an emergency."

Louise glanced around the room. "An emergency? Where's the dog? In the car?"

Nancy's nostrils flared as she jerked her head sideways. "I don't have time for this chit chat either. Who are you anyway? I need to talk to Bob. He'll know what this is about."

Louise tapped her name tag. "Who am I? I'm Dr. Louise Miller. My colleague here, Dr. Daphne Carling, and I own the Black Creek Animal Hospital. Now, you said that you have an emergency with your dog. Generally when there's an emergency people either call ahead, or they at least bring the dog with them. Did you forget Scarlet at home?" The question might increase the woman's ire, but it would also ease Shirley's tension. She stole a glance at Shirley. It worked. Shirley was smiling.

Nancy started towards the exam room. "It's not that kind of emergency. Where's Bob?"

Louise relaxed her shoulder muscles. The emergency didn't involve the well-being of the dog. "Like your dog, Dr. Kurt is not here right now,"

Daphne, who had been quietly standing beside Louise, let out a little snorting laugh, covered her mouth, and retreated to the treatment area. Louise pressed her lips together, suppressing her own amusement at Daphne's reaction. While many people found Louise somewhat witty, Daphne often burst into uncontrollable giggles at a comment Louise had made. That was one of the many things that Louise appreciated about their friendship. Who wouldn't like to be around someone who appreciated your odd sense of humor?

Nancy scowled. "There's no need to be rude."

Louise stepped closer to Nancy and spoke softly. "I completely agree, so if you'd like to be civil, I'd be happy to start over and discuss the emergency you are having with your dog. If the dog is sick, we will gladly have a look at her this morning."

Nancy threw her hands in the air. "I'll call Bob on his cell.

I thought he was supposed to be here on Tuesdays—that's why I stopped in."

"He was, but now that Dr. Carling is back, he'll only be here four days a week. He's off today, but in tomorrow." Mary offered the information in a friendly voice, only to be met by a cold, angry stare from Nancy.

Louise clapped her hands. "There you have it, Ms. Wells. You're welcome to make an appointment with Dr. Kurt for tomorrow, since it's not a real emergency."

Nancy flung her purse under her arm. "That won't be necessary. I'll call Bob and we'll get this all sorted out. You'll see." Nancy spun around and stomped out of the clinic.

Louise pressed a hand to her forehead. "Wow."

Mary shook her head. "I agree. Wow."

Louise was happy for the interruption to her earlier conversation with Daphne. Now they had a new topic of conversation. Who was this woman? She had been livid with Cliff at the dog show. Did she follow-up her rant with something more sinister? And what, exactly, was her relationship to Bob?

Chapter 16

LOUISE AND DAPHNE had agreed not to bother Bob on his day off, but when the next morning rolled around, Louise was eager to talk to him about Nancy Wells. Upon arriving at the clinic, she went directly to her office, assuming that Bob would be there. He wasn't. She did find Rita waiting for her.

Rita rose from Louise's desk. "I knew this AI stuff was going to bring trouble."

Louise scratched her head. What could be bothering Rita? There had been a few small bumps, but those were expected with any new program. Rita knew that.

Louise removed her jacket and hung it up. As she did every morning, she passed her desk and went straight to the coffee maker to put on a fresh pot. "Come on, Rita. I was hesitant myself at first, but so far there haven't been any real issues. Sure, a lost slide here, a little misplaced sperm there, but nothing serious. We found everything, and Molly Begley will be having her pregnancy ultrasound in a couple of weeks."

Rita plucked a file folder from the top of a pile on Louise's desk. "Ha. Ha. Very funny. And the slides weren't lost. I put them in the sharps container because they had been left unattended in the pharmacy area. They should have been upstairs in the lab."

"Yes, they should have been, but as Heidi was heading upstairs she was called into the treatment area to help with an emergency."

Rita ran the toe of her grey runners over the floor. "I know that now."

Louise sat at her desk and turned on the computer. "That's not what you're upset about, is it? It all worked out. Luckily Molly was still in the clinic, and we were able to get another swab for cytology. Once we knew she was ready for breeding, everything went smoothly after that."

Rita plopped down on Daphne's chair. "No, that's not it. You're right, Molly is fine. I did a follow-up call with the Begleys yesterday, and they said that she is doing well. They're very excited about the possibility of pups, as they'd been trying for so long. Not just with Molly, but with two of their other Springer spaniels."

"Glad to hear it. They're a really nice couple. I do have to admit that Bob has brought a few A-plus clients to the practice." Rita frowned, and Louise tilted her head. "What's up?"

Rita removed an inventory list from the file in her hand and, after setting it in front of Louise, pointed to the middle of the page. "See here? It says we should be getting six vials in today from England, but there are eight vials in the canister that arrived this morning."

Louise scanned the document. "Probably a typo. Or maybe six Canadian is eight British?" She laughed at her own joke.

Rita didn't laugh. She snatched the document off the desk. "That's what I thought last week when we received two more vials than we should have. Now it's happened again."

Louise glanced at her schedule on the computer monitor. Her first appointment was in ten minutes and she hadn't had a chance to talk to Bob yet. *Where is he, anyway?*

Before Louise could respond to Rita, Heidi entered the office. "Did I hear you talking about extra vials? That's weird that it's happened again. When I mentioned the extra vials to Bob last week he said that he'd check into it. Later he told me that he recounted and only found the six that we had ordered. I thought that was odd, because I learned to count long ago, but when I checked again later, there were only six."

Rita shook her head. "There were six in the canister, but after you had told me about the mix-up, I found two vials in the vaccine fridge in one of the exam rooms." She turned her gaze to Louise. "I assumed then that we had a typo, but this is now the second time the numbers are wrong. It can't be a typo again."

Louise furrowed her brow. "Why were there semen vials in the vaccine fridge?"

Rita gathered her other files from Louise's desk. "I thought that was odd too, so I asked Bob about it. I wondered if there was an insemination appointment that hadn't made it onto the schedule. He was in the AI lab when I approached him. I must have startled him, because boy, did he jump."

Heidi laughed. "He is a bit jumpy sometimes. Ever walk into a room when he's on his phone? Acts all paranoid."

Louise frowned, her suspicious nature kicking in again. The altercation she'd witnessed between Bob and those two men at the dog show drifted through her mind. "Did he have an explanation?"

Rita shrugged. "Sure, he always has an explanation for the things he does. He said he forgot they were in his pocket until he was heading into an appointment, so he popped them into the fridge. Guess he forgot they were there until I called him about it the next day."

Louise rose and made her way to the coffee pot. Bending down, she opened the small fridge to retrieve the milk. "It's a good thing all that time in his pocket didn't ruin the semen."

Grasping the container, she turned back to face Rita and Heidi and jumped, spilling drops of hot coffee onto her hand. She set her cup down and shook the assaulted hand. "Bob! Good morning." *How long was he was standing there?* "We were just talking about you." *Better to admit that it in case he thinks we're gossiping about him.* They hadn't said anything wrong, but she still felt uneasy because this was the first that she had heard that he'd been pocketing the semen vials. Someone with his experience in artificial insemination should know better than to do something so careless. She wanted to ask him right then and there why he'd do it, but it was better to wait until no other staff were present. For now she'd stick with the other questions she had for him. The ones about Nancy Wells.

"How was your day yesterday? Did you get any interesting phone calls?"

Bob grinned. "Yes, sorry. I should have warned you about Nancy. She's well respected in breeding circles and her dogs are top of the line, but she is a bit... how do I say it?"

Louise retrieved her coffee mug and sipped at the hot liquid. "No need to say it, Bob. We met her yesterday."

Heidi stepped to her left to let Bob farther into the office. "What was her big emergency?"

Bob shifted his weight and cleared his throat. "Oh, no big deal. She thinks everything's a big emergency."

Louise pursed her lips. *Why would such an innocent question warrant such an uneasy response?* Louise studied Bob's face for a clue but saw nothing.

Bob sat at Daphne's desk and pulled up the appointment schedule. "One of her neighbor's dogs got into the yard with a female of Nancy's. Nancy was worried about mongrel pups, but it turned out not to be an issue because the female wasn't in heat. I calmed her down." He tapped the computer monitor with his finger. "Look at that. Busy day. Better get started." He rose, then grabbed his lab coat and stethoscope from the hook on the door. "I suspect my first appointment is here." Bob made a quick exit.

Rita sat at Daphne's desk and stared at Louise. "If the dog is not in heat, there's no risk of pregnancy. Wouldn't you think that a breeder as experienced as this Nancy Wells is supposed to be would know that?"

Staring at the doorway, Louise grabbed a paper towel and wiped her hand. "Yes, I would definitely think that."

Chapter 17

AT THE END of Louise's shift, her clients and patients taken care of, she scrambled to get to the grocery store. Prior to the excitement of the past few weeks, she had invited Alex, Daphne, and Joe for dinner on this particular evening. She had forgotten about the invitation until Daphne mentioned the need to arrange a babysitter for Ella and Ben. Louise didn't want to cancel on her friends, but did she have anything to serve her guests? She didn't know if she had enough food to feed herself.

She had forgotten to shop on the weekend, and when she arrived at the grocery store, it seemed that she wasn't the only one. The aisles were bustling with families, seniors, and a few other single adults who were rushing about as though they were also expecting company that evening. Not having a list, Louise scurried up and down the aisles randomly plucking items that looked interesting from the shelves. Once her cart was full, she headed to the checkout where she was met by long line-ups.

Louise waited patiently for her turn to pay for her items, then packed them up and bolted for her car only to be stopped by a client. A six-and-a-half-foot tall, husky man with a full beard and a bandanna on his head swung his tree-trunk leg over his motorcycle, stood, and waved. "Dr. Miller. How are you?"

Louise sighed internally, but smiled outwardly. "Mr. Candor, hello. I'm fine. How are you? And how's Mr. Muggles?"

As she approached him, Mr. Candor extended his hand. "I'm good. So's the little guy. I think he's lots happier without all those rotten teeth. I didn't know it was so bad."

Louise shook Mr. Candor's hand. "It's amazing how much discomfort dogs and cats will live with."

Mr. Candor removed his keys from the ignition. "I can't tell you how grateful I am. I'm not so sure Mr. Muggles will show his gratitude next time he sees you. He's only got the one tooth left after the dentistry, but that silly chihuahua still thinks he's a tough guy."

Louise shifted the bag she was holding from one hand to the other. "I'm sure you're right, but let's keep the fact that he's harmless now our little secret. We don't want to hurt his pride."

Mr. Candor threw his head back and let out a belly laugh Santa Claus would have envied. "Can I help you with those groceries?"

"No. Thank you, though. My car is right over there." Louise motioned to the car with her head. "I'm sorry to have to rush off, but I'd better get going. I have company coming. It was nice seeing you."

"You too, Doctor. And thanks again."

After shaking Mr. Candor's hand, Louise dashed for her car. Before she reached it, a white van parked two lanes over drew her attention. It looked familiar. Was it the one she'd seen at the dog show? She opened her hatch, frantically unloaded her shopping cart, then retrieved her phone from her bag, clicked on the camera app, and casually strolled past the door to her car. She stopped behind a black Ford Escort SUV parked kitty-corner to the van and peered around it. She didn't know who the men she'd seen shoving Bob that day were, and she didn't want them to see her poking around their vehicle. Unfortunately, she couldn't see the plate from that position. She straightened up and sauntered past the SUV. She caught her breath. The plate read ADST 289. The first three letters matched. Why did it matter? She rubbed the back of her neck. The opportunity to ask Bob about the incident was long gone, but she snapped a photo of the plate and the van anyway. She may need it later.

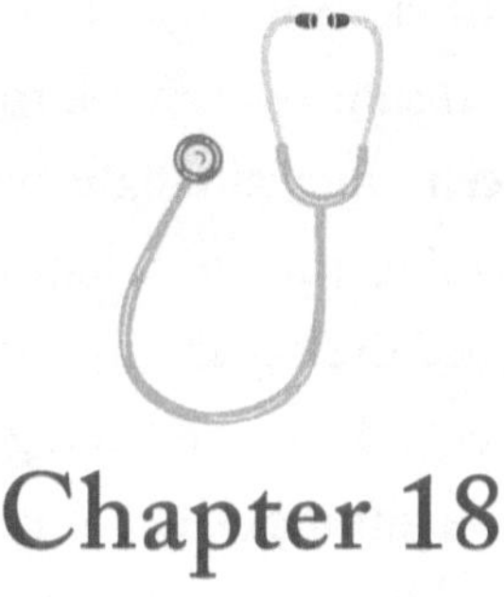

Chapter 18

LOUISE'S HOUSE WAS a traditional two-storey brick nestled on the bank of the creek that ran through Coverdale. The house needed more renovations than she could handle with her busy work load, but she hadn't been able to resist buying it. She'd always wanted a home near water, and with the market the way it was at the time, it was too good a deal to pass up. Her realtor had advised her that the house would not be on the market long. Her home sat on a half of an acre of land that boasted a small wooded area and beautifully manicured gardens. When pulling into the driveway, visitors were treated to a visual delight created by a rock-bordered garden overflowing with hostas, petunias, various annuals, and a large pine tree that leaned to the north. Louise didn't know if the angle of the tree was something to be concerned about, but it wasn't leaning towards the house, so she chose not to worry about it. The driveway was constructed from the same red bricks as the house. As she drove up it, she noticed weeds poking between the bricks and sighed. They weren't too high yet—perhaps she'd find time next week to remove them.

The traffic had been unusually light on her way home, but Louise was still unloading the car when Alex pulled into the driveway. Louise plopped the bag she had been holding back into the trunk, then watched as he parked and got out of his car.

"Perfect timing." Grinning, she pointed to the bags before heading to the house. *Feminism is over-rated.*

After retrieving the keys from her pocket, she unlocked the door and stepped in. The entryway opened to a small hallway. Louise had painted the walls a soft grey to complement the grey swirls in the vinyl plank floor that covered the entirety of the main floor. From her position in the hallway, she had a clear view of the kitchen to the left and the living room to the right. Between the two rooms a staircase led to the upper level that housed three bedrooms.

Louise made her way to the dining room through the living room, where she deposited her backpack and keys on a side table. She paused to admire the garden that was clearly visible through the window above the table. Then, remembering that her guests were due to arrive soon, she headed into the dining room where she gathered the plates, cups, and utensils she would need to entertain them.

The front door banged. Louise jumped. It was Alex, carrying all of the groceries. She met him in the kitchen.

"Thanks." She relieved him of two of the bags he was struggling to lift onto the counter.

Alex set the remaining four bags on the floor. "What is in here?"

Louise shoulder bumped him. "A few essentials. Milk, potatoes, ice cream."

"Ice cream is an essential?"

She lifted a container from one of the bags and spun toward the refrigerator. "When it's chocolate, it is."

Alex tugged a pack of frozen potato wedges from a bag. "Do you want any of this left out for tonight's dinner?"

Louise glanced at the clock. "I don't think I'll have time to cook dinner. Maybe we should order a pizza. What do you think?"

Alex held up two cans of peas. "You know I never say no to pizza, but what's all this food for if we're ordering out?"

Louise studied the cans in Alex's hands. "Peas? Daphne doesn't like peas." She clapped her hands. "Pizza it is."

"You're goofy."

"Thank you." She stuck the ice cream into the deep freezer, then nudged a few of the cans on the counter aside to make room for more. "This will all last. It's mainly cans and freezer foods. I still need to get changed. Do you mind calling PizzaLand?"

"Will do."

Louise left Alex to put away the groceries and order dinner while she changed out of her work clothes. When she returned to the living room, she found him stretched out on the sofa with Oscar sitting on his chest. They both had their eyes closed—Oscar's head raised in reaction to the massage Alex was giving him. Louise paused. A warm feeling grew in her chest. Her two favorite fellas.

The doorbell rang and Oscar jumped into the air. Alex groaned when the cat landed on him. Louise laughed.

Alex clasped his hand over his chest. "Not funny." He pulled out the neck of his dress shirt and glanced down. "He scratched me."

Louise stuck out her lower lip. "Poor baby. You'll live."

Alex laughed. "The little furball's lucky I'm so fond of him."

Louise headed to the front door. "That'll be Daphne and Joe. There are Band-Aids under the sink if you need one."

Once the pizza arrived, the two men loaded up their plates and headed into the dining room. Alone in the kitchen, Louise signalled for Daphne to join her at the kitchen table.

"I saw the van again."

Daphne placed a piece of pizza on her plate, then sat at the table. "Are we not eating with the fellas?" She bit into the pepperoni-laden slice. "Hmm. This is good. What van?"

"The one we saw at the dog show."

"Were those tough-looking guys around?"

Louise rose and helped herself to another slice and a can of pop. "No. I didn't see them, but the license plate was the same. I took a photo."

"Did you ever mention to Alex what happened that day?"

Louise shook her head. "No. With the excitement of the baby, it slipped my mind. When I remembered later, I didn't see the need to bother him about it. We don't know what it was all about."

Alex called from the dining room. "Are you two going to join us?"

Louise pushed her chair back and stood. "Guess we'd better keep them company."

She and Daphne gathered up their plates and drinks and headed into the dining room.

Joe pulled a chair out for Daphne. "Alex was telling me about a fire last night down at the docks."

Using his foot, Alex reached under the table and pushed an empty chair out. Louise eyed him playfully. He shrugged and grinned.

Louise positioned her dinner on the table, then sat in the proffered chair. "Was anyone hurt?"

Alex swallowed a bite of pizza. "No, thankfully. It was one of the long-abandoned warehouses—seemingly forgotten when the company that owned it went under. They've been used by homeless people, but with the good weather lately the building was empty at the time of the fire. There is evidence though that it had been used for other purposes." Alex waved his finger from Louise to Daphne. "I do need to talk to you two about it."

Louise excused herself and headed to the kitchen to get some napkins. When she walked into the room, she lifted a hand. "What would we know about goings on at an abandoned warehouse?"

"Probably nothing, but you will know about this." Alex removed a photo from his pocket and placed it on the table.

Louise glanced at it. "It's a picture of a pen. So?"

"Look closer."

Louise picked up the paper. Her eyes widened. She handed the photo to Daphne. Daphne set it on the table and tapped on it with her finger. "That's one of our pens."

Louise swung her gaze to meet Alex's. Where was this

going? "We have hundreds of those pens. We've been handing them out to clients for a couple of years."

Alex's eyes locked on hers. "I was concerned that the pen may have been left there by Eric."

Louise stiffened. "As I said, we've given out hundreds of them. It could have come from anyone. I'm sure clients leave them lying around and other people pick them up."

Daphne pressed her lips together and pushed the photo back to Louise. "Um. Look closer, Louise. This is one of the new pens. The color of the logo is wrong. We were going to return them, remember? We haven't given any of them away yet. The only people with access are you, me, and the staff."

Louise shoved her plate away, her appetite gone. Eric would have had access to the new pens. Had he been at the warehouse when the fire broke out? What would he be doing there? He used to spend time at the docks with his old crew, but he stopped hanging out with them after they duped him into being the get-away driver for their pharmacy break-in. That was years ago. Weren't the ring leaders still in jail? But Alex had said that Eric was with one of them the night Cliff was murdered. Louise surveyed her guests' faces. They all appeared to be as concerned as she was. No. She trusted Eric. He had never willingly broken the law, and she couldn't imagine he would now.

Louise returned her attention to Alex. "Eric's not the only one who would have had access to those pens. Bob might have taken one." Her voice rose and she waved her arm through the air as though warding off an invisible being. "He wouldn't have known we meant to return them. He probably used one, then passed it on to someone else."

Alex raised his hands. "Why would you suspect that your associate would be involved in burning down a warehouse?"

Louise stared at him, brow furrowed. "I said he may have passed it on to someone else. Besides, you have no more reason to suspect that Eric's involved than I do to suspect Bob might be."

"Eric has pulled a disappearing act. That's suspicious behavior."

Louise sighed. "It's *concerning*, yes, but we don't know where he is. He could be in trouble."

Daphne touched Louise's shoulder. "Tell him about the van. And what happened at the dog show."

Alex set his plate to one side, then folded his arms and leaned on the table. "What van? What happened at the dog show?"

Louise stood. "I need a coffee."

Alex followed her into the kitchen. "What is Daphne talking about?"

Louise took three cups out of the cupboard and filled them. "Bob was at the dog show. We didn't talk to him, but we saw him. A couple of guys were shoving him. I didn't see where Bob went afterwards, but I watched the other two guys after they went out to the parking lot. They got into a white van. I was going to tell you about it, but then Daphne went into labor and Cliff was killed." Louise bit her bottom lip. "I figured it was probably nothing, but now I'm wondering."

Louise handed one of the cups to Alex before carrying the other two into the dining room. After setting one in front of Joe, she returned to her seat. "That's not all that happened there. That breeder woman I told you about, the one that made a scene at the clinic? She was there and obviously upset with Cliff. And Tim Gates, the president of the NKC, was nasty to Cliff too. That's two people who were mean to Cliff the very day he was murdered. And we know that Nancy has a connection to Bob." Louise turned to Daphne. "I told you how nice Tim's office was, remember? Maybe he's up to something illegal. How else could he afford such décor? I looked him up on the Internet. He doesn't have another job. Just the NKC."

Alex rose, pressed his palms against the table, and bent closer to Louise. "Tim Gates has a nice office? How do you know that? When were you there?"

Louise swallowed hard. She'd said more than she'd meant too. "I stopped by the other night."

Alex wrinkled his brow. "You stopped by? You stopped by a crime scene?" His voice rose. "Why? How did you get in? And what were you doing there?"

Louise spun her plate in circles with her finger. "I wanted to see if there was something that could clear Eric as a suspect."

Alex shook his head. "Unbelievable. I'm not sure if I should be insulted that you don't trust me and my colleagues to do a thorough job or worried that you're going to get yourself into trouble." He dropped back onto his seat.

Louise stared at her plate. "Sorry. It's not that I don't trust the police. I have a lot of respect for your department, you know that, but I want to help Eric. Anyway, we had a plan."

Alex shot Daphne a look. "We? You didn't go too, did you? You're supposed to be the responsible one."

Louise crossed her arms. "Hey!"

Joe tossed the crust he'd been chewing onto his plate. "Daphne? You went to the NKC offices?"

Daphne shook her head. "No."

Joe exhaled loudly. "That's a relief."

"Louise didn't pick me up."

Joe rubbed his forehead, but before he could speak, Louise leapt from her seat and snatched up the bag she'd placed under the desk earlier.

She dug out a Ziploc bag that held a torn piece of paper and offered it to Alex. "Look at this. I do trust your department, but in this case, I think they may indeed have missed something."

Alex studied the partial document. "It looks like a receipt."

"That's what I thought." Louise pointed to the reddened corner. "And I think that might be blood."

Alex rubbed his chin. "I think you're right. Where did you find this?"

Louise rocked back on her heels. "Under a filing cabinet. I slipped it into the plastic bag in case there might be finger-prints or DNA evidence."

Alex stood. "Did you find anything else?"

Louise smirked. "No."

Alex sighed. "Well, you're right that Tim Gates doesn't make much money. You'll be happy to know that we have looked into him already. The person who finds the body is always a suspect. Other than some fancy furniture in his office, we haven't found anything suspicious."

Louise frowned. "He's been cleared already?"

Alex shoved the Ziploc bag into his coat pocket. "I didn't say that."

Daphne rose and drifted into the living room to make herself comfortable on the recliner. "Speaking of DNA, do you think someone might have been cheating the system and Cliff found out?"

Alex narrowed his eyes. "Cheating what system?"

Daphne pulled the lever to raise the chair's footrest. "Cliff told me that the NKC has fairly strict guidelines. To be certified with them, breeders have to prove the pedigree of their dogs with DNA testing, not just breeding certificates."

Louise narrowed her eyes. "Really?"

"Yes." Daphne frowned at Louise. "I didn't think you were listening at the time. Anyway, he told me that in the past some breeders would get their semen from sources akin to puppy mills, then present fake documents claiming that it came from champion dogs. Depending on the breed, the NKC rules dictate which diseases the breeding dogs must be screened for. Now that AI is so prevalent, and documents are so easy to forge, they had to come up with a more reliable way to ensure that the unscrupulous breeders weren't cheating the system."

Alex removed a notepad and pen from his pocket. He sat at the end of the couch, close to Daphne. "Why are they so worried about pedigree? A dog's a dog."

Daphne lowered the leg rest. "As Cliff explained, when a dog is registered with the NKC, the buyer of a pup can be assured that the pup's parents were screened for diseases that are common to that breed."

Joe sat beside Alex. "Then why would a breeder cheat? Following the rules means they will have healthy pups and happy clients."

Louise set a plate of cookies on the coffee table. "I suspect because semen from NKC-registered dogs is more expensive than it would be from non-registered dogs. Those receipts I was looking at the other day, Daphne, for the semen from England, indicated that they cost a thousand dollars per vial."

Daphne snagged a cookie. "I believe it. From what Cliff

told me, it can sometimes be more expensive than that. The NKC has offices in Canada, the US, and Europe. They have an international registry of canine DNA. Semen is shipped fairly regularly between countries."

Alex and Joe shook their heads simultaneously.

Daphne glanced at the clock on the wall. "We'd better get going, Joe." She held up the cookie in Louise's direction. "Our sitter needs to be home early tonight. She has an exam in the morning."

After seeing Daphne and Joe to their car, Louise and Alex deposited themselves on the porch off the kitchen. The sun was setting behind the pleated clouds—the sky reminded Louise of the remnants of a campfire after the flames were gone, but the wood still glowed red and orange. She loved this time of day, when the shifting clouds and setting sun worked together to demonstrate the beauty of God's creation. The effect was enhanced when the sun dipped closer to the horizon, the brilliant colors intensified behind the black silhouettes of the trees on the nearby hill.

Louise filled a glass from the pitcher of iced tea she'd brought outside. She handed it to Alex then poured a glass for herself.

Alex clinked his glass against hers. "Cheers."

"Cheers."

He leaned his head against the back of the chair and inhaled deeply. "The air this time of night is so fresh. So relaxing. So much nicer out here than in town. And so quiet."

Louise nodded. "I love it. I couldn't imagine moving back into town. You should get a place out here."

Alex emptied his glass and sat it on the arm of the Adirondack chair. "I think about that sometimes. About possibly making some changes. If we lived closer together, we could spend more time together."

Louise refilled his glass. "True. We'd still have to go into town to go to restaurants or movies, though. I guess we could carpool instead of meeting up. And you could come over after work and tell me about your cases."

Alex slumped his shoulders. "Sure. Or if we…"

Louise shifted on her chair to face him. "The talk about cheating on DNA testing and scamming the NKC has gotten me thinking about Nancy Wells."

Alex rubbed his forehead. "That's the breeder who made a scene at the clinic? You think she's scamming the NKC?"

"I don't know. After her appearance at the clinic, I did a little digging into her background. I checked out several kennel clubs and breeder sites on the web."

Alex shook his head. "Doing a little investigative work, are you? I really wish you'd call me when you have concerns about things. That is my job, you know."

Louise frowned. "At the time I thought she was merely a difficult client. It's only this evening that I'm wondering if she's up to something."

"Did you find anything interesting? Or helpful?"

Louise tugged a blanket free from the back of the chair and covered her shoulders. "No. Her website is basic breeder info. She's been breeding Spaniels for a few years. Most of her dogs are champions. There are loads of photos of the dogs, usually with Nancy or the judges. No other people in the pictures, though, which I did think was odd."

Alex tilted his head. "Why is that odd?"

"I don't know. Where are her family and friends? Her fellow breeders? I couldn't find any trace of her on any social media sites. That was odd too."

"Not everyone is internet friendly. She may not like computers."

"Maybe. I really hope she's not a scammer, but…"

"How could she scam the NKC if DNA tests are confirming the source of the semen?" Louise watched a dove land on the railing that wrapped around the veranda. It drew her attention to the chipped paint. "I don't know. I also found out today that Bob has been acting strangely, and that there has been more than one mix-up with our semen shipments."

Alex sighed. "Now you think your associate is scamming the NKC too?"

"I hope not, but why the bizarre behavior?"

Alex raised his empty glass. "What about the paperwork that comes with the shipments? The place of origin should be recorded on the shipping label."

Louise emptied the last of the iced tea into his glass. "You're right. It is. I was looking at Bob's records the other day. England is definitely recorded as the place of origin for all of the shipments we've received so far."

The paperwork might look okay, but something was amiss. How could she convince Alex that Nancy or Tim were more probable suspects for Cliff's murder than Eric? And what about the men from the van? What was their role in all this? Or were they simply a couple of guys that Bob cut off on the highway the day of the dog show? Road rage or conspiracy?

Her hand fell to the side of her chair. It brushed passed Alex's. His fingers slowly caressed hers. She started to pull away then stopped. Where was their relationship going?

Her stomach ached. She didn't want to risk the fun they had together. Romantic relationships were hard, and if they failed, the friendship would be lost. And worse, what if something horrible happened to him? She blocked out the terrifying thought. His skin felt soft against hers, and her anxiety lessoned as warmth filled her chest. She circled her index finger around his. Her phone buzzed.

Louise leapt to her feet. "Um. Who could that be? I'll… I'll be right back." She flew through the door and found her phone. A text from Jenny. Louise's heart sank. The screen door slammed. She turned to look at Alex, her knees weak.

He set the iced tea pitcher onto the counter. "Anything important?"

Louise scratched her head. "Jenny texted me. Her boyfriend Roger called her a few minutes ago. I think He works night shift at the docks. Eric's down there."

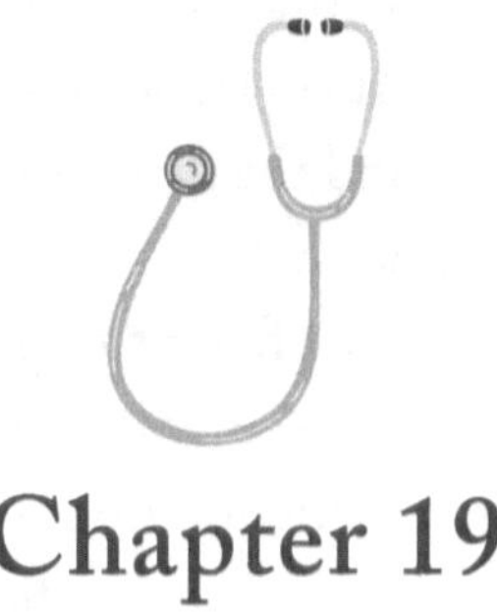

Chapter 19

IT WAS THAT time of year again. Pansy was happy that her mother seemed to be doing well. Mommy had been in the hospital for a few weeks after her sickness, but now she'd been home for months with no setbacks.

As Pansy headed out the door, her mother called to her from the kitchen. "Pansy, be sure to come straight home after school. We'll go shopping for your birthday dress tonight."

Pansy was so excited at the idea of shopping with her mother that she danced all the way to the school bus. The day seemed to last longer than other school days. Pansy had kept a close eye on the clock, but the hands moved as if they were stuck in molasses. When the final bell rang, Pansy raced to the bus stop. She studied the road to the right and to the left. Where was the bus? She jumped up and down as she watched for it. It appeared at its usual time, but young Pansy was sure it was late. No matter. It was here now. She found her seat and closed her eyes, willing the bus to fly to her house.

When the bus turned the corner onto Pansy's street, her excitement was dashed. An ambulance sat in the driveway. As soon as the bus stopped and the driver opened the door, Pansy sprinted to the front of her house.

Her father met her at the front stoop. He grabbed her arm and moved her away from the entrance. "Step aside, Pansy. You're in the way. The paramedics need to get by."

Paramedics? What was a paramedic? Pansy understood when she saw the two uniformed men from the ambulance wheel her mother by. They lifted the stretcher down the stairs, then headed for the ambulance. Pansy tried to follow, but her father held her in place.

Pansy's heart sank as she watched the two men lift her mother into the back of the ambulance. What was happening? Her mother was happy before she had left for school. Her mother wanted her to get home quick so that they could go shopping.

"Daddy, where are they taking Mommy? We're supposed to go shopping now. I came home right away so we could go. Didn't I get here fast enough?"

Her father crouched in front of her. "Hush up. We've no time for that now."

Pansy could smell that now familiar scent on his breath. She didn't know what it was, but he was like a different person when she smelled it. It made her sad.

Her father let go of her arm and nudged her into the house. "Go make sure your little sister is okay."

Pansy blinked away tears as she ran into the house. She could hear her little sister crying in their room. She rubbed her eyes with her fists and headed upstairs.

When Pansy opened the door, Li'l Sis ran to her. She threw her arms around Pansy's waist and held her tight. "Mommy's sick again."

Pansy rubbed the back of Li'l Sis' head. "Everything's okay." Pansy didn't know if everything was okay, but she had to say something. Her eyes felt heavy. She sniffled. It wouldn't be good to cry in front of Li'l Sis.

The two girls remained home alone for several hours. The sun got lower and lower in the sky and it started to get dark outside. Dinner time came and went. Pansy's stomach had started making noises earlier, but now it was achy. If she was hungry, Li'l Sis must be hungry too, but Pansy was terrified to go into the kitchen alone.

Li'l Sis, who had been sleeping on the couch, raised her head. "My tummy is hungry. Where's mommy?"

Pansy sat beside her little sister and hugged her tight. "Don't worry. I'll get us something." She stood and forced herself to walk toward the kitchen. She paused at the entryway. It didn't look so scary. Her mother let her get things out of the refrigerator sometimes. The stove and toaster were the problem. She wouldn't go near them. And besides, the rule was that she wasn't to go into the kitchen when she was home alone. Pansy shoved back her shoulders. She wasn't alone. Li'l Sis was with her.

Pansy found the peanut butter, jelly, and bread and made sandwiches for supper. After eating, she helped Li'l Sis into her pajamas and tucked her into bed. Pansy returned to the main level. The house was quiet. She checked the front and back doors. They were both locked. She turned on all of the lights, then sat on the couch and pulled her knees to her chin. Grabbing the blanket from the back of the couch, she covered her head and body. Her arms and legs trembled. She couldn't stop the tears this time, but it didn't matter. No one could hear her crying.

The door banged and someone yelled. Pansy's father. He yanked the blanket off of her and threw it across the room. It landed on the floor near the kitchen.

Her father scowled. "What are all these lights doing on? Can't I leave you alone for a few minutes?" He stumbled towards the front door and fell against the wall. He reached up and turned the light off. "Get to bed!"

The next morning Pansy rubbed her eyes against the bright sun shining into her bedroom. She heard a woman's voice. Hoping it was her mother, she bolted upright. The woman spoke again and her chin dropped to her chest. That was her Aunt Quinn's voice. The little remaining hope that her birthday party would still happen, even without a new dress, faded. It didn't matter. She didn't want a party anymore now that her aunt and her cousin Blair were there. Last year she'd had a party. Her friends all arrived on time, but Aunt Quinn had sent them home an hour later. She spent her birthday visiting her mother in the hospital. Is that what would happen this year?

The door to Pansy's room flung open. Aunt Quinn stood in the doorway, her arms crossed. "When are your friends arriving?"

Pansy was speechless. She stared at her aunt.

Aunt Quinn stepped into the room. "Well? I asked you a question. What's wrong with you this morning?"

Pansy's heart skipped a beat. Maybe she *would* get a birthday party. "At lunch time, 'cause it's Saturday."

"Fine." Aunt Quinn spun around and started towards the staircase. "I'll make some hot dogs." She paused and glanced over her shoulder. "How many kids?"

Pansy jumped out of bed and yanked open her dresser drawer. "We're having pizza this year. Mommy promised."

"Pizza's too expensive." Aunt Quinn scowled at Pansy.

Pansy leaned a hip against the dresser. "Oh." She fought the tears again. She didn't want Aunt Quinn to see her cry. Hot dogs would be fine if she got to see her friends. "Five friends."

"Get your sister dressed and get downstairs. And be quick about it." Aunt Quinn made her exit.

As the lunch hour approached, Pansy anxiously awaited the arrival of her friends, but no one knocked on the door. Aunt Quinn fed Li'l Sis and Blair. Pansy insisted on waiting for her guests. At two o'clock she had to admit to herself that they were not going to show up. She ran to her room, slammed the door, and crawled into the closet. The tears returned.

"I knew it." Her cousin Blair pushed her way into Pansy's room. "You don't have any friends. It's 'cause your folks are crazy."

Pansy leapt to her feet and threw the closet door open. She waved her fist at Blair. "They are not. You're just mean. I don't want you here."

From the corner of her eye she caught a glimpse through her open bedroom door of Aunt Quinn standing on the landing, eyes narrowed and lips turned down. "That's fine, young lady. You're as ungrateful as your parents. Come, Blair. We're going home."

Blair jerked her chin in the air and turned away from Pansy.

A familiar ache settled in Pansy's stomach. "I haven't eaten yet."

Aunt Quinn waved her hand in the air and started down the stairs. "Well, whose fault is that? I called you an hour ago for lunch and what did you do? You sat there by the door like a poor sad mongrel dog. Your father can feed you and your sister when he decides to drag himself home."

Pansy stood in silence watching her aunt and cousin put on their coats, pack up their belongings, and leave. The door slammed. She made her way downstairs. Li'l Sis had eaten lunch, so she didn't have to worry about that. She would cut them each a slice of birthday cake. She smiled at the idea. With no adults in the house, they could have as big a piece as they wanted.

Pansy found Li'l Sis sitting in the kitchen licking ketchup off a fork. "Do you want a piece of cake, sis?"

Li'l Sis set the fork down. "I do. What cake?"

Pansy ruffled her sister's hair. "My birthday cake, silly. I saw it in here earlier." She opened the fridge.

Li'l Sis shook her head. "No. No cake anymore. Auntie took it."

Pansy sank to the floor. This had to be the worst birthday ever. At least next year couldn't possibly be worse.

Chapter 20

LOUISE PUSHED THE end call button on her phone. She rested her elbows on the desk and closed her eyes. Daphne was going to be late. Ella had a cough and refused to allow Joe to administer the cough syrup. How did Daphne do it? Juggle work and family? The responsibilities of running a veterinary clinic gave Louise an occasional sleepless night. How did her colleagues with children find enough time in the day to take care of their family and work full time? How did they balance the worries of their personal lives with the worries of the work day?

After the text from Jenny last night, Alex had morphed into detective mode. He had called his office and asked them to send backup to the warehouse. Louise had frowned. Why would he need backup? What did he expect to find? It was Eric. Harmless Eric. Louise had followed Alex to his car, planning to accompany him to the docks, but he wouldn't allow it. It could be dangerous, he'd told her, but he promised to call her as soon as he had something to report.

When she had awoken on the couch that morning and realized she hadn't heard from him, she called his supervisor who assured her that Alex was fine. That was all the woman would tell her. It was now eight in the morning and he still hadn't called.

Where are you, Alex? Why haven't you called? Why won't they tell me anything?

Louise poured a second helping of coffee into her mug then dragged herself to the treatment room to assess the day ahead. Heidi and Jenny had already admitted several patients to the clinic.

Heidi was washing her hands. She tilted her head towards the smaller kennels. "We have a few admits this morning. We've just finished getting a recheck blood sample from Henry Shaw, the Persian in the cage over there." Heidi pointed to the line of cages near the entrance to the surgery suite. "Bob admitted him yesterday. Kidney failure."

Louise scanned the kennels. "And who is this handsome fellow?" She poked her finger between the metal bars of the cage to rub the chin of a long-haired orange tabby cat.

Heidi dried her hands with a towel before retrieving the cat's file for Louise. "His name is Snuggles Harris. He was transferred from the emergency clinic this morning after being admitted there overnight. He was blocked—poor cat couldn't pee. The transfer report says his bladder was huge on presentation and that his kidney values were up. The catheter was still in when he got here."

Louise opened the kennel door and cupped her hand under Snuggle's abdomen. "His bladder is empty. The catheter is patent." She scanned the file. "It says here he produced a normal amount of urine overnight, but I don't like the look of it. Too dilute. Let's get a blood sample and recheck his kidney values."

"Will do." Jenny made a note on the white board. The in-clinic patients were listed on the board, allowing the staff a quick reference to the diagnostics and treatments the doctors had ordered for them. "He's next on the list. We were going to get him out and flush the catheter. Do you want us to pull it?"

Louise shook her head. "No, not yet. Let's wait and get the blood work done first. If his kidneys are looking okay, we'll pull the catheter and monitor him through the day. Hopefully he can go home this evening. I'm sure his family is pretty worried about him."

Heidi retrieved a handful of vials from the cabinet above the sink. The lids were different colors to denote their purpose. Vials with white lids indicated a biochemistry profile. Those with red lids were for a CBC. "After Snuggles was admitted, the Henry's returned with coffee for everyone. Isn't that sweet?"

Louise forced a smile. "Sure is. Are there any surgeries today? I don't see any listed on the board."

Jenny handed her a clip-board that held the surgery check-in list. "We haven't had a chance to write them there yet. We have two cat neuters, one cat spay, and a hernia repair on a Norwegian elkhound. Pretty light."

Heidi slapped her forehead. "Great. You just jinxed us."

Jenny covered her mouth and giggled. "Oops, sorry. Especially when we're short two vets."

Louise snapped to attention. "Short two vets? Where's Bob?"

Jenny transported Snuggles to the treatment table. "He

hasn't come in yet. He's usually here before everyone else, but not today, and it's his surgery day."

Louise took a deep breath. Was it a coincidence that Bob was late the day after Eric was spotted at the docks? "Jenny, when Roger saw Eric last night, did they talk?"

Heidi inserted a needle with a Vacutainer into Snuggles' leg, then snapped on a white-capped vial. Once she had the sample she needed, she removed the needle, and Jenny applied pressure to the puncture site. "No. I don't think so. Roger said that Eric was talking to some woman. Roger didn't know who she was. He was going to go over and say hi until he noticed that the woman was crying."

Louise walked over to the treatment room sink and turned on the hot water. "What was he doing down there?"

Jenny returned Snuggles to his kennel. "He makes deliveries there a lot. Last night he had a delivery then he was going to meet up with a buddy who works in one of the factories near the docks. They get together at a sports bar when there's a game because they like to watch the big screen. His buddy never showed."

Louise put her hand under the water, then pulled it back. "Ouch!" She fanned her assaulted hand before turning on the cold water. "Not Roger. Eric. What was *Eric* doing down there?"

Jenny removed a Y-tube from a hook on the wall near the surgery suite and attached it to the anesthetic machine. "I don't know. Roger said once he realized his pal wasn't gonna' show up, he wasn't keen on sticking around too long. There's been a couple of shifty guys hanging around the docks the past few months. Word is they're the ones that burned down that warehouse. They were seen driving around in the same van that was parked outside the building the day of the fire."

Louise dug her phone from her pocket and opened the photo of the van. She held the phone up. "Is this it?"

Jenny tilted her head and squinted at the screen. "I don't know. I wasn't there."

Louise rubbed her forehead. "Right. Sorry. If I send this to you, can you forward it to Roger and ask if it looks like the same van?"

"Sure. If he saw it."

"Thanks." Louise sent the photo to Jenny.

Mary buzzed from the front office. "We have an emergency coming in. Old dog. Collapsed at her water bowl."

Louise sighed. "How far away are they?"

"They're in the parking lot—they didn't call ahead. One of the owners came in a minute ago and told me they were here. It's a big dog—I can see them struggling to get her out of the car."

Louise yanked a stethoscope from a hook on the wall and wrapped it around her neck. She sent Heidi and Jenny a knowing look. "Better get the stretcher. Sounds like we're going to need it."

Louise rushed into the front office, soon followed by Heidi and Jenny. A man and woman were struggling to carry a large brown dog with long hair into the clinic. Louise approached to help, then stopped. The smell was familiar and nauseating. Could this morning get any worse? If this was what she feared, the dog would need surgery as soon as possible.

Mary motioned for Louise to join her at the other end of the counter. "Here's the file. We haven't seen this dog since she was here eight years ago for her puppy vaccines. She's not spayed."

Louise took the file. "I was afraid you were going to say that. She's got to be what, 60 pounds?"

Mary lifted a shoulder. "At least."

Louise returned to the clients. Heidi and Jenny had lifted the dog onto the stretcher. Louise motioned for them to take the patient to the treatment room, then turned her attention to the very exhausted-looking couple. "What's going on with…" She glanced at the file. "Tiny? Mr. and Mrs. Jay, is it?"

The man wiped his hand on his pants. "Yes, that's us. She was fine last week, but the other day we noticed she was kind of smelly."

His wife handed him a wipe from her purse. "Really smelly. It was so disgusting we had to make her sleep in the garage. She had this thick, gross discharge from… well… from you know, her private area. It lasted a few days, but then we thought she was better."

Louise made a note on the file. "Why is that?" *Because the discharge stopped?*

Mrs. Jay sat and wiped her brow. "The gooey stuff stopped. And she started drinking a lot. We figured that was a good sign. You know, if she was drinking okay."

"Was she eating?"

"I don't think so. We keep her bowl full, so it's hard to say. This morning she couldn't get up so we rushed her right over. What do you think is wrong with her?"

Louise hated this part of the job. She didn't know these people and didn't want them to feel bad, but she had to be honest with them about the seriousness of the situation. "I suspect she has a condition called pyometra. It's an infection of the uterus. The gooey discharge is the first sign. Once the gooey discharge disappears it can mean she's fought off the infection on her own, but, sadly, that's rarely the case. No more discharge is usually a bad sign."

Mr. Jay lowered himself into the seat beside his wife and held her hand. "Meaning?"

Louise pulled a chair closer and sat facing the couple. From her position she could see into the parking lot. She scanned for Daphne's car, but it wasn't there. This was a surgery for Daphne or Bob, except that Bob wasn't there either. The muscles in her neck stiffened.

"My concern is that Tiny's condition has deteriorated since the discharge stopped. She can't get up on her own, and she's drinking and urinating a lot. That means that the cervix is closed and the infected material can't get out. What happens in that case is that the uterus fills with pus and leaks toxins into her bloodstream. It's life-threatening and must be treated quickly."

A tear slid down Mrs. Jay's cheek. "Can you give us antibiotics for her?"

Louise paused. How often had she had this conversation? Clients with seriously ill pets who wanted to go home with antibiotics, hoping that a pill would fix everything? "I'm afraid medication alone won't help. At this point in the disease, surgery is the only viable treatment. She will need to be spayed, but first we'll have to do X-rays or an ultrasound to confirm the diagnosis. We'll also need to run some blood work to assess the health of her kidneys, liver, and a few other things."

Mr. Jay's face reddened. "And I suppose this is going to cost us a ton of money. That's why we didn't ever get her spayed. Just a scam for you vets to make money."

Louise rubbed the back of her neck. The accusation was uncalled for, but Mr. Jay was upset about his dog. This wouldn't be the time to point out that spaying a dog at the age of six months was not only cheaper than spaying a dog with pyometra, but it was safer and would have prevented the very disease that Tiny now had.

She turned to Mary. "Can you ask Rita to create a quote for a pyo workup and spay please."

As she shifted to face the Jays, Louise caught sight of a white van in the parking lot. Her stomach tightened. It was the same one she'd seen at the dog show, she was certain of it. Her eyes met the driver's. He was clean shaven, wearing a red ball cap, and appeared to be in his forties. He leaned back, out of her line of vision, allowing her a glimpse of the man in the passenger seat. He also had a red ball cap on, but long, scraggly hair flowing down his back. He looked younger than the driver, although they had similar eyes and cheek bones. Were they brothers? More importantly, what were they doing out there?

Louise felt pressure on her left shoulder. She leapt to her feet and spun around, dropping her clipboard.

Rita stood in front of her, head tilted. "Sorry. I didn't mean to frighten you, but you didn't answer when I said your name. Are you okay? What are you looking at out there?"

Louise retrieved her clipboard then glanced out the window. The van was gone. "Nothing. I was wondering if Daphne made it in yet, but her car isn't out there."

Rita kept her focus on Louise. "Not yet, but she called not long ago. She'll be here soon." She leaned in to whisper. "Are you sure you're okay?"

Louise nodded. "Yes. Thanks." She offered her hand to

Mr. Jay. "Our office manager, Rita, will go over the quote with you. I can't make the decision for you, but Tiny is very sick."

Mrs. Jay glared at her husband. "I don't think we'll be able to afford it, but we'd like to see the quote." She pressed a hand to her chest. "Poor Tiny. She's had such difficulty getting up for several months now, especially when it's raining or cold. I don't want to give up on her but… I don't know."

Louise touched Mrs. Jay's arm. "We'll work together to make the best decision for Tiny. I'll have our techs set her up on IV fluids, then give her pain medication to make her more comfortable." Louise repressed a sigh. They would do what they could to make things easier for Tiny and her owners, but the outcome was unlikely to be a happy one.

Chapter 21

LOUISE UNLOCKED, THEN yanked open, the filing cabinet drawer marked Personnel. It couldn't be a coincidence that the van showed up on the same morning Bob was late. She had to find out what was going on, and she knew where to start. Bob's resume in hand, she closed the office door and plunked herself at her desk. She browsed the paper until she found the corner where she jotted down the number for the Edmundston clinic, then punched the numbers into her phone. What would she say? They wouldn't tell her anything the last time she had called.

A woman's voice. "Edmunston Animal Hospital."

Louise needed to speak the clinic owner. Vet to vet. Clinic

owner to clinic owner. "Hello. My name is Dr. Louise Miller. I own the Black Creek Animal Hospital in Cloverdale. I was hoping to speak to Dr. Dowling. It's fairly urgent."

"I'll see if she's in. Please hold."

Louise tapped her pen on the file folder as she waited, then forced herself to stop and close her eyes. *God, please help me. I don't want to cause trouble for anyone, but something is not right. Protect Eric, Father. And Alex. I don't know where they are, but you do.* Louise opened her eyes when a new voice came over the speaker.

"Hello. This is Dr. Dowling. Dr. Miller?"

"Yes. Thank you for taking my call. I hope I'm not interrupting. I'm sure you're busy."

"That's fine. I suspect you're calling about Dr. Kurt? My associate shared with me that you called a few weeks ago. There really isn't much we can say."

"That's part of my concern. Generally, if there are no problems with someone, a person would simply say so. I don't want you to share anything you're uncomfortable sharing, but unusual things have been happening around here the past couple of weeks. One of our staff members is missing."

Dr. Dowling gasped. "Oh my, that's terrible. I can't imagine that Bob, for all his failings, would be involved in someone's disappearance."

"All his failings? You wouldn't want to elaborate on that, would you?"

"I do need to be careful. I can let you know that Dr. Johnston, the previous owner of this clinic, had been under investigation for forging rabies certificates and possibly Coggins test documents. He had friends in the horse racing industry."

"I read about the rabies certificate allegations on the CVO site, but not the Coggins."

"There wasn't enough evidence for them to proceed with a Coggins investigation, but there was for the rabies. Before the case against him proceeded, Dr. Johnston chose to retire and sell the clinic."

Louise propped her elbow on the desk and rested her forehead on her hand. "Wow. A sad way to end a career. What about Bob? I know he and Dr. Johnston were friends."

Dr. Dowling hesitated, as though measuring her next words. "They were friends. When this all came about… well, there was speculation that Bob was involved. We found out that the individual who was creating the forged documents was a friend of his. No one found evidence of his involvement, but after Dr. Johnston left, Bob handed in his resignation."

"Bob only graduated a couple of years ago. How could he have been that deeply involved already?"

"Oh, Bob's known Dr. Johnston a long time. He worked here at the clinic during summer breaks when he was in the pre-vet program. Dr. Johnston helped Bob get into vet college."

Louise's lower jaw dropped. Bob was Dr. Johnston's protégé in veterinary medicine. Was he also his protégé in crime? Louise thanked Dr. Dowling for her help and ended the call.

Louise resumed her pen tapping as she stared at the far wall. Their veterinary software prevented tampering with dates on the rabies certificates, so she didn't have to worry about that. They didn't do any horse work, so Coggins certificates were not a concern. But something still bothered her. What had Daphne been saying at dinner last night? Louise pounded on her desk. *That's it! DNA.*

A knock on the door returned Louise's mind to more immediate concerns. "Come in."

Rita edged the door open and popped her head into the room. "Everything okay?"

Louise nodded. "Yup. What's up?" She wasn't ready to let Rita know that her initial mis-trust of Dr. Kurt might have been well founded. She had no evidence of wrongdoing. She'd need proof.

Rita entered the room and handed a paper to Louise. "The Jays have elected euthanasia for Tiny. They'd like to be with her when the injection is given."

Louise accepted the paper and stood. "I thought they might. That's why I had Heidi place the IV catheter. We can leave that off the bill. Keep the fees to the exam and euthanasia, and…"

"They chose communal cremation. They said they had loads of photos to remember her by and didn't want her ashes back. I offered them time alone with her beforehand, but they'd rather not delay it."

Louise inhaled deeply. Tiny was suffering, but ending the life of a beloved family member was never easy. Each euthanasia, no matter the circumstances, weighed heavily on the hearts and minds of Louise and her team, a burden they shared with the rest of the veterinary community.

Louise removed the empty syringe from the catheter Heidi had placed in Tiny's right forelimb. The large dog, who'd been close to moribund on her arrival, had drifted away peacefully, her human family stroking her head, as Louise injected the blue fluid into her vein. Mr. and Mrs. Jay requested a few moments alone with Tiny after the procedure.

Louise turned the lights to the exam room low, and quietly closed the door behind her. After leaving Mr. and Mrs. Jay in Mary's capable hands, Louise marched to the treatment room. She needed to talk to Heidi about Bob and the AI shipments. Heidi had worked with Bob more than the other staff members. Had she noticed anything odd other than the erroneous vial numbers? They could talk while performing the surgeries. Since no one else had shown up yet, she'd have to do them.

She flung open the door ready to ask Jenny to set up for the first procedure and stopped short at the sight of Bob in scrubs—performing surgery on the Norwegian elkhound. Jenny was assisting him.

Louise caught Heidi's attention and threw her hands in the air.

Heidi approached Louise. "He showed up while you were in with the Jays. He said he'd do the surgeries, and I didn't think you'd object."

Louise narrowed her eyes and glared at Bob. "Hm. Perhaps he's hoping to hide behind the mask." Heidi smiled and Louise let out a breath. She'd made the remark out of frustration, but Heidi seemed to find it humorous. "Actually, this is good because I wanted to talk to you privately."

Heidi furrowed her brows. "Sure. I was heading up to the break room. We could talk there."

Louise smiled. "Don't worry. It's nothing for you to be concerned about. I have a few questions regarding the AI shipments."

Heidi laughed. "Phew."

They arrived in the break room to find Daphne steeping a cup of tea. Louise joined her at the counter. "How's Ella?"

Daphne removed the tea bag and added milk to her cup. "She's fine. When she's sick she gets needy. She's a lot like her father that way." Daphne laughed at her own joke.

Louise reached for a glass on the shelf above the sink. "Poor Joe. I'm glad she's okay. I'm also glad that you're here. I've asked Rita to join us too." As though they'd planned it, Rita entered the room at the same time her name was voiced. "Perfect, we're all here." Louise opened the refrigerator and stared at the contents. "Does anyone want a cold drink? Heidi?"

Heidi raised her hand. "Sure. I'll have a cola. It'll complement my chips perfectly."

Louise glanced over her shoulder. "Rita?"

Rita dropped the stack of files she'd been carrying onto the lunch table and flopped into a chair. "No thanks."

Louise grabbed two colas and joined the others. She eyed Daphne, who was watching her intently with a furrowed brow. No doubt her business partner was wondering why Louise had called this impromptu meeting. Normally they would discuss any clinic related happenings privately before involving the staff, but this situation was urgent and Louise wanted to take advantage of Bob being busy with surgeries. "I called the Edmunston clinic again. This time I spoke to Dr. Dowling, the owner. I'll fill you in on the conversation later, Daphne, but for now I wanted to ask Heidi and Rita about their thoughts on the AI program and how it's going."

Rita lifted the stack of files and tapped them on the table to align the bottoms. "If we're being honest…" She eyed Louise. Louise nodded. Rita inhaled deeply. "It's been a lot of work. We have all these new clients, which is great for business, don't get me wrong, but it means a lot of paperwork. Well… it did."

Louise stole a chip from Heidi. "What do you mean 'it did'?"

Rita shrugged. "We were working out a system, then one

day Bob decides that he'll handle all of the paperwork." She nudged Heidi's elbow. "Do you know why?"

Heidi lowered her can of cola. "No, but not long after that we noticed the error in the number of vials on the shipment labels. And then there was the day I couldn't find the two vials for the Begley dog. I think they were they the ones that Bob popped into the vaccine fridge."

Rita slapped the table. "Yes. You're right, they were. And speaking of the Begleys, I overheard Bob on the phone the other day talking about missing vials. I guess he thought he was alone in the storage room, because he seemed startled when I came out from behind the food shelves."

Heidi stood and went to the refrigerator. She helped herself to another cola. "Yeah. Remember, Louise? I mentioned before that he acts all antsy sometimes when he's on the phone."

Louise pursed her lips. "I remember. Are there more vials missing? I thought the Begley dog was pregnant. Why would they be ordering more semen?"

Rita lifted a palm in the air. "She is. That's why I was confused when I asked Bob about more missing vials and he said he had been talking to Susan Begley. It annoyed me, and I reminded him that the missing vials were his fault, not mine." Rita rapped her finger on the table. "And that's not all, I'm sure he referred to the person he had been speaking to as Nancy, not Susan. I asked him about that too. He said that he must have gotten Mrs. Begley's name wrong." Rita rolled her eyes.

Daphne sipped her tea. "Rita, why didn't you mention any of this before? It obviously upset you."

Rita dropped her chin. "I was embarrassed afterwards by how I handled it. I wasn't eavesdropping, I just happened to be in the room, but I should have let him know I could hear him sooner than I did. And something about his tone of voice intrigued me. He sounded really nervous, so I couldn't help myself. I kept quiet until I heard him talking about missing vials, then I got upset and confronted him. It wasn't very professional."

Louise couldn't disagree that listening in on someone else's conversation was rude, but she had been guilty of it herself recently, so she chose to wear her friendship hat instead of her employer one. "It's okay, Rita, I think any of us might react in a similar fashion. What made you think that Bob was nervous?"

Rita played with a paper napkin on the table, crumpling it and flattening it again beneath her palm. "The things he said, like 'don't worry, I'll find them.' I can't remember it all, but he spoke in a shaky voice. More than you'd expect for missing semen."

Heidi bumped Rita's shoulder with her fist as she returned to her seat. "Well, if it was Nancy *Wells* he'd been talking too, that would make anyone's voice shaky."

Nancy Wells! Was that who he'd been talking to about missing vials? What were the two of them up to? Louise played absently with the tab on the top of her can. "Heidi, where are the shipments coming from?"

"The paperwork says England."

"That's what I thought." Louise eyed the clock on the wall. "They'll be done the surgeries soon. Heidi, perhaps you should get downstairs and see if Jenny needs any help."

Heidi crumpled her empty chip bag and tossed it into the garbage can on the other side of the table. "Two points." She rose.

Louise rubbed her chin. "And Heidi, let's keep this conversation between the four of us for now."

"Sure."

Rita slid her chair from the table. "I have to get the order in before noon."

Heidi and Rita made their exit. When they'd gone, Louise stood and paced the room. "So, in four weeks, we've hired Bob and started a breeding program. A program that seems oddly busy for such a short time period. In that same amount of time, we've had too many vials, too few vials, strange phone conversations, odd behavior by our new associate, Cliff Mariner's murder, Eric's disappearance, Bob's connection to two known forgers, and a mystery van showing up in our parking lot. And let's not forget that in the past few weeks a pharmacy and two veterinary clinics have been broken into."

Daphne set her mug of tea down so hard that it sloshed over the rim and splattered on the table. "The van showed up here? When? What forgers?"

"I spotted it this morning while talking to a client. It had to be the one I saw at the dog show, and the guys in it had to be the two who were shoving Bob. They looked so familiar, it had to be them."

Louise's phone vibrated in her pocket. She tugged it out and opened the text app. "It's from Alex. He needs to talk to us. He'll be here in about twenty minutes."

Daphne grabbed a napkin and dabbed at the puddles of tea on the table. "Did he find Eric?"

Louise frowned. "He didn't say, so I suspect not." *I hope not.* If Alex had found Eric alive and well, not to mention innocent, Alex would have indicated that in his text. Not finding Eric had to be better than the alternative.

Chapter 22

LOUISE SAT WITH her elbows on her desk, alternating her gaze between the window and the clock. It had been twenty-five minutes since she'd heard from Alex. *Where is he?* In the time since she'd received his text, she'd seen a client with two dogs who were due for their yearly examination and vaccines, and another whose cat had been sneezing. The cat's file was open on her monitor waiting for her to input her exam findings, but she struggled to remember what she and the client had discussed. *Where are my notes?* She pawed her pockets in search of her scribblings. *Argh. Must have left them in the exam room.* She cupped the edge of her desk and pushed her chair back, startling Daphne.

"I'm sure Alex will be here soon."

"It's not that. I forgot my notes downstairs." Louise rose and rushed into the hallway. As she rounded the corner, she found herself face to face with a figure standing at the top of the staircase. She jumped back and screamed.

Alex stepped into the light from the dark landing. "Sorry. I didn't mean to startle you." He jerked a thumb over his shoulder. "You really should get a light installed in the stairwell. The light at the bottom doesn't help much up here."

Louise inhaled deeply, still shaking. Her reaction surprised her—it wasn't the first time she'd almost run into someone on the landing, but Alex was right, they needed to get a light installed.

"No worries. My mind was elsewhere." She waved him into the office. "Where have you been?"

Alex nodded at Daphne, then moved a chair from the corner of the room closer to Louise's desk. "As you know, I went to the docks last night after you received that text from Jenny."

Louise tried to ignore the dueling butterflies in her stomach. "And?"

Alex shook his head. "He wasn't there."

Louise and Daphne both slumped in their chairs, then Daphne edged around Louise and made her way to the coffee maker where she filled a large mug with the dark, hot liquid.

Louise eyed her friend. "When did you start drinking coffee?"

Daphne retrieved the milk from the refrigerator and added a splash to the cup. "This is for you. That scream a few minutes ago tells me you need it." She positioned the cup on the desk in front of Louise.

Louise scooped it up and held it close. "You know me so well. Thanks."

Daphne held the carafe in Alex's direction. "Alex?"

"No thanks." Alex glanced over his shoulder towards the hallway. The door to the office was open. "I don't have much time. Where's Dr. Kurt?"

Louise rested the mug on her desk. "Why?"

Alex got up slowly, as if attempting to be quiet. He examined the length of the hallway, then closed the door to the office. "I told you about the pen they found at the warehouse."

Louise tilted her head. "Yes. We discussed that. It could have come from anyone. You can't assume that it was Eric simply because…"

Alex raised his hand. "Hold on. We lifted a fingerprint from it and had it analyzed. Eric's prints are in the system from his arrest a few years back. They didn't match the print on the pen found at the warehouse."

Louise slid to the front of her chair. "That proves he wasn't there the night of the fire."

Alex returned to his seat and leaned closer to Louise. "It proves it wasn't his pen. Or that he had been wearing gloves that night. No more than that, I'm afraid. A security guard at the docks identified Eric from a photo. He was there last night with a woman. The guard's description is similar to the one Roger gave us."

Louise let out a loud breath and glanced at Daphne. Her friend had a hand over her mouth. Eric was okay physically, but why hadn't he contacted them? Who was the woman he was with? He'd never mentioned having any family in the area. He did have a sister, but she lived on the west coast. And if it was her, why the secrecy? Maybe he had a girlfriend who'd gotten him mixed up in something. Louise let go of her mug and pressed her palms to her face. Were her cheeks as red as they felt?

Alex cleared his throat. "We need to check the fingerprint

against someone else here at the clinic, and for that I need your help."

Louise eyed Alex. *What is he up to?* "How?"

"I need something that Bob Kurt has handled recently. Something small, like a scalpel, that would have his fingerprints on it. Was he doing surgery today?"

Daphne eased past Alex and made her way to the small trash can beside the filing cabinets. "Yes, but he would have been wearing gloves."

Louise shook her head. "Seriously. What kind of operation do you think we run here?"

Daphne smiled. "Gloves, masks, gowns. It's a top-notch, modern hospital, this one."

Alex lowered his head. "Sorry. My mistake. Can you think of anything else?"

Louise pointed to Daphne's computer. "I think he was using that keyboard earlier."

Alex scrunched his nose. "I need something small enough to put in my pocket."

Daphne yanked a tissue from the dispenser on the counter, then reached into the garbage can. "How about this?" She held up an empty gum container. "I thought I saw Bob toss something in here earlier today, and he's the only one who chews gum."

Alex jumped up. "That's perfect." He produced a plastic evidence bag and held it open while Daphne dropped the item in. Alex zipped the bag closed and wrote the date and clinic name on the orange label, as well as the letters BK, before tucking it into his inside jacket pocket.

"I'll let you know what I find out." Alex strode toward the door and turned the knob. Daphne sent Louise a pointed look.

"You should tell Alex about the van and the information you got from the Edmunston clinic."

Alex returned the door to its closed position. "The van you saw at the dog show and the grocery store?"

"Yes. It was in the parking lot for a few minutes this morning, then it was gone."

Alex's eyes widened. "Did you get a look at the occupants?"

"They looked like the same fella's who were pushing Bob around at the dog show. Why? You didn't seem too interested in them last night."

"I ran the plate information you gave me. I can't say much, but those guys roughing up your associate… well, that's one reason we're interested in Dr. Kurt's prints." Alex reached for the door knob.

Louise leapt to her feet and, before Alex could make his escape, situated herself between him and the door. "What did you learn about them? Are they dangerous? Who are they? Should we be worried?" She peered over Alex's shoulder at Daphne. The color had drained from her friend's face. Louise tried to crack the tension. "Maybe I should get a gun."

A grin crept across Daphne's face. "You'd need a fashionable holster."

"No. I'd stick it in the back of my pants like on TV. That's what the cool cops do."

Alex stepped back, narrowly avoiding Daphne who was still standing behind him. "You're not a cop. And you don't need a gun."

"Besides…" Daphne said, "It could be dangerous."

Alex filled his lungs with air. "Guns *are* dangerous."

Daphne returned to her desk and sat. "I mean, sticking one in your pants. What if it went off accidently?"

"Oh. Right. I hadn't thought of that." Louise waved her hands in the air. "Nix the gun idea."

"Ladies, this is serious. I know you like to joke around, but this really isn't the time."

Louise hadn't intended to upset Alex, but humor was her way of coping with stressful situations, and Daphne could always be relied upon to play along. "You're right, but sometimes it helps to forget things are serious, if only for a few seconds."

Alex rolled his eyes and almost cracked a smile. "Okay. But promise me you'll both be careful. If you see that van or the guys who were in it around here again, call me right away. We still haven't caught those responsible for the pharmacy and clinic break-ins."

"We will." Louise shared the specifics of her conversation with Dr. Dowling as she escorted Alex to the stairwell. After he left, she reheated her coffee in the microwave and returned to her desk.

Daphne glared at her. "Why do you give him such a hard time?"

Louise waved her free hand in the air. "We both gave him a hard time. It's just nerves. I'm sure he's used to it by now."

Daphne furrowed her brow. "I'm talking about more than the teasing and joking around. He really cares about you, but you push him away."

Louise tugged on her scrub top, then grabbed a file from her desk. "I can't talk about this right now." She glanced at the clock on her phone. "We should be getting back to—"

The intercom buzzed. Louise hit the button. "What's up? Is my next appointment here?"

Mary's voice came over the speaker. "No, but that van is back."

Chapter 23

LOUISE GRABBED HER phone and opened the camera app—she planned to be ready this time. She raced down the stairs with Daphne close behind. When they arrived at the landing, instead of turning left towards the front office, Louise went to the right and opened the side door. She paused and pointed to the reception desk. "You watch them through the front window in case they take off before I get to them."

Daphne grabbed Louise's sleeve. "What are you going to do? We need to call Alex."

Louise patted Daphne's hand as she guided it away from her arm. "That's a great idea. Ask Mary to call and let him know what's going on." Louise bolted out the door, slowing only when she got to the corner of the building where she pressed her back against the brick wall. After catching her breath, she risked a peek around the corner. The van was still in the front parking lot. She held her phone far enough past the wall to get a picture of the suspect vehicle hoping not to attract attention, then, pressing it tight to her wrist with her fingers, slid it up her sleeve. She peered around the corner again. The van was parked facing away from Louise, so she couldn't see who was in it. Daphne's dark blue SUV was parked on the other side of the lot. Louise took a deep breath then rounded the building and strolled past the white van without glancing at it.

Daphne didn't usually lock her door, and Louise prayed she hadn't randomly decided to that morning. When she arrived at the car, Louise tried the passenger side door. It wasn't locked. *Thank you, Daphne.* She climbed into the car and acted as though she was searching for something on the floor. After shuffling through empty water bottles, ketchup packets, and what seemed to Louise to be an unusually large amount of cookie crumbs, she sat up, clutching a pack of baby wipes. Both passengers in the van were clearly visible in Daphne's side mirror and Louise was able to sneak a photo of their reflection.

After pocketing the phone, Louise opened the car door and got out. *Don't look directly at them or they'll know you're watching them.* She couldn't help herself—her line of vision shot directly to the driver. He stared back at her, one side of his upper lip lifting to reveal a blackened tooth. Their eyes locked and Louise froze. *Now what?* Regaining control of her limbs, she tossed the pack of baby wipes into the air as nonchalantly as possible and caught it as she approached the white van. The driver's window was open and she forced a laugh when she reached it. "Babies. They're always making a mess. I thought I'd forgotten these at home. Phew." *Are they buying it?* "Do you gentlemen have a pet? Do you need an appointment?"

The driver had a deep, irregular scar on his face stretching from his left cheek bone to the middle of his chin. What would cause an injury like that? Louise decided she didn't want to know. The man behind the wheel glared at her without speaking, shifted the transmission into drive, and pressed down on the accelerator. Louise stepped back as he shot by and drove out of the parking lot. She watched as the van disappeared on a side street that led to the highway.

Her heart still pounding in her chest, Louise entered the clinic through the front door. Daphne met her at the threshold, her arms crossed. "What was that? Why did you go out there?"

Louise held her breath for a few seconds to steady her nerves and slow her heart rate. Thankfully, the waiting room was empty. "I wanted to find out what they were doing here. Alex did warn us that we could be a target for drug dealers. They might be the guys who broke into the other clinics."

Daphne's face reddened. "So what was your plan, to ask them if they were drug dealers?"

Louise grinned at her friend. "Of course not. I'm fairly certain that if they *were* drug dealers, they would have lied about it."

Daphne shook her head, uncrossed her arms, and started towards the exam room. "What *did* you find out about them?"

Louise followed. "Nothing directly. They weren't big on talking, but look what I got." She showed the photos she had snapped to Daphne.

Daphne plucked the phone from Louise's hand and studied the pictures. "Great. You have pics of a couple of possible drug dealers. Now you know what they look like, and they know what you look like. What now? What if they come after you? You should have waited for the police."

Louise took back her phone. "You're right. It was impulsive, and not the wisest thing I've done today, but these photos may be helpful. I'll show them to Alex. If these guys have committed other crimes, the police may be able to identify them from their records." She dropped the device into the pocket of her white lab coat. "Did you talk to Alex?"

"No. The dispatcher said he was on a call. They're sending a patrol car over."

"Okay, good." Louise rubbed the back of her head as she followed Daphne into the exam room. "It just occurred to me... I haven't seen Bob since he was in surgery earlier. Where is he?"

"He's upstairs in the staff room." Rita joined Louise and Daphne. "I went in there to start the dishwasher shortly after the two of you ran down here. Bob was standing to one side of the window, peeking out as though he was afraid to be seen. When I said hi to him, he almost jumped out of his shoes. It's like Heidi said earlier—the guy is really flighty sometimes."

Louise bit her bottom lip. The first time the van had shown up in their parking lot, Bob had been late for work and didn't show up until the van left. When he did arrive, he rushed into surgery and, even after the surgeries were completed, he was like a ghost—she knew he was in the building, but was never quite sure where. From Rita's description, it sounded like he was cowering in the staff room, out of sight, when the van reappeared.

Louise sat on the stool beside the examination table and tapped her finger on the stainless steel. "Did he say anything to explain his behavior?"

Rita leaned a shoulder on the door frame. "Not voluntarily,

but I did ask what he was looking at. He said a friend had told him that an ex-girlfriend had been trying to find him and he thought he'd spotted her car in the parking lot. I didn't buy it."

Louise continued her tapping. *I don't buy it, either.*

Daphne placed her hand over Louise's to steady it. "Perhaps you and I should head upstairs and have a chat with Bob. We may get more answers by asking him directly rather than speculating."

Louise sighed. "You're always so practical. Okay. Let's get to it."

When Louise and Daphne arrived at the staff room, they found Jenny and Heidi sitting at the lunch table. Daphne joined the two veterinary technicians, but Louise checked the doctor's office, the AI room, and the storage room, before joining them.

"Do either of you know where Bob is? Rita said he was up here a little while ago."

Heidi sipped her cola. "He was when we first came in, but he said he had something to check on in the AI room. We heard him rustling around in there for a bit, then I think he went down the back stairs."

Louise contemplated the can in Heidi's hand. Who consumed more caffeine in a day—her with her coffee, or Heidi with her colas? Shaking her head to clear it of distractions, she wandered over to the window and peered out at the parking lot. Bob's car was gone. Rubbing her temples, Louise turned and leaned against the window. Something was definitely going on here. Their associate veterinarian was clearly involved in something bad. Something potentially far worse than forging a few rabies certificates.

Chapter 24

LOUISE BOLTED UP in her bed. A loud bang, followed by the sound of breaking glass, echoed from the lower level of her home. She froze, straining to hear in the darkness. A brief moment of quiet, then another crashing sound. She lunged across the bed to her nightstand on the far side and patted the surface for her phone. It wasn't there. Her heart pounding against her sternum, Louise threw off the covers and lowered her feet to the cold hardwood floor. She crept to the window for a clue as to the source of the noise. The porch light, forgotten the night before, illuminated the driveway where her car sat alone.

The first glimmer of sunlight appeared above the horizon

giving her a view of the street—all seemed quiet. Louise estimated the time to be approximately six-thirty. She jumped at the sound of something else falling. It had to be an intruder and she needed to call the police. Enough natural light in the room now, she could see the contents of the night table. Her earlier assessment had been correct, her phone wasn't there. *Now what?*

Louise tiptoed to the closet and gripped a baseball bat. *I knew this would come in handy some day.* She held the bat over her shoulder while slowly prying the door open, then paused and listened. Scuffling noises came from the back of the main floor, then nothing except for the humming of the refrigerator.

Minutes passed before Louise dared to move from her position. She closed her eyes. *God be with me, and please let the intruder be gone.* She crept down the stairs then glanced into the kitchen. Her phone lay on the counter where she had left it after talking to her sister, Maryanne, the previous evening.

The L-shaped kitchen could be accessed from Louise's current position at the foot of the stairs or from the living room. She scurried to the counter to retrieve the phone. As she lifted it, she spotted movement in the living room.

Squeezing the phone to her chest, Louise crouched behind the island. She'd always wanted a kitchen island, and now was doubly grateful for this one. More banging. Why would an intruder be trashing her living room, and why were they so noisy? Did they think she wasn't at home? She rested the bat beside her legs and held her index finger on the home button to unlock the phone. Before she had a chance to dial 911, she heard what sounded like the toppling of a table then something flew over the island and her head, landing on the opposite counter. Louise bent her knees to her chest and held her breath.

The object regained flight. When it landed on Louise's

knees, she screamed. Her muscles tensed, but she felt no pain, only faint vibrations and... soft fur. Oscar rubbed his chin against Louise's, then gave her a head butt.

She clasped her hands around Oscar's thorax and held him out in front of her. "Oscar! What are you doing?" He wiggled against her grip. She lowered him to the floor, then rose to her feet. "Crazy cat. Oh well, better a crazy cat than an intruder." She scooped up the bat and let out a sigh. "I'm so glad you're the only one to witness my reaction."

Louise made her way to the living room and flipped on the light. She could see that Oscar had been on top of the corner cabinet—he had knocked over a glass dog figurine. It lay shattered into thousands of pieces on the floor, the mess partially covered by the papers that had been on the coffee table. The TV, still standing, had been moved twenty degrees from its normal position—that had been a close call. The small table that normally sat under the window now rested on its side. Louise had witnessed a similar scene in the past when Oscar went mad chasing a fly or a mouse. Once he got his prey in sight, he didn't stop until he caught it.

She leaned down and patted him on the head. "Nice work, buddy. You've really outdone yourself this time. I suppose you think I should feed you now?"

Oscar licked his lips and ran to his food bowl. Louise tossed the bat onto the couch and followed him into the kitchen. After dropping a spoonful of canned cat food into his bowl, she checked the doors and windows. Satisfied that everything was secure and the entire episode had been the work of Oscar alone, Louise retrieved a broom from the coat closet and swept up the broken glass. Bending over the garbage can under the sink, she dumped the remnants of the figurine into it. Someone pounded on the door. Louise straightened and glanced at the clock on the stove—six-forty. Who would be knocking at the door this early? She leaned the broom against the wall, retrieved the bat, and made her way to the front door. A curtain covered the window in the front door—Louise moved it far enough to peek out before releasing the breath she'd been holding. Alex.

When Louise returned to the kitchen after changing out of the tracksuit she slept in on cool nights and into a pair of scrubs, Alex was pouring hot coffee into her favorite mug. "If I thought you stopped by this early to make me coffee, I'd be grateful, but something tells me this isn't a social visit." Louise added milk to her coffee then lifted the mug to her lips. "Just what I needed. Thanks." She sat at the table and eyed Alex. *This can't be good.*

Alex filled a second mug for himself before returning the carafe to its base. He joined Louise at the table, placed his mug on the table, then dug his hand into his coat pocket. He produced what appeared to be a sports card and dropped it onto the table. It landed face down. "Do you recognize this?"

Louise shook her head. "Should I?"

"Sorry." Alex flipped the card over. "Now?"

Louise gasped. The baseball card she'd given Eric as a gift several years ago. She snatched the card up and studied it. "Where did you find this?"

Alex rubbed the back of his neck. "A witness came forward yesterday morning and provided us with a description of the getaway car involved in the pharmacy robbery. Video surveillance taken around the time of the vet clinic break ins showed a car of the same color, make, and model near the clinics."

Louise leapt up. "That's great news. You know what type of car they drive." She pried open the plastic container that held a half dozen blueberry muffins. "Muffin?"

"No, thanks. We have more than the description of the vehicle because the department's video technician captured the license plate from one of the videos. I received the report after I left the clinic yesterday. Using the plates, we were able to get a name and address for the owner of the car."

"Did you make an arrest?" Louise glanced out the kitchen window. The shadow of the house darkened the porch, but the water in the creek glistened as the sun reflected off the ripples. Oscar had perched himself on the window ledge—his attention fully on the squirrel climbing the short pine tree at the water's edge.

"We did. The owner of the car was home when we arrived with a warrant to search the premises. Since they live on the fourth floor of an apartment building, they were unable to make an escape."

Louise cut the muffin she was holding and applied a dollop of butter. "They?" *Why is he telling me this?* Even if she'd been the one to supply him with details, Alex didn't usually discuss an ongoing investigation with her. She set the muffin on the counter, her hunger waning.

"The car is owned by a young man named Keith Giles. He and his roommate, Terry Roberts, have an extensive record for robbery and break and enter."

Louise slumped into her chair. "Why do those names sound familiar?"

Alex tapped the baseball card on the table to the rhythm of Oscar's wagging tail. "Because they're the guys that Eric had been hanging around with when he had been arrested years ago."

Louise straightened. "They're the ones who tricked him into being the getaway driver. He doesn't associate with them anymore." She shot a look at the card in Alex's hand and her stomach tightened.

Alex raised the card in the air, and rested his elbow on the table. "We found this in Giles and Roberts' apartment." He rotated the card through his fingers. "You gave this to Eric *after* he graduated from the veterinary technician program at college. That was three years after his arrest. Three years *after* he'd promised you, Daphne, and me, that he would have no further involvement with his old crew."

Louise swallowed hard. "Four, actually. It would have been be four years since Eric's arrest." She bounded to her feet, sending her chair crashing into the wall beneath the window ledge. Oscar rocketed into the air, landed safely on the floor, then scurried into the living room. Louise waved her hand in the air. "They probably stole that card from Eric. I paid a hundred dollars when I bought it. Maybe it's worth a lot more now."

Alex shook his head. "They didn't steal it, Louise. Why would they do that? How would they even know he had it unless he's been in contact with them?"

Louise grabbed a paper towel from the dispenser under the upper cabinets and dabbed her eyes. "I don't know. There has to be an innocent reason, because you're right, it's been years since Eric's arrest, and in all that time he has never been in trouble. *Something* is going on."

Alex stood and returned the card to his pocket. "There is definitely something going on, but the more evidence we find, the more it seems that Eric is involved in whatever this *something* is."

"What did those two guys say? Did they implicate Eric?"

Alex zipped up his jacket and headed towards the front door.

"They aren't talking. *Look*, I shouldn't be telling you all of this because it's part of an active investigation, but I don't want you doing anymore of your own digging. You could get hurt. I'm hoping that if I tell you what's going on, you'll let the department handle it. We *will* find Eric."

Louise followed Alex to the front of the house. "You're basing Eric's involvement on a baseball card. That's not much evidence."

Alex turned towards Louise and placed his hands on her shoulders. "There is more evidence. Like I said, I shouldn't be telling you this, but… we also have video surveillance of Eric with Giles and Roberts."

Louise froze. They must be mistaken because Eric promised…

Alex released Louise's shoulders and grasped the door handle. "The video is from a security camera at a store across the street from the NKC offices where Cliff Mariner was murdered, on the same night as the murder, around the same time. "I'm sorry to drop this on you and leave, but I have to get going. You can't repeat what I've told you to anyone, okay?"

Louise slowly nodded. "Okay." Holding the door open, she watched Alex as he walked to his car, got in, and drove away. She'd promised she wouldn't repeat what he'd told her, but she didn't promise that she would stop investigating on her own. She closed the door and headed into the living room. The glass was cleaned up—the rest of the mess could wait. She needed to get to the clinic and go over the paperwork for the AI shipments. This whole situation had started when Dr. Bob Kurt and his breeding program came to town. *What did he get Eric mixed up in?*

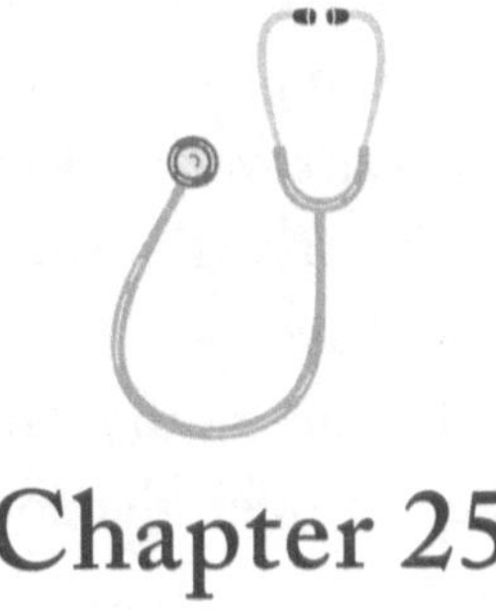

Chapter 25

PANSY WOKE EARLY and ran downstairs because she could hear her parents in the kitchen. Last year her birthday had been horrible. This year had to be better because her mother had been doing well the past few months and yesterday they had gone shopping for her birthday dress. After finding the perfect dress, Pansy and her mother had gone to a restaurant for pizza and ice cream—a rare treat since Pansy's father stopped working.

Yesterday had been the best day Pansy could remember in her nine years. A gift from heaven—her mother all to herself, a fancy new dress, and her favorite meal all in one day. She'd gone to bed last night smiling and looking forward to today.

Her heart sinking, Pansy slowed her pace as she descended the staircase. Loud voices emanated from the kitchen.

"You were out all night," Pansy's mother ground out the words. "Where were you?"

"Ah, you know nothing about nothin'." Her father slurred his words as he always did when his breath smelled funny. "I work hard and you just keep picking on it."

"Work hard? You haven't worked in months." Her mother's voice broke. Was she crying? "And you're out drinking away the little money we have."

Pansy reached the bottom of the stairs and crept towards the kitchen. She peeked through the door that separated her from her parents. Her mother shoved an empty jam jar in her father's face. "That money was to pay the rent."

Her father flung his head back and stumbled against the counter. "Ha. Thought you could hide it, eh? It's my money too. You didn't mind spending money on a stupid dress yesterday."

Pansy pushed the door fully open and ran into the kitchen. "Please stop fighting. It's my birthday."

Pansy's mother stared past Pansy with eyes that she hadn't seen in a long time—not since the last time her mother had been quiet and taken to the hospital. Her mother threw the jar at her father. It crashed to the floor—the broken pieces scattering around the kitchen. "Now look what you've done," her mother hollered, then ran out of the kitchen in tears.

"Yeah, yeah. Everything's my fault. Nothing's your fault." Pansy stared at her father. She hadn't seen him this lopsided before—he seemed to have trouble standing. She'd witnessed that before, after he'd been drinking whiskey, but he never acted this way before lunch. Pansy glanced at the clock on the wall— eight o'clock in the morning. Her father turned his unfocused eyes in her direction. "You're old enough to know. Your mother's gone wacko. I'm going out." He threw open the back door to their home and left. Would she ever see him again?

Pansy clasped her hand over her stomach. She scanned the kitchen floor then carefully made her way to the broom propped in the corner. Li'l sis would be down soon. If she stepped on the glass, she'd get hurt. Pansy swept every inch of the kitchen floor, then swept it again. *That should do it.* She returned the broom to its resting place before heading upstairs to check on her sister and her mother.

The door to her parents' bedroom faced the top of the staircase. As Pansy reached for the doorknob, her heart started pounding. Was that what a heart attack felt like? Could someone her age have a heart attack? She'd heard the term on TV right before actors would grab their chests. She cracked the door open. "Mom? Are you okay?" She rapped on the door. "Mom?"

Not getting an answer, Pansy opened the door fully and entered the room where she had shared so many good times with her mother learning makeup tips and talking about her friends at school. When they had arrived home from shopping yesterday, she and her mother came to this room to hang up her birthday dress so Li'l sis wouldn't find it and mess it up with her dirty fingers.

Their mother was sprawled on the bed. She still had her shoes on, and she lay very still. Pansy froze for a moment, then ran to her mother's side. She rubbed her mother's face and shook her shoulders. Something seemed terribly wrong. "Mom! Mommy! Mommy, wake up!"

Her mother didn't respond, so Pansy ran downstairs to call 911. Li'l sis sat at the table eating dry cereal. "What's a matter, Pansy. Where's Mommy?"

Pansy inhaled deeply. "Everything's fine." *I hope.* "Finish your cereal and stay here. I have to make a phone call. Do *not* go back upstairs, okay?"

Li'l sis shrugged and ate a spoonful of cereal. Pansy used the cordless phone to call 911. The ambulance arrived a short time later, sirens screaming and lights flashing. Li'l sis continued to eat her cereal while Pansy followed the EMTs to her parents' room. When they pulled the sheet over her mother's head, Pansy's knees weakened. She knew what that meant—she'd seen it on TV.

The taller of the two EMTs crouched in front of Pansy. "Do you have a family member you can call to come pick up you and your sister?"

Pansy couldn't find the words to answer, so she shook her head.

The EMT straightened and clasped Pansy's shoulder. "I see. Well, we're going to take your mother to the hospital." He nodded at a police officer in the doorway. "Officer Smith will take you and your sister somewhere safe. Would that be okay?"

Pansy nodded. She didn't know if that would be okay, but she didn't know if anything would ever again be okay.

Pansy followed the officer downstairs, then watched the EMTs load the stretcher carrying her mother into the ambulance. Pansy couldn't hold back the tears any longer—would she ever see her mother again?

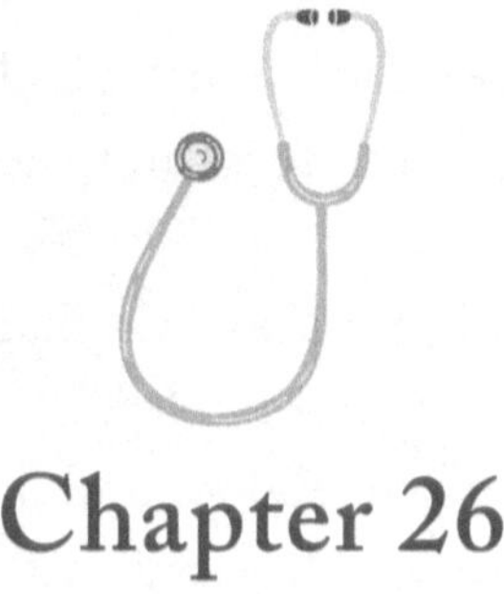

Chapter 26

LOUISE HEADED STRAIGHT to the treatment room upon her arrival at the clinic—she wanted to talk to Heidi about the change in who had been overseeing the semen shipments. When she opened the door, the sound of barking dogs and meowing cats greeted her. Heidi, her back against a kennel door, her left hand blocking the feline patient's escape, rolled a towel against her hip, sighed, then flung it across the room towards the laundry basket.

Louise followed the towel as it made its way onto the top of a pile of dirty towels. "I think you may have missed your calling. Have you ever thought of a career in basketball?"

Heidi sighed, then closed the kennel door and walked over to the basket.

Louise perused the white board. "What's going on? I thought we had a light day today."

Heidi pushed down the towels in the basket before lifting it. "So did I."

Louise approached the kennel Heidi had cleaned. The cat was now pawing at the bars, and she scratched his head. "Who's this?"

"Lincoln Webb. He got into a cat fight last night and now he has a swelling on his right hind leg."

Louise opened the kennel door and lifted Lincoln into her arms. She gently palpated his leg as she carried him to the treatment table. Heidi joined Louise and held onto Lincoln, allowing Louise to carefully investigate his lesion after shaving the swollen area. "He has a nice cellulitis going on, but no abscess we can lance at this point. We'll clean up the bite wounds, and while we're doing that, I need to ask you more questions about the AI shipping orders."

"Sure, what's up?"

"I'm wondering why Bob started overseeing the shipments."

"Like I said the other day, I have no idea, really. All I know is that I was happy to let him. He seemed to be trying so hard to be my buddy. I gotta' be honest, it was getting creepy."

Louise discarded the soiled gauze squares into the kidney bowl before washing her hands. "Did you mention his behaviour to Rita?"

Heidi shook her head and scooped Lincoln up, cradling him in her arms. "No, 'cause once he took over the paperwork and unpacking of the shipments, it stopped. I thought maybe it was my imagination, so I let it go."

"Have you noticed anything else out of the ordinary? Other than the number of vials being inaccurate? Did the shipping forms appear to be doctored at all?"

Heidi furrowed her brow. "No, but I didn't look at them *that* closely." She shifted Lincoln to her other arm. "Wait. I'd forgotten about this, but…"

"But?"

"The other day, after our chat in the staff room, I got curious, so when the next shipment arrived, I counted the vials and compared them to the shipping labels. The shipping label matched, so I checked our inventory chart. I hadn't thought to do that the last time. There were *four* extra vials this time. What do you think is going on?"

Louise combed her fingers through her hair. The vial numbers matched the shipping labels this time, but not the chart that Rita had insisted on creating to ensure that they were charging the breeders for the right amount of product. Louise's chest tightened. "I'm sure it's nothing." *I hope.* She drew one cc of an antibiotic into a syringe. Did Bob know about Rita's inventory chart? "Is Bob here yet?"

Heidi cupped her hand under Lincoln's chin and held his head close to her chest. "I haven't seen Bob yet, but I was getting the surgery patients ready when Lincoln came in. It's been a bit hectic this morning. Anyone could have passed through here unnoticed by me. Shirley said she'd come back and give me a hand once admissions were done, but the phone hasn't stopped ringing."

"What about Jenny?"

Heidi returned Lincoln to his kennel and gave him a bowl of water. "Jenny isn't scheduled to come in for another hour."

"Who's on surgery today? It isn't me, is it?" Louise winced. It wouldn't be the first time she'd forgotten her own schedule.

"No, I think it's Bob's day today. Nothing too big. A couple of cat neuters and a dog spay. Daphne showed up this morning. It's her day off, but Joe's taking his mother home, and he took the kids with him so they could visit their grandpa. Daphne said she's going to use the time to get caught up on her files."

Louise clapped her hands. "Perfect. I'll be in the office if you need me. Let me know when Bob arrives if he comes in here before he goes upstairs."

Heidi sprayed disinfectant on the exam table and wiped it clean. "Sure, but he should be here already." She shrugged. "If he's not upstairs, then I guess he's late. Again."

Louise found the office door closed when she arrived on the upper level of the clinic. The door across from the office, the entryway to the AI room, stood closed as well. Her stomach growled—missing breakfast after she'd set down her muffin was catching up to her. She made her way past both closed doors and headed towards the staff room to forage for a snack. When she reached the entryway, she stopped. Bob stood to one side of the window, his head tilted so that he could see out without being seen. Louise frowned. Rita had described him doing that the other day. *What is he hiding from?*

Louise stepped through the doorway and crossed her arms. "Bob?"

He spun around, lost his footing, and fell against the windowsill. Heidi hadn't been imagining things—he really was jumpy, and why was he still wearing his jacket? His bag sat unopened on the staff table, as though he had recently arrived at the clinic and gone straight to the staff room. Had he snuck up the rear stairwell? Mary and Shirley hadn't seen Bob when Louise inquired a few minutes ago.

Louise squinted. "What's going on? What are you staring at out there?"

Bob regained his composure and straightened his tie. "Me? Oh, nothing. I'm… um… looking to see if an ex-girlfriend is out there."

Louise furrowed her brow. "Is that something we should be worried about? Should we notify the police?"

His cheeks blanched a little as Bob retrieved his bag from the table. "No, of course not. We broke up last night and I'm a little worried she might show up here today and make a scene. That's all."

Louise lowered her arms. Was this guy serious, or not quick enough to make up more than one lame excuse for sneaking around? "Two breakups in one week? That's unfortunate."

Bob cocked his head. "Sorry?"

Louise smiled grimly. He obviously didn't remember his conversation with Rita earlier in the week. "Where have you been? Poor Heidi's downstairs trying to prep for surgery and handling a walk-in cat bite abscess all on her own. I believe we've explained that when the staff are overworked, we vets help them out. We don't leave all the dirty work for them to do on their own."

Bob swallowed hard. "Of course not. I'm happy to help out. Like I said, I wanted to make sure I hadn't been followed before getting started on my surgeries." He rotated his shoulders as if trying to release pent-up tension. "All clear out there—no psycho ex-girlfriends." He inclined his head towards the window.

The change in posture wasn't lost on Louise. Could there be at least a grain of truth in what he said? Perhaps he really was worried about being followed. But by whom?

Bob threw his bag over his shoulder and headed for the door. He paused when he reached Louise. "You know, I did see something going on in the parking lot that you should know. Eric was out there."

Louise strode to the window and scanned the parking lot. "Eric? Where?"

Bob shrugged. "Oh, he's not out there anymore. I saw him pull up, but before he got out of his car, some woman—she was crying—showed up and got into the passenger seat. I couldn't see too well, but they both looked pretty intense. Then they drove away."

Louise eyed Bob. Was he telling the truth? "When?"

Bob waved his hand in the air. "Right before you came in." He paused and averted his eyes. "Poor kid. I hope he's okay."

Louise wanted to maintain eye contact with Bob, but that was impossible when he refused to look directly at her. Should she fire Bob right now? No, she'd have to discuss it with Daphne first. Besides, her suspicions regarding their associate's off-work activities weren't a justifiable reason to fire him... not to the labor board. Not yet, anyway. Louise needed more information, and the best way to get that might be to keep Bob around. His veterinary skills were excellent, so keeping him on for a while longer didn't pose any danger to their patients.

Louise's stomach growled again. She walked over to the counter and helped herself to a double chocolate donut out of the box someone had left there. "Speaking of cars in the parking lot, Bob, I didn't see yours out there."

Bob's shoulders slumped. "Um... my car? No, you're right,

it's not there." He straightened his tie again. "It… it broke down last night. I had to drive a rental today."

Louise returned to the window and scanned the parking lot. "Which car is your rental? I don't see a strange car out there."

Bob stalked towards the hallway. "I parked across the street this morning. Thought I'd get some exercise. Anyway, off to start on the surgeries."

Louise sat on the windowsill and stared at the empty doorway. Why would he park across the street? Not for the exercise, that's a certainty. If he was lying about that, he could be lying about Eric too, but why? And Bob had mentioned a woman getting into Eric's car. Had Bob overheard her, or the others at the clinic, talking about a mystery woman? If Bob knew that Eric had been hanging around with an unknown woman, then he must know where Eric was.

Louise grabbed a second donut before heading to the doctor's office.

Daphne was seated at her desk, a large pile of scrap paper in front of her. When Louise entered, Daphne raised her head, then returned her gaze to her monitor. "Good morning. I see you found the donuts."

Louise raised the sweet treat in the air. "I did, thanks. You've no idea how much I needed one this morning." She sniffed the air. "And you started the coffee. I didn't know that you knew how to operate a coffee maker."

Daphne thrust her shoulders back. "I'm trying to expand my skill level. Veterinary surgeon, mother of two, and before long, coffee maker extraordinaire." She threw a chef's kiss into the air. "The donuts are from that new coffee shop that opened near our place last week. I couldn't resist."

Louise poured herself a cup of coffee. "No explanation

needed." She sat at her desk and opened her laptop. "I ran into Bob in the staff room. Remember what Rita had said about him sneaking around earlier in the week? He was doing the same thing when I caught him." Louise relayed her conversation with Bob.

"I wonder what's troubling him?"

Loiuse watched a fly as it flew against the window, trying to make its escape to freedom. Was Bob trying to make an escape? "I'm not sure, but it must have something to do with the semen shipments. Heidi told me earlier that the number of vials in the last shipment matches the shipment labels, but not the records Rita has been keeping."

Daphne rose from her desk and opened the window to let the fly out. "Do you think he's purposely ordering larger volumes than needed? I can't imagine why he would do that." After returning to her desk, she tapped a few keys on her keyboard then positioned her monitor so that Louise could see it. "I found this on my computer this morning. Someone has been searching for cheap flights."

"To where?"

Daphne scrolled through the search history. "Nowhere specific. It appears that the goal is to find a cheap flight to anywhere."

Louise felt light headed. Had Eric been at the clinic using Daphne's computer to find a means of fleeing the police? If he'd been involved in multiple robberies, and his accomplices had been arrested, he would need to get away from town. He had a sister living out west. Would he try to make his way to her? "Do you think Eric may have done this?"

Daphne shook her head. "If he snuck in here last night to use the computer, why would he come back this morning while we're all here?"

Louise rubbed her neck. "You're right. That makes no sense. Maybe Bob did it. It's possible he's in need of a flight from something… or someone."

Daphne reopened the veterinary software program and started typing. "I think he's simply, you know, being Bob. I'm sure you're imagining things."

A door across the hallway creaked then slammed closed. The office door swung open and Bob stuck his head into the room. "I have to go. Sorry." As quickly as he had made his entrance, Bob disappeared.

Louise eyed Daphne. "Still think I'm imagining things?"

Daphne twisted her lips. "Perhaps not. Guess I'll scratch my plans to do paperwork all morning and perform a few surgeries instead. Unless you'd like to be surgeon today?"

"No. Surgery is all yours. And I do appreciate you doing it on your day off. I have a few appointments this morning and should head downstairs." Louise grabbed the stethoscope she had draped over her monitor the day before and slung it around her neck.

Daphne did the same with her stethoscope. "I'm right behind you."

As the two practice owners approached the door to their office, Heidi appeared in the entrance and they both stopped. "Have you seen the AI room? I came up to grab a cola, and after our chat, Louise, I thought I'd glance in there on my way by. It's a mess. Someone trashed the place."

The three of them rushed across the hall.

Daphne raised her hand to her mouth. "Oh my. Do you think Bob did this?"

Louise stepped into the AI room, avoiding the glass shards.

"How could he have? We would have heard something. We were sitting merely a few feet away."

Daphne made her way to the far end of the room where several cardboard boxes had been torn open and emptied. The contents lay scattered on the floor. "The door was closed when I came in this morning."

Heidi pressed a hand to her forehead. "And I was in here right before leaving yesterday. It was neat and tidy. It sure didn't look like *this*."

Daphne examined the lock on the window. "Someone must have broken in last night, but the alarm didn't go off, and this window is secure. I didn't get a call from the security firm." She turned to Louise. "Obviously you didn't either."

Louise shook her head. "No. I would have called you right away if I had." She joined Daphne at the window. "So how did they get in? Mary would have said something if the entry doors had been tampered with when she arrived this morning. You don't think…"

Heidi lifted a hand. "Don't think what?"

Daphne frowned. "No, you're being overly suspicious again."

Heidi crossed her arms. "Suspicious of what? This is turning into one of those conversations where the two of you speak in code."

Daphne pushed one of the empty cardboard boxes with her foot, revealing a small pool of beige liquid. "Eric wouldn't do this. Why would he make a mess in here?"

Louise rubbed her temples. "I don't know, but he did disappear, then weeks later he's seen at the docks. And after his old buddies get arrested, they find the baseball card I gave him in Keith Giles' apartment."

Daphne, who had been dabbing at the beige liquid with a paper towel, shot a glance at Louise. "What did you say about Eric's friends getting arrested? And what about the baseball card?"

Louise's eyes widened. "Um… let's pretend I didn't say that. Alex stopped by the house this morning, but he made me promise that I wouldn't repeat what he'd told me."

Daphne stood. "Why is he sharing information with you that I can't know? I care about Eric too."

"Of course you do, but Alex knows that you won't do anything foolish to try to find Eric. At least, that's what he thinks. He seems to have more faith in your common sense than in mine."

Daphne snorted. "That is completely understandable."

Louise made her way to the door, avoiding the glass and other objects on the floor. "We have to admit it, as much as we want Eric to be innocent of the robberies, he did take off. It's just so … strange."

Heidi retrieved a handful of garbage bags from the one cupboard that hadn't been emptied. "True, but Bob has been acting strangely too. Don't forget that. Besides, if Eric was searching for drugs, he wouldn't have to do this. He knows where the controlled-drug cupboard is."

"We can't jump to conclusions," Daphne tossed the paper towel into a trash can. "About either of them"

Louise reached for the phone in her pocket. "I'd better give Alex a call." She pointed to the bags in Heidi's hand. "I think it's best not to touch anything yet in case there are fingerprints." Louise scrolled to Alex's name in her contact list and hit the enter key. She listened for a few rings, then tapped the end button. "Alex isn't answering. I'll try again, but in the meantime, we should get an idea of what is here in case something has been stolen. Heidi, do you need to go downstairs to set up for surgery?"

"No. Jenny should be here by now. She's on surgery today. I'll buzz down and let her know what's going on up here."

Daphne handed a pen and pad of paper to Heidi. "Let Jenny know that we've had a change of surgeons today. She's probably already set up for Bob, but my hands will swim in those size eight gloves he wears."

"Will do."

While Heidi left to go to the doctor's office, Louise and Daphne picked their way carefully around the room, assessing the damage, which was extensive. The liquid nitrogen tanks had been emptied of their vials, as had the freezer and refrigerator. The vials lay smashed on the floor. Louise pressed a hand to her roiling stomach. The ruined samples splashed across the floor represented thousands of dollars worth of product. The supplies in the cabinets had been tossed onto the counters and floor, some of the materials broken, and most of the sterile packaging torn.

After returning to the AI room, Heidi picked up the one unbroken vial. "This is all garbage now. Even if not broken, we have no idea how long these specimens have been sitting out."

Louise held up her palm to Heidi. "Remember not to touch anything."

Heidi returned the vial to the spot she had found it. "Oops. Sorry." She worked her way to the new tanks. "One of the shipping containers is missing. There was a new shipment early last week, and I'm sure it was sitting right here by these other two."

Daphne made a note of the missing container. "Heidi, why don't you and Rita pull all of the shipping records. You'll need to match up what's still here with the delivery and patient records."

Louise slapped Daphne on the shoulder. "That's a great idea."

Daphne grinned. "And let's see if any of the semen for the Wells' dog is missing."

Heidi donned a pair of exam gloves. "Why the Wells' dog?"

Daphne clipped her pen onto her clipboard. "Because, as far as I can tell, all of these odd goings on started after I left for maternity leave and Bob introduced the AI program. And of all the new clients he has introduced to the clinic, Nancy is the most concerning."

Heidi's eyebrows rose. "Better be careful, Daphne. You're starting to sound a lot like Louise."

Louise feigned a scowl. "Really, Heidi? And who's the one wearing exam gloves to examine the crime scene?"

Daphne giggled. Louise's mood lightened, happy that they could still laugh together despite all the craziness. She tried Alex's number again and this time he answered, but it was a short conversation.

"Alex can't help. He's busy with something urgent right now, although he couldn't tell me what. He said to call 911." As she was returning her phone to her pocket, Louise caught sight of a familiar item on the floor under the window. Why hadn't she noticed it before? Remembering her precaution to Heidi, she bent down to view the document without touching it. The color of the paper and the font tickled her memory. Where had she seen this before? After studying it for a few seconds, Louise gasped—it resembled the bloodied paper she had found in Tim Gates' NKC office the night she had snuck in.

On the bottom right corner of the page, the number one thousand had been entered in numerical form, but the last zero looked unusual. Louise squinted. Was that a dot over the middle of the zero? Had a third zero been added over top of a period? If so, then the original sum would have been one hundred, not one thousand. Louise retrieved her phone and opened the album app. She flipped through the photos until she found the picture she had taken of the evidence she had since given to Alex. There it was. One hundred dollars printed in numerical digits on the bottom right corner, in the same font and size.

She studied the words in the photo. In the same position on the document on the floor that she read 'shipment', was the partial word 'ipmen'. That made sense. It was a shipping invoice. What about the other partial word—'razi'? The document on the floor had the word England in the corresponding location of the word 'razi' on the NKC document. England had been entered as the origin of the shipment. That made sense because Bob had told her that many of their AI products came from England, but what did 'razi' mean?

Two officers from the Bathurst Region Police Department responded to the 911 call from the Black Creek Animal Hospital. Rita's propensity for keeping detailed records on clinic supplies, including those needed for the AI program, proved to be invaluable in assessing the financial extent of the damage done in the AI room. The two police officers, Brian Tomlin—a five-year veteran with the force, and Wayne Carter, a seven-year veteran—initially suggested that the vandalism could be the result of the actions of a group of neighborhood kids. Their interest in the case increased, however, not only when Louise explained to them that Detective Alex Haines had two of the clinic's employees under investigation, but also once Rita explained the large sum the insurance claim would be for.

The officers recorded statements from the staff who had

been in the building that morning, as well as taking multiple photographs of the crime scene. At Louise's insistence, they promised to send a CSI team to take fingerprints.

Louise escorted the officers to the front office as soon as they completed their tasks. Mary and Shirley had been busy during this time rescheduling the day's appointments. Louise watched as the officers piled into the cruiser and drove away. She sighed and leaned on the counter in front of Mary. Just as quickly, she straightened. Bob was back already?

Mary ended the call she had been on, then followed Louise's gaze to the parking lot. "Well, well. Look who's back."

Did Mary share Louise's suspicion that Bob's return *after* the police had left was an unlikely coincidence? Louise kept her eyes on Bob as he walked into the clinic, but mental fatigue kept her quiet. She let Mary lead the inquisition.

Mary leaned back in her chair and crossed her legs. "Well, hello, Dr. Kurt. You have amazing timing. How is it you missed the visit from the police department?"

Bob offered an unconvincing look of surprise. "The *police*? Why were they here? When?"

Mary narrowed her eyes. "Just now, before you walked in. Almost like you planned it that way."

Bob's nostrils flared. "Why would I do that?"

Mary straightened. "Chill, man, I'm kidding"

Bob's laugh sounded forced. "Right. Sure." He nodded stiffly at Louise. "Um… I'd better get started on those surgeries."

Louise stared at Bob. "No need. Daphne finished the two cat neuters while I was dealing with the police. I believe she's finishing up the dog spay as we speak."

Bob shifted his bag from one shoulder to the other. "Okay. Guess I'll go see if they need any help."

Keep it cool, Louise. Bob knew that Louise and Daphne were good friends with Alex. She didn't want to let on to him that he might be a suspect in a police investigation. "You do that. I'm sure Daphne would appreciate it."

Bob retreated through an exam room, heading towards the treatment area.

Shirley shook her head. "What's up with him today?"

Mary shrugged. "Beats me, but I'm starting to wonder if he's on something."

Louise didn't think that Bob indulged in mind-altering drugs, but at this point, nothing was off the table. She'd been suspicious of his involvement with Eric's disappearance and the recent break-ins, but what if she was wrong about *how* he was involved. Was he a thief? A suppler? A buyer and user? The thought made her stomach lurch again. She couldn't let this man have uncontrolled access to the clinic. She needed to confront him to ensure the safety of her staff and patients, even if it compromised Alex's investigation.

Louise marched towards the treatment room, but she found Bob in the clinic pharmacy. That might be good—she could speak to him without the presence of any staff members—or it might be bad. Why was he loitering around the drugs? On the other hand, as Heidi had pointed out about Eric earlier, Bob knew the location of the cupboard with the controlled drugs. Nothing in the clinic pharmacy would entice a drug addict with a DVM degree – he would know that the controlled drugs are kept in a secure location.

Louise positioned herself directly in front of their new hire. "Where did you go? What's with taking off like that?"

Bob adjusted his tie. "Sorry, family emergency."

Louise eyed Bob's tie—he adjusted it a lot. What was that, a nervous habit? If he wasn't careful, he'd choke himself with the thing. "Really? And what type of emergency makes you rush off from your job? You know, your *job*." When he didn't reply, Louise inhaled deeply. "You don't say anything, no details. Such a big rush to get out, then you're back not even an hour later ready to work? Seriously? What's really going on?"

Bob lifted both hands. "I'm sorry. I'll explain it all later. It was… a family thing."

Louise stepped closer to him. "What do you know about the mess in the AI room? You were in there right before you ran off."

Bob stepped back. "No, I wasn't in there this morning. I told you Eric was sneaking around the parking lot earlier. Maybe he'd been in there? That woman he was with, she probably put him up to it."

Louise leaned on the counter. She didn't like confrontations like this, but she was sure he was hiding something. "Put him up to what? If you hadn't been in the AI room, how would you know that there was something to put Eric up to? Where did you go after you left the staff room earlier?"

Bob glanced at his phone. "I was… down the hall. In Rita's office. I was checking through the big bags of dog food to see if I could find the new weight loss diet."

Louise furrowed her brow. "You're late for work on a busy day and you take the time to do inventory?"

Bob's face reddened. "A friend of mine was asking about it on the weekend. His dog is overweight and he's worried about her health."

Louise rolled her eyes. "Well, Daphne has likely finished the surgeries you were supposed to do today, and we're light on appointments this morning, so you're free to attend to your *emergency*." Would he give something away by reacting to her offer?

Bob batted away the suggestion. "No need. It's all taken care of, for now."

Louise raised her eyebrows and crossed her arms. "Wow. Gotta love those quick-to-fix emergencies. Did it have anything to do with Nancy Wells? She has emergencies that aren't really emergencies too."

Bob's skin flushed an even deeper red. "Um, no. I haven't seen Nancy in a while. Anyway, I have some files to write up. How about I go do that and we can talk later?" He backed up, towards the staircase.

Louise continued to stare at him. That was a strong reaction to the mention of Nancy's name. Louise had suspected that Nancy might also be involved in whatever Bob was up to, but now all doubt vanished. "Sure, Bob. You do that."

Louise watched Bob scurry up the stairs, then she made her way to the X-ray room where they kept the safe that housed the controlled drugs. She turned the dial until she heard the click that assured her the lock was fully engaged. After informing Daphne and the technicians that the safe was now locked, she headed to her office. If she'd ever needed a coffee, the time was now, although, given the level of adrenaline coursing through her, perhaps decaf would be a good idea.

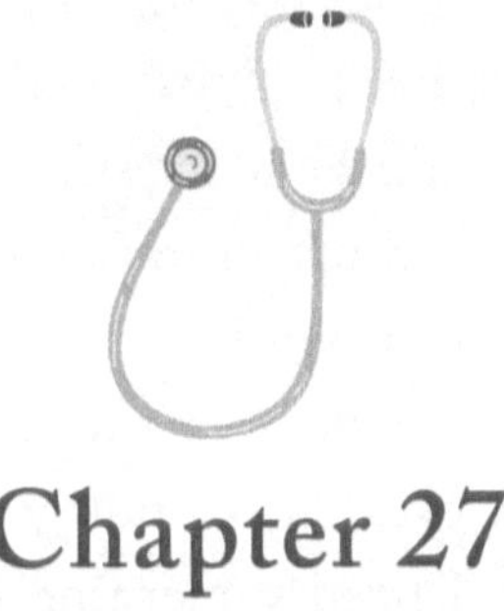

Chapter 27

LOUISE GLANCED UP at the clock on the office wall, expecting to see the little hand pointing to the four, but it seemed to be stuck at the eleven o'clock position. Was it broken? It felt like hours had passed since she'd last tried to get Alex on the phone, but the second hand skipped along at the proper pace. Louise inhaled deeply and rose from her desk. Where could he be and why wasn't he checking his messages? Had he been informed about the extent of the break-in at their clinic? She shook her head. If he had, he would have called.

She lifted her phone to see if she'd missed a call. Her shoulders slumped at the lack of red dots that would have indicated a message was waiting. Gripping the phone tighter, she dragged herself to the window and rested her forehead on the cold glass. Another deep inhalation of room air did little to calm her nerves. She pulled her arm back a little, resisting the urge to slam the phone against the wall. *Where are you, Alex?*

"How are you doing?" Daphne tapped Louise on the shoulder before making her way to her desk.

Louise shook her head. "Frustrated and worried. Being friends with a police officer is stressful—you never know if they are safe or not. I don't know how anyone can handle being in a relationship with one."

Daphne raised her eyebrows. "Hmm, good thing you're not."

Louise rolled her eyes. "Let's not get into my friendship with Alex right now. I need something to take my mind off everything that's going on. What's happening downstairs?"

"Nothing much. I'm concerned that the person who ransacked the AI room might return, so I've asked Mary to reschedule the remainder of today's appointments. We sent the two cats who were neutered home, but Lincoln and the dog spay are still here. Having a quieter morning will give us a chance to get the AI room cleaned now that the police have finished in there. Every surface is coated with black debris from the fingerprint dusting."

Louise pocketed her phone and clapped her hands. "That's a great idea, and while you are doing that, I'll head to the office supply store and then the bank. I need a distraction."

Without waiting for a reply from Daphne, Louise gathered up her bag and bolted out of the office.

The westbound traffic on Highway 401, Canada's busiest roadway, was thick with transport trucks and passenger vehicles. The traffic volume was typical for this time of day on a late summer Friday—a mixture of people heading to work or meetings, others heading home after an over-night shift. Lots of them would be cottagers getting an early start on what might be the last nice weekend of the year. Finding herself behind a transport truck in need of a tune-up, Louise switched on the air conditioner and changed the air flow setting to recycle. It was a cool September morning, but weathering a few chills was more appealing than breathing in the choking exhaust being spewed from the semi in front of her.

She didn't have to endure the discomfort for long—less than a mile later she signalled a lane change and exited the highway. Going through a memory-dependent inventory of what they might need at the office supply store, Louise was struck with the tiniest pang of guilt for leaving Daphne and the staff to clean up the mess in the AI room. *But someone has to purchase the printer paper.* Louise conveniently chose to forget that Rita, as office manager, would normally order their office supplies over the internet.

The sought-after store was housed in a strip mall a few blocks east of the Bathurst Center where Louise and Daphne had met Cliff Mariner at the dog show. Driving past the large arena, Louise's heart felt heavy. The world had always been a dangerous place, that's why she'd stopped watching the news several years ago—to avoid the early morning barrage of vio-lence and tragedy that it brought to her mind, not a positive way to start the day. At the time she'd decided that it would be healthier to spend that time praying for her friends and family, but the truth was that she hadn't really followed through with that. Most mornings were spent frantically getting ready for work after hitting the snooze button one too many times.

When Cliff Mariner was murdered, and Eric disappeared, it was as if the worries of the world she had been trying to avoid had run up and smacked her on the side of the face. Was her response adequate? What had she been doing the past few weeks? Louise slowed the car and turned into the parking lot, then quickly found a spot near the office supply store. After shifting the car into park and pressing the engine button, she leaned back in her seat and closed her eyes. *What have I been doing? Running around trying to find Eric, but how often have I prayed about it?*

When she opened her eyes, the storefront for a travel agency loomed before her. A colorful poster in the window offered customers the mountain adventure of a lifetime—an adventurous trek through a rain forest followed by a lesson on base jumping and wing suit flying. In the photo, a young man stood on the edge of a cliff, wearing a suit that would have made him look like a bat if it was black instead of neon orange. Louise recoiled at the thought of jumping from such a height and putting her life into the hands of the suit makers, but why did that scene seem so familiar?

Her gaze froze on the mountain scene and the young man for several minutes. Something was nipping at her memory, but what was it? From the corner of her eye, she spotted a man leaving the variety store carrying a large jug of chocolate milk. He appeared to be in his mid-twenties and had short brown hair. When he opened the jug and lifted it to his lips, Louise held her breath. Eric drank the same size jug of chocolate milk almost daily, and he'd do it in one sitting.

Her eyes darted to the poster as she was reminded of the unusual dream she'd had about veterinary college. She'd had that dream four weeks ago, the same day that Bob Kurt had started working with them at the animal hospital. So much had happened since the dream that she had completely forgotten about it.

She and Daphne had spoken about the details that day at lunch—when Bob had pulled his first disappearing act. *That was our first clue that something was up with that man.* She had asked Daphne's opinion regarding God speaking to people through dreams. Had He been speaking to her? Was God warning her that Eric was in trouble? No. There was something else.

Louise lowered her forehead to the steering wheel and replayed the dream sequence in her mind. Dream-Daphne had reminded her of something important—the need to forgive. *Is that what the dream was about, Father? Were you preparing me to be ready to forgive Eric again? What could he possibly do to cause me to waver on forgiving him?* Louise's chest tightened. *Or are You telling me I will need to forgive someone for hurting Eric?*

Chapter 28

TEN-YEAR-OLD PANSY KNEW it was safe to get Li'l sis up and dressed when she heard movement and talking in her foster parents' room. Before rousing her sister, she wiped the tears from her eyes and blew her nose—she didn't want to upset Li'l sis. Remembering the past caused Pansy to ache all over, so she tried not to remember, but once a year that last day with her mother overwhelmed her senses.

You don't need a new dress, Pansy, or a birthday party. Those things are for babies. You're not a baby.

Pansy gripped Li'l sis's shoulder and gave her a gentle shake. "Hey, kid, wake up."

Li'l sis rolled onto her back and pushed Pansy's arm away. "No. I'm sleepy still."

Pansy shot a glance at the clock on the desk, then shook Li'l sis again. "Come on, Li'l sis. We're going to be late for school. The mom and dad slept in again." Pansy glared at the closed door—she could hear their foster parents on the other side. They were the adults. Why weren't they the ones making sure that she and Li'l sis got to school on time?

It was getting harder and harder to make up excuses for their tardiness without telling the teachers what was really going on, but Pansy feared that if she told the truth, there would be trouble. Her foster father scared her. If he got mad enough, would he strike her or Li'l sis? Would they have to go to a different foster home? Pansy had heard stories about foster homes that were worse than this one. Here they had clean clothes and dinner every day, and they did get to go to school, even if they were often late. Pansy's worse fear was the possibility that she and Li'l sis might be separated and sent to different foster homes—their foster father had told them that he could make that happen if they misbehaved. Li'l sis was the only family Pansy had left—they had to stay together.

The following three years had been difficult, but the foster home had become Pansy and Li'l sis's new normal. They had settled into the strict, cold routine of life with their emotionally distant foster parents by creating their own happy world within the confines of the small bedroom they shared.

Their world was thrown into upheaval again one day when Pansy was thirteen. She arrived home from school to find her and Li'l sis's clothes packed in garbage bags and sitting on the front porch. Her foster mother, who had been reclining on the porch swing, rose and met Pansy at the front door.

"You and that kid sister of yours are moving out today."

Pansy's throat went dry. "But… why?" What about school and her friends? What about her room and the secret treasures she had collected and hidden away over the years? Would she and Li'l sis still be together? Pansy sniffed but fought back the tears—she didn't want to cry in front of her foster mother— she wasn't going to show weakness to this woman.

The mother moved in front of the door, blocking Pansy from entering. "We're tired of sharing our home with kids that aren't even our own. And now that you're a teenager, it's not worth the little bit of money we get to put up with, well, you know… all that hormone stuff. Your social worker will be here soon to pick you up."

Pansy stared at the woman who had fed and clothed her for four years. This was the only home she and Li'l sis had known since their parents left them. What would they do now? Who was going to take care of them?

Pansy glanced at the two green garbage bags that held everything she and her sister owned. When she was younger, at home with her real parents, she had toys and books that she could call her own. She treasured some of those toys, but after her mother's funeral her Aunt Quinn told her that she couldn't keep anything.

Aunt Quinn had hosted a large gathering of people in Pansy's childhood home after the funeral. The guests, most of whom Pansy didn't know, ate, drank, and laughed as though they were at a celebration. Pansy hid in her room. Why were these people having a party when her mother was dead? Why weren't they all crying and screaming and slamming doors like she wanted to?

Once the house was quiet, Pansy crept downstairs. She found her Aunt Quinn and cousin Blair sorting through her mother's china cabinet and wrapping the plates in paper before placing them into a box.

Pansy crossed her arms. "Those are my things."

Aunt Quinn glared at Pansy. "Your things? My dear, you have no things. Anything here worth anything is mine now. I lent your parents money a few years ago, money I never got back, so once you and your sister are gone, I'll be having a garage sale."

Pansy stomped her foot. "Li'l sis and I aren't going anywhere. This is our house."

Blair laughed. "You're such a dumb kid. You can't live here without adults. You need money. You don't have any." She stuck her tongue out at Pansy.

Pansy furrowed her brow. "I can have my own garage sale. I know what that is. And I'm not dumb. You are."

Pansy had tried to stand her ground, but she soon learned that Blair had been correct—the child welfare people would not allow a nine-year-old and a four-year-old to live alone together without an adult. The day after her mother's funeral, Pansy and Li'l sis watched as their Aunt Quinn packed two small gym bags, one for Pansy and one for Li'l sis. Each bag contained two pairs of pajamas, two outfits, underwear, and socks.

When the social worker arrived, she lifted the two bags and eyed Aunt Quinn. "Is this all they have?"

Aunt Quinn nodded. "Yes. That's it. They're kids. That's all they need."

Pansy stared at the stranger on their lawn. She had kind eyes, and when she noticed Pansy watching her, she smiled before crouching to match the young girl's height. "Hello, Pansy. You and … what do you call your sister?"

Pansy smiled. "Li'l sis, cause when she was a baby, she was so little."

The lady extended her hand to Li'l sis. "That's a sweet nickname. You two can call me Ms. Lori. I'm going to take you to your new home." Ms. Lori rose and took a few steps toward her car, then stopped and turned back to address Aunt Quinn. "It is generally preferable for children to stay with family members."

Aunt Quinn sneered. "Preferable for whom?"

Ms. Lori didn't answer, only strode to the car and opened the back door for Pansy and Li'l sis. Pansy sighed. She didn't know what the future held, but she did know that she didn't want to live with her cousin Blair.

That had been four years ago. Now their things were packed into bags and they were, once again, awaiting transport to a strange new home.

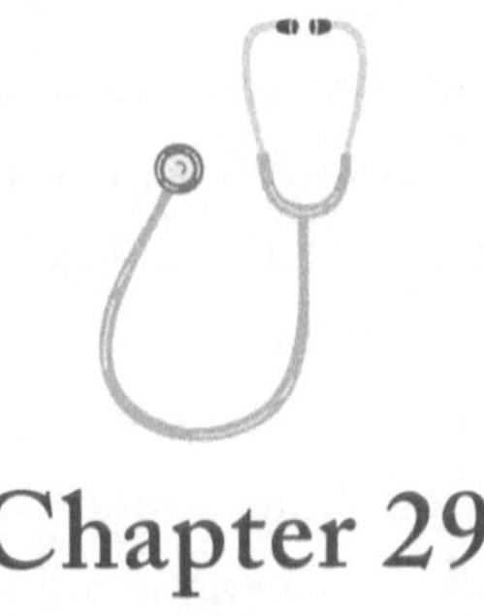

Chapter 29

L OUISE RAISED HER head from the steering wheel and gasped when she saw the man with the jug of milk standing outside her window, staring at her. She lowered the glass an inch.

The young man tilted his head and leaned in closer. "Are you all right, miss?"

Louise forced a smile. "I am, thank you. It's been one of those, you know… days."

The curly-haired good Samaritan nodded. "Oh yeah. We all have them kinda days."

Louise contemplated him as he laughed. He seemed to be a deep soul for someone who looked so young.

"Anyway, I'm glad you're okay." He indicated a car across the lot. "My ride is here. I hope the rest of your day is better."

Louise waved. "Thanks. You have a great day yourself."

Staring into the rear-view mirror, she watched him walk toward a car parked on the street side of the lot. A couple in the bus station lot across the street caught her eye. They were too far away for a clear view of their faces, but the man's jacket... *That's Eric's jacket.*

Louise started her car and slammed the transmission into reverse while decreasing the pressure on the brake. The back-up alert screamed at her. She instinctively slammed her foot down and stole a glance in the rear-view mirror. The elderly man who appeared in the reflection waved a cane in the air, his eyes narrowed. Louise rotated her head to make eye contact with him, and mouthed *sorry*. He shook his head and continued on his way—slowly. Louise inhaled deeply, held her breath, and counted to ten.

As soon as her potential victim had safely made his way past her car, Louise checked for other obstacles, then pulled out and spun her car ninety degrees. The traffic light at the exit to the strip mall turned red. *Figures.* She came to a full stop then, tapping her fingers on the steering wheel, scanned the lot across the street for the guy wearing the familiar jacket. Passengers poured off a recently arrived bus, and others were lining up to board it, making it difficult to see the couple she had spotted earlier. The man had been with a person of slight build and long hair. Was that the woman Roger had seen Eric with at the docks?

The light changed to green and Louise eased her car across the street and into the crowded parking lot. She drove towards the entrance to the building, hoping to spot the jacket, but as she drew closer to the passenger loading area, a barrier loomed in front of her, preventing her from proceeding. She was forced to turn right and travel west between two other cars that had also been diverted. Gripping the steering wheel tighter, Louise leaned toward the dash and scanned the crowds, careful not to hit the car in front of her. A horn sounded from behind, returning her attention to the driveway. She was in no danger of crashing into the car that had been in front of her because it was now several car lengths ahead. Glancing in the rear-view mirror, she noted that the female driver of the car behind her appeared to be upset. Once again, in less than ten minutes, Louise found herself apologizing for bad driving. She waved at the woman and increased her speed to meet that of the vehicle ahead.

As the line-up of cars rolled past the end of the building, Louise caught a glimpse of a passenger parking lot to her left. Not wanting to upset the lady behind her, she scanned the lot without slowing down. There it was—the red and blue leather sports jacket that Eric always wore at this time of year. The wearer had his back to her, but he was the right height with the right hair color and hair style. It had to be Eric.

Without thinking, Louise hit the brake. The horn behind her sounded louder and longer this time. *Stupid. This is not the time to cause an accident.* She waved another apology and pressed lightly on the accelerator while searching for a way into that area of the parking lot. The horn behind her didn't stop. Were there now multiple horns? The man in the jacket raised his head and glanced over his shoulder in the direction of the noise. It *was* Eric and the car he stood next to was his, but another barrier prevented Louise from entering that lot from her current position. The exit she was being forced to wouldn't allow her to turn left—she'd have to turn right on to the main road, then circle around the bus station to get in the vicinity of Eric and his companion. She lowered her window, waved her arm, and called his name, but no one would have been able to hear her at that distance with all the honking horns.

As she approached her exit lane, Eric's car pulled out and headed to a left turn exit. Locating Eric and catching up to him would be nearly impossible—traffic was heavy and they were going in opposite directions. *Nuts. Now what. Go to the bank? Call Alex?* There was no convenient or safe place to pull over, so Louise turned right. At the next intersection she signaled a right turn that would take her to the bank two towns east. She'd call Alex from there.

The bank used by the Black Creek Animal Hospital was situated on Main Street in Georgetown, east of Coverdale. Two blocks west of the bank, Louise passed the Georgetown Veterinary Clinic on her right. The urge to stop and say hi to her friend and colleague Dr. Cheryl Smith came and left quickly. She needed to call Alex about her Eric sighting, and she'd now been gone from her own clinic for over an hour. Though her business partner hadn't called, Louise suspected that Daphne was starting to wonder what had become of her.

After the break-in at Cheryl's clinic last month, Cheryl closed the Georgetown clinic for a few days to clean up the mess the thieves had left behind. Were they the same people who had broken into Louise and Daphne's clinic last night? In Cheryl's case, they targeted the pharmacy and tried to open the locked cupboard that housed the controlled drugs. They were unsuccessful in that endeavor, but they did find the five-hundred-dollar cash float hidden under the front counter, prompting Cheryl to insist that their cash float now be stored in the clinic safe.

It didn't make sense that people who were after cash and drugs would focus on the AI room at Louise's clinic. Why hadn't they searched elsewhere if what they were after wasn't in the only room they ransacked? Had they been interrupted by something? Or perhaps by someone? If so, who? Did they find what they were looking for? What could that possibly be? How did they get past the clinic's alarm system? Louise clenched a fist and tapped it against the side of her head. So many questions. Eric and Bob both had a code to deactivate the system, but according to the alarm company, neither of their codes had been used.

Louise signaled a left turn, then drove into the bank's parking lot. Normally she would go into the building to say hello to the small staff, one of the perks of living in a small town. Everyone working there knew who she was, making a work task feel more like a social encounter. Peering at the clock on her dashboard, Louise was reminded of the time and how long she'd been gone from the clinic. She'd use the drive-thru to make her deposit then call Alex and Daphne before heading back to Coverdale.

As she maneuvered her car around the corner of the build-ing to access the ATM, she spotted movement at the town-houses across the street. She slowed to get a better look. It was Eric. Louise knew that Eric had friends living in Georgetown, but she didn't know exactly where. Was this their place? If he was on the run from the police, would he go to a friends? The woman from the bus station was still with him. Louise wanted to get over there and confront them, but couldn't easily back up from her current position in the one-way laneway, and a blue Honda Civic in front of her prevented her from moving forward. Not wanting to leave her car unattended in the drive-thru, she was forced to watch the action across the street from her current position.

Eric raised his hands and slapped them to his cheeks. The woman removed something from her pocket and dabbed at her eyes. *She must be crying.* Eric reached into his own pocket and retrieved his cell phone, then handed it to the attractive, blonde woman. She tapped on the screen before pressing the phone to her ear.

What's going on? Louise opened her door and started to get out of her car. *What are you doing Louise?* She stood frozen for a moment. Should she call Alex? Or should she go over and question Eric? She had promised Alex that she wouldn't do anything foolish, and if Eric was involved with drug dealers, it could be dangerous to confront him. She didn't know whose townhouse that was — what if there were criminals inside? *Why isn't the Honda moving forward?*

Louise gently compressed her horn to encourage the vehicle in front of her to move. It was parked in front of the ATM, but she hadn't seen anyone in the car use the automated teller. Still standing part way out of her own car, she leaned to the left to get a view of the occupant. From her position, she couldn't see anyone in the driver's seat, so unless the driver was really small, no one was in the vehicle. *Great!*

Louise stepped out of her car, slammed the door, and marched to the driver's side of the Honda. The door was slightly ajar and papers were strewn all over the floor and seats. Louise glanced to her right and left before striding around to the front of the bank, hoping to see the driver of the blue car. She was alone in the parking lot. She was tempted to enter the car and examine the papers to see if she could find the owner's name or phone number, but she successfully resisted the urge to unlawfully enter. If she got caught, she'd have a hard time explaining her snooping to the police, especially one detective in particular.

Thinking that the driver must have gone into the bank, Louise went in herself to ask him or her to move the car, but when she passed through the entry doors, it was obvious there were no other customers. *Oddly quiet over the lunch hour.* Louise made her way to the teller to let him know that a car was blocking the drive-thru. Before she left the building, she used the inside ATM to make her deposit. When she returned to her car, the blue Honda was still at the outside ATM, but Eric was gone.

I should have walked over there and talked to him when I had the chance. What is he up to? Louise retrieved her phone and tapped on the contacts list. She scrolled to Eric's name, then clicked on dial and waited. It rang twice before the voice mail came on asking her to leave a message.

"Eric, I don't know what's going on, but at this point I'm just glad to see you're alive. Please, please call me back."

Louise ended the call and returned her phone to her pocket. She'd call Alex when she got back to the clinic. Still blocked in by the Honda, she carefully reversed out the laneway before starting her return to Coverdale.

Chapter 30

WHEN LOUISE OPENED the back door to the clinic, the sound of loud, exaggerated voices drifted from the front office. She dropped her bag to the ground and scurried to see what the commotion was all about. Expecting to find a celebration, or possibly a disgruntled client, Louise was surprised to discover Mary and Shirley alone at their stations.

They were laughing, and their hands were dancing through the air to the pattern of their speech. Mary slapped Shirley on the shoulder. "That was wild. You crack me up sometimes."

Louise stepped out of the exam room and approached the counter. "What's so funny? I thought there was a party going on up here."

Shirley averted her gaze. "Um. Just a little goofing off. Too much caffeine for lunch, I think."

Mary plopped into her chair. "I didn't know Shirley was so good at impressions. She cracked me up."

Shirley shot a knowing look in Mary's direction. Louise wasn't concerned that they might be shirking their duties—they were two of the most reliable receptionists she'd ever worked with. However, the news that Shirley did impressions, and the look she sent Mary's way, piqued Louise's suspicion that something more was going on. Perhaps if they shared what it was, it would lighten her own mood.

Louise leaned on the counter and caught Shirley's eye. "I love a good impression. Lay it on me."

Shirley returned to her seat. "The moment has passed."

Louise tilted her head and smiled. "You weren't mimicking me, were you?"

Shirley's eyes widened. "No. Of course not. Just… well… Nancy Wells was in earlier and…"

Mary scooped up a small pile of pens and deposited them into a container on the counter. "Not long after you left, Nancy Wells showed up with her dog Scarlet and insisted on seeing Bob. She said she'd been trying to call him on his cell all morning, but that he wasn't answering. In her usual nasty manner, she insisted on seeing Bob *immediately*." Mary rolled her eyes.

Mary and Shirley were both skilled at staying calm in a storm—it was unlike them to react in an unprofessional manner towards a difficult client. Still, Nancy Wells *had* been excessively difficult in the short time they'd known her.

Mary straightened a pile of file folders on the desk. "Bob wasn't busy, but I told her he was. Sorry. I couldn't resist. In truth, I wasn't really sure what he was doing. The surgeries were done and we'd canceled all the appointments for the day like Daphne had asked us to do. Bob must have been hiding upstairs."

Louise rubbed her chin. Mary's choice of words was interesting. Bob had been hiding when Louise encountered him earlier in the day. Was he indeed still hiding? "Did Bob see Nancy?"

"He sure did." Mary's hands became animated again. "Nancy was getting red in the face. She insisted that she had an AI appointment with Scarlet, but we didn't have anything booked for her. When that finger of hers approached my face, I buzzed Bob to let him know she was here."

Shirley slapped the desk with her palm. "And bam! He was down here in a shot. I've never seen him move so fast. He popped his head out of exam room one and motioned for Nancy to join him. She went in and the door slammed shut. To be honest, I was a little worried that Bob might be in danger."

Louise removed one of the pens from the container and clicked repeatedly on the spring end. One of their pens had been found in the burnt-out warehouse, but it wasn't one of these. The one the police found had a defect so they hadn't made those accessible to clients.

Louise inhaled deeply. "Why is that?"

Shirley straightened in her seat. "It was wild. Nancy was screaming at him, then he'd tell her to shush and keep her voice down. It would be quiet for a while, then their voices would rise again."

"Did you hear anything specific?" Louise asked.

Shirley shook her head. "Only a few bits and pieces. Like Bob saying 'stop worrying, I've got it under control' and at one point Nancy said, 'I don't get it, what do they want?'"

Shirley had indeed done an impressive impression of both Bob and Nancy, but her last comment caused Louise's heart rate to increase. To whom was Nancy referring?

"It didn't make any sense. No *sense*, but *intense*." Mary patted her own shoulder.

Mary seemed proud of her little rhyme, but the humor was lost on Louise. The van had shown up in the clinic parking lot earlier and at the dog show at the same time that Nancy was there. Had Nancy been talking about the men Louise had seen in the van?

Louise glanced in the direction of exam room one. "Is Nancy still here? I don't hear her."

Heidi joined them.

Mary smirked. "No, she left the dog and took off. When I asked her when she was coming back for Scarlet she scowled at me and bolted through the door. No surprise there. Then Bob came out and said that Scarlet would be staying for a couple of hours."

Heidi handed a clipboard to Shirley. "When I saw Bob putting Scarlet into a kennel in the dog room, I asked him why Scarlet was staying. He didn't even answer me. Just shrugged and went upstairs. Mary told me about Nancy's claim that there was an AI appointment, which I thought was odd since Bob knows that all of the semen is ruined."

Louise rubbed her forehead with the side of her hand. "Where's Bob now?"

Mary raised her hands. "Probably still upstairs. We haven't seen him since Nancy left."

Louise started for the staircase. She needed to call Alex right away. She still hadn't told him about seeing Eric in Georgetown, and now she had to update him on Bob's behavior. "I'll be in my office. I need to call Alex as well as chat with Daphne about a few things. Is she still here?"

Heidi handed Louise the file she'd been holding. "No. Once the dog spay was recovered, she went home for lunch. She said she'd stop by later to help with the clean up in the AI room. We're still working on that. We were a little distracted when that white van followed Nancy out of the parking lot because it looked like the one you asked us to watch out for."

The van was here again? Louise dropped her keys on the counter. "That's not good. When was this?"

Shirley glanced at the clock. "Not long after you left, so about an hour and a half ago?"

Louise retrieved her phone. "I need to let Alex know about the van, among other things. What type of car was Nancy driving?"

Shirley met Mary's eyes then shifted her gaze to Louise. "It was blue."

Louise's shoulder muscles tightened. "A blue what?"

Shirley went to the window and scanned the parking lot. "Sorry, I'm not sure. I'm not into cars." She pointed out the window. "It was a small one, kinda like that one parked next door."

Louise joined Shirley at the window. There was only one car in the adjacent lot, a gray Honda Civic. *Oh no. It can't be.* Louise scooped up her keys and ran to her car. The car in front of her at the bank drive-thru. Was it Nancy's car—how was that possible? It would be too much of a coincidence. The Civic was one of the top sellers in Canada—there had to be hundreds of them in Coverdale alone. But the car at the bank had been abandoned. An image of papers strewn across the front seats flashed through Louise's mind. Had there been a struggle? *I should have looked at those papers when I had the chance.*

Louise peeled out of the parking lot. On her way to the bank, she instructed her Bluetooth service to call Alex, but the call went to voice mail again. She left a message. "Alex, I need to talk to you ASAP. Please call me as soon as you get this."

When Louise arrived, the blue car was gone. Maybe it hadn't been Nancy's car after all. Louise's shoulders relaxed. The worst that had happened was that she had wasted time returning to the bank. Nancy was probably off somewhere ruining someone else's day.

Standing in the parking lot, Louise's gaze was drawn to the townhouse where she had seen Eric earlier. What if that had been Nancy's car here earlier, so close to the spot where she had seen Eric. A paralysing cold penetrated Louise's bones.

Chapter 31

WHIPPING AROUND THE corner of the clinic, Louise narrowly missed marking her SUV with white paint from an exiting delivery truck. Hal, the clean-shaven, slim gentleman behind the wheel was friendly as a rule, but the contortion of his face told Louise that he wasn't impressed by her current driving. She smiled shyly at him and waved. She'd have to grab a gift card from the local coffee shop to give him when he made next week's delivery.

Hal maneuvered between Louise's car and the red-brick building with impressive skill. Once the way was clear, she shot into the nearest parking spot and leapt out of the car, eager to get to her desk and call Alex. He still hadn't returned her call and, already high on an adrenaline rush, she didn't want to call him while she was on the highway.

The growling of her stomach reminded Louise that she hadn't had lunch yet. That thought was soon forgotten when she spotted Alex's car a few spots over. *What is he doing here? Why didn't he simply call me back?* Certain that something must be terribly wrong, Louise snatched her bag from the passenger seat and hurried in to see what bad news awaited her.

When she flung the back door open, she saw the back of the man she'd been worrying about all day. Her fingers trembling, Louise dropped the bag onto the floor, creating a clattering noise when the keys attached to it rattled onto the tiles. Alex spun around. Louise rushed to him and flung her arms around his broad shoulders.

Alex placed his arms around Louise's waist. "This is nice. I could use a greeting like that more often."

Louise pulled back and slapped his shoulder. "Where have you been? I've been calling you all day."

Alex sighed. "That didn't last long."

Louise crossed her arms. "Did you get my messages?"

"That's why I'm here. I need to speak with you and Daphne. Is she here?"

Louise retrieved her bag and turned to the stairs. "I'm not sure. Come up to the office."

With Alex close behind, Louise led the way to the upper level, her feet pounding a rhythm of anxiousness on each step. What now? A month ago, the most exciting thing that would have happened by 1 pm on a Friday would have been a cat bite abscess. Now confusion was the order of the day. She knew how to treat an abscess. Clean it, dispense antibiotics, and watch for skin necrosis. The events of the past few weeks were unlike anything Louise had experienced before. She was used to solving mysteries, but veterinary mysteries, not criminal ones.

If one thought of the patient as the victim, the disease as the perpetrator, other diseases as the suspects, and the symptoms as clues, being a veterinarian wasn't much different than being a homicide detective. Her patients couldn't speak to her directly any more than murder victims could speak to Alex. Of course, she had the promise of curing her patients, or victims, of disease, whereas Alex didn't have that luxury. He was an amazing detective, but after the crime was solved and the perpetrator arrested, the victim was still gone. Maybe she shouldn't be so hard on him.

Louise stopped at the entrance to the office and touched Alex's elbow. "I'm sorry."

He squinted. "For?"

"For being mad at you a minute ago. You didn't deserve that. I'm sure you have a lot on your plate and, it's, well… so much is going on right now."

Alex smiled. "You were mad at me? I didn't notice."

Louise playfully swatted him on the arm before entering the office.

Daphne, who was sitting at her desk, threw her hands in the air. "There you are. What's going on? Mary said you took off without saying a word." Her tone was uncharacteristically stern.

Louise shook her head gently while giving Daphne the eye, hoping that Alex wouldn't notice the exchange. "Nothing." Louise moved closer to Daphne and whispered, "I was following a lead."

She felt Alex's breath on her neck and turned around. *Man, he moves fast. And he has good hearing.*

Alex drew in a deep breath, then released it slowly. "A

lead? I follow the leads, remember?" He pointed at his own chest. "Detective." Then at Louise's. "Veterinarian. You treat sick animals and I catch the bad guys."

Alex took a step closer, forcing Louise to step aside to avoid being forced to sit on Daphne's desk. "I wanted to find out if the abandoned car I'd seen earlier today at the bank was Nancy Well's, but it was gone by the time I got back there."

Alex raised his hands, palms up. "Why are you looking for Nancy's car?"

Louise made her way to the coffee pot and grasped the urn. "Coffee?"

Alex shook his head.

Louise poured herself a cup and feigned a sip to mask her words behind the ceramic. "Because Mary and Shirley thought she was being followed by that van."

Alex cocked his head. "Excuse me? Did I hear that correctly?"

Louise's eyes darted around the room. "I don't know. What did you hear?"

"Something to the effect of the van returned, it followed Nancy, and you went after it?"

Louise gulped the coffee, giving herself a moment. "Umm. Yes. That sounds about right."

"So, you're out chasing after a mystery van? Why would you do something so dangerous?"

Louise studied the steam rising from the cup in her hand. "I did try to call you. Remember? I left multiple messages." He'd have to wait to hear about Eric. First she needed to know what he wanted to speak to her and Daphne about. "You said downstairs that you had something to discuss with us?"

Alex narrowed his eyes. "I hope you have a lot of appointments today."

Louise sat at her desk. "We canceled the rest of the day's appointments after we discovered the break-in. Why?"

"So I won't have to worry about you running around town trying to solve a crime, like on those murder mysteries you like to watch."

Louise slapped the desk. "Seriously? I know this isn't fiction. I'm not going to try to catch a murderer." She caught Daphne's eye and grinned. "Not without a gun, anyway."

Alex slapped his palm to his forehead. "When did you get a gun?"

"I haven't… yet. I was joking the last time I mentioned it, but now I'm wondering if I should."

Daphne stood and shook her index finger at Louise. "No, you shouldn't."

Alex stared at Louise. "I hope you're *still* joking about getting a gun, but in case you're not, I'm glad you have someone rational here to keep you grounded when you're having one of your impulsive moments."

Heat flushed through Louise's body. "I'm not impulsive. And I don't need a baby sitter." She opened the desk drawer, shuffled the contents, and reclosed it. "When have I ever been impulsive?"

Alex rolled his eyes. "Oh, I don't know. When was it you went to a crime scene in the middle of the night, alone, and broke into someone's office? Let's see… I think that was…" Alex raised his right hand, then bent his fingers one at a time while mouthing the days of the week. "Four days ago."

Louise raised her shoulders and whispered, "Besides that."

Daphne lowered herself onto her chair and motioned for Alex to have a seat in the chair opposite her desk. "What did you need to speak to us about?"

Alex retrieved his note pad from his jacket pocket, then sat. "I need to formulate a time line of Cliff Mariner's movements the day he was killed. The two of you interacted with him at the dog show. His boss, Mr. Gates, was surprised that Mr. Mariner was at the NKC offices that night as there was no reason for him to be there. Mr. Gates was unaware that Mr. Mariner had a key to the office. Did Mr. Mariner say anything to the two of you about going to the office that night?"

A knot formed in Louise's stomach as she exchanged a look with Daphne. "I think we've already established that a key wasn't necessary to get into Tim Gates' office. Cliff's the one who told us that the lock was broken."

Alex made some notes. "Why would he tell you that?"

The knot tightened. Were they providing Alex with information that may darken Cliff's memory? "He had forgotten the certificates he needed for the winners of the competition scheduled the following day. He'd forgotten previously and didn't want to embarrass his boss again."

Daphne leapt up. "That's right. That's the reason Tim Gates was yelling at Cliff when we were by the show ring. He was really angry."

Alex made another note. "Cliff was angry? Because Mr. Gates yelled at him?"

Daphne made her way over to the window and sat on the ledge. "No, Cliff wasn't angry, Tim was. After Tim walked away, Cliff laughed and said that had Tim not yelled at him he would have forgotten that he'd forgotten the papers."

Louise was reminded of Cliff Mariner's laugh and gentle demeanor—though their acquaintance was short, he had struck her at the time as someone who was truly happy and content. Someone who enjoyed his role at the dog show, even if it meant putting up with a cranky boss. "Cliff didn't seem at all phased by Tim's behavior. He simply let it go and came up with a solution to the problem at hand. We spent less than an hour with the man, but I left there respecting him. I wish I had that type of control."

Alex caught Louise's eye. "I wish you did, too."

Louise chose to let that last comment slide, in honor of Cliff, who certainly would have.

Alex flipped back a few pages in his notebook and tapped a page with his pen. "Daphne, you mentioned the other night that the NKC was concerned that some of their breeders might try to cheat the system by falsifying breeding certificates. Mr. Gates suggested that Cliff may have been in the office that night covering up for an unscrupulous breeder. Apparently Cliff had broken into the desk drawer where confidential documents were stored."

Louise shook her head. "Cliff? Cheating the system? No way he was involved with anything like that."

"I agree with Louise," Daphne said. "If he was helping breeders to falsify documents, why would he have told me about the DNA testing? He sounded very proud of their organization and its strict guidelines." She rose and started for the doorway. "I don't think I have much more to offer, Alex. If you don't mind, I need to head down and check on Edwina, the dog I spayed earlier."

Alex nodded. "I don't want to keep you from your patient. You know how to reach me if you think of anything else."

After Daphne left them, Alex repositioned himself in her office chair. "Much better. You really should think about the comfort of your visitors. That old chair is horrible on the back."

Louise shrugged. "We don't get many visitors. Anyway,

back to Cliff. After he died, I tried to find out more about him because Daphne and I wanted to attend his funeral, but we couldn't find any details on when and where it was to be held. When I searched online, the only thing that came up was an obituary for a Linda Mariner, which indicated that she left behind a husband, Cliff, but no other relatives. It's so sad to think that the poor man was all alone in the world, had to deal with a nasty boss, and then was murdered. He told us that he was retired before joining the NKC, but I couldn't find out what from."

"He was a clerk at a grocery store for thirty-years. After his wife passed away, he retired, sold their home in Ottawa, and moved here. He was renting a small apartment in Amherst."

Louise's jaw lowered as she stared at Alex.

Alex smiled and pointed at his chest. "Detective. Remember?"

Louise shook it off. "Sorry. I guess I do get caught up in the moment sometimes and forget about common sense. It sounds like Cliff lived a pretty simple life." The computer monitor flashed on when Louise's hand grazed the mouse. Her attention was drawn to a calendar pop-up that reminded her of the need for a new night stand. She studied the screen. "Tim Gates, on the other hand, had all that fancy furniture in his office. I bet his house was well decorated too." She paused to give Alex a chance to confirm her suspicion. He remained silent. "Money is always a motive." Louise grinned at Alex. He'd often teased her about her CSI mind and love of detective shows. "That's what they say on TV, anyway."

Alex flipped his notebook closed. "And sometimes Hollywood *is* spot on. So, as nice as Cliff was, if he needed the money…"

Louise raised her hand. "No. I don't believe he'd do something so unethical." She propped her elbows on the desk and tented her fingers in front of her. "What if he was doing his own investigation and stumbled onto something?"

Alex massaged his chin and contemplated her. "Maybe."

Chapter 32

THE CAR RIDE lasted over an hour. Pansy yawned and stretched out her left arm. Her right arm was trapped at her side by the body of her sleeping sister, whose head rested on Pansy's shoulder. After they'd left the foster home, Ms. Jane treated them to dinner at a roadside diner. Li'l sis filled up on French fries and a milkshake, but Pansy had only picked at her food. Her stomach hadn't stopped flipping since she'd spotted the garbage bags holding their meager belongings on the front porch of the house she had called home for the past four years.

Garbage bags. When Aunt Quinn kicked them out of their childhood home after the death of their mother, she'd packed a few clothes into a gym bag for each of them. Now the gym bags were gone, and their belongings were stuffed into garbage bags. Is that all they were to their foster parents? Garbage? Pansy sniffled and wiped her eyes.

The sky was a brilliant blue, free of clouds, and the sun-rays blasted through the windshield. Pansy squinted. Were the sunglasses a friend had given her in the garbage bag with her belongings? The brightness and warmth of the sun made her sleepy. Pansy closed her eyes and lowered her head onto Li'l sis' head, but sleep didn't come. Instead, in the darkness behind her eyelids, she saw visions of her mother and father and the friends she'd left behind four years ago. Now she was leaving behind her new friends. Pansy grasped Li'l sis' hand with her own and intermingled their fingers. *I won't let you go. No matter how many people come and go, we have to stay together.*

Ms. Jane had assured Pansy that she and Li'l sis wouldn't be separated, but as they continued the drive into the unknown Pansy struggled with trusting adults. Ms. Jane was the third social worker they'd had since entering the foster care system. She seemed really nice, but she was an adult, and so far, all of the adults in Pansy's life had let her down.

The back passenger-side wheel hit a pothole, jolting the car, and Pansy's eyes shot open. Her gaze met Ms. Jane's in the rear-view mirror.

Ms. Jane smiled at Pansy before returning her attention to the road. "Sorry about that. This road is notorious for pot-holes. It won't be long before we get to your new home. I think you will be pleasantly surprised."

Pansy studied their surroundings. They had left the city limits a while back and she was happy that they were still in the country. They passed farm after farm—each with a large brick house and barns. Almost every property had a tall, round building that she had never seen before. She loved watching nature shows on TV, but she had never been out in the country before today. Her foster dad said that driving to the country was a waste of gas and time. She had given up hope of ever seeing a barn or a cow or a horse in real life, but now they were driving past lots of them. Pansy's stomach quieted.

Would they be staying in the country? She hated the city—crowded with mean and angry people. Pollution filled the air, while litter cluttered the sidewalks and parking lots. People rushed about, focused on themselves with little regard for others. On TV, the country people were always friendly. Perhaps it was the clean air and open spaces? Pansy knew that not everything on TV was real, but a part of her wanted to hope that there was a better place than the places she'd known so far.

She shook her head and sank down into the seat. *Don't be foolish. You'll be back in a city again soon.* The butterflies in her stomach returned, but only briefly. When Ms. Jane slowed the car and turned into a long country lane, Pansy shot up, stopped only by the seatbelt.

Li'l sis woke up when her shoulder pillow moved. "Where are we?"

Pansy rubbed the kinks out of her right arm. "Is that where we're gonna' live?"

Ms. Jane maneuvered her car to a spot on the grass beside a rusty, red pickup truck. "Yes, Pansy. I think you and Li'l sis will be very happy here. Mr. and Mrs. Wick are looking forward to having you stay with them. They have a lot of animals and a lot of space to run and play."

As soon as Ms. Jane removed the key from the ignition, Li'l sis tugged on the lever to open the door. "Oh boy! Look Pansy, there's a dog over there."

Ms. Jane reached over the back of her seat and motioned to Li'l sis. "Hold on there, young lady. You'll get to meet the dog soon enough. You girls wait here while I go and let the Wicks know that we're here."

Pansy watched Ms. Jane make her way to the front door, happy to stay in the car because she wasn't sure what to think about the big dog that Li'l sis was so excited about. After the social worker entered the house, the dog rose to its feet, stretched, and headed towards the car. Pansy was certain that if she got down on all fours, the dog would be bigger than she was. He had long black fur, an enormous round head, and his pick tongue hung out one side of his mouth. From the tip of his tongue ran a long string of thick, clear goo. *What is that? Spit?*

Pansy's eyes widened. Rabies? She'd seen a documentary on TV about a girl that got rabies from a bat. Didn't they say that dogs could have it too, and one of the signs was that they have a lot of drool? Pansy's heart raced. Why would they bring her and Li'l sis to a place that had a vicious dog with rabies? She leaned into the front seat and locked the doors.

Li'l sis spun around. "Hey! Why'd you do that?"

Pansy swallowed. "That dog is vicious. We can't let it in the car."

Li'l sis stared at Pansy. "Can dogs open car doors?"

Pansy furrowed her brow. "Shut up! I'm keeping you safe."

When the big black dog reached the car, he rose up onto his hind legs and rested his forepaws on Pansy's window. She screamed and grabbed Li'l sis into a bear hug. Li'l sis screamed too.

A tall, slim man with a healthy head of brown hair and a moustache came out of the house. He wore a red plaid shirt and overalls. The man retrieved a rope from the floor of the porch and put his hand to his mouth. "Come over here, you big bear, and let them little girls be."

The dog returned his front paws to the ground and raced to the porch where he sat in front of the man. The curly-haired stranger attached the rope to the dog's collar. Ms. Jane and a tall lady with short, golden-blonde hair came out of the house and made their way to the car. Ms. Jane tapped on the window and motioned for Pansy to lower it. She rolled it down an inch.

The lady smiled. "Well, you must be Pansy, and what is it they call your sister?"

Li'l sis puffed up her chest. "I'm Li'l sis. That's what Pansy named me."

"It's good to meet you both. I'm Mrs. Wick, but you can call me Olive." Olive gestured to the porch. "You don't have to be afraid of the big guy over there. He's well trained, quite friendly, and loves children. Oh, and the dog is pretty nice too." Olive wiped her hands on her apron and held one out.

Pansy laughed and lowered the window farther. She took the lady's hand and shook it. "Nice to meet you."

"And it's very nice to meet you, Pansy." Olive leaned into the car. "How about you two come into the house. Ms. Jane tells me you've already had dinner, but dessert is ready. I hope you like pie."

Pansy couldn't remember having pie that she didn't like, but when was the last time they'd had pie? She forgot about the big scary dog and jumped out of the car, followed by Li'l sis. As they got closer to the porch, Li'l sis slipped her hand into Olive's and gazed up at her.

Olive squeezed Li'l sis' hand. "What is it?"

Li'l sis' eyes sparkled. "Is there ice cream too?"

On their way into the house they were introduced to Mr. Wick, who insisted that they call him Hugh. "Mr. Wick is my father." Hugh patted the dog on the head. "And this here is Indigo."

After dessert, including ice cream, Pansy and Li'l sis were shown their new room. Twin beds, two dressers, and an open toy box filled with dolls and other items that would delight any little girl filled the bright space. A desk by the window played host to a laptop computer, and next to it was a shelving unit filled with a variety of books. Pansy reminded herself to breathe. This couldn't be real. Was it a trick?

When it was time for Ms. Jane to leave Pansy, Li'l sis, Olive, and Hugh walked her to the car to say goodbye. Pansy gave her a hug. "Thank you." Maybe some adults weren't so bad.

The next day Olive treated the girls to a trip to a shopping mall to purchase clothes for school and church. "You'll need some work clothes too, because on a farm we all have to help out."

Pansy narrowed her eyes. Were she and Li'l sis there as cheap labor? It didn't take Pansy long to learn how fun it could be to milk a cow and feed the chickens. She enjoyed most of her assigned farm tasks. It was fun being part of a family that worked together and who helped each other out.

Despite Pansy's initial hesitation, she and Indigo soon became constant companions. They spent hours together investigating the nearby woods and ponds and even a few deserted barns. Pansy and Lil' sis made friends at school, and for the first time in years, Pansy got to go to a friend's birthday party. This party was different than any she had remembered from childhood. There were boys at this party, and dancing. She was happy to celebrate her friends' birthdays, but she didn't talk about her own, as it would lead to disappointment and sadness.

Eleven months after arriving at the farm, Olive joined Pansy on the front porch where she had been combing Indigo. "So, Pansy, you'll be 14 years old next month. That's a big deal, my dear. We'll have to see what we can do about celebrating."

Pansy ceased brushing her canine companion. "Really?" Was this a trick?

Olive brushed a strand of Pansy's hair away from her eyes. "Of course. You invite a few friends over next Saturday, and we can have a barbeque. How does that sound?"

Pansy stared at Olive. "Really?"

Olive squinted and ruffled Pansy hair. "Yes. Really. Silly girl. Make a list of guests, then after dinner we'll go shopping. Maybe a new dress for your birthday?"

Pansy froze. Her mouth dried, but her hands dampened. She examined the floor of the porch for the right words. "I don't think I need a party. Maybe we could just go for dinner—the four of us?"

"Are you sure? You were so excited a minute ago. Why the change?"

Pansy shrugged. Why didn't she want a party anymore? Who doesn't want a party? But when Olive mentioned a new dress, Pansy's excitement vanished. Would this wonderful woman go away on her birthday?

Chapter 33

ALEX FOLLOWED LOUISE across the hall to the AI room. "I want to have a look in here to see if there may be any connection to the break-in at Bob's boarding house before talking to him about it."

Louise spun around to face Alex, blocking his access to the room. "There was a break-in at Bob's place? When?" Was that why he ran out of the clinic earlier? Had there really been an emergency? But why wouldn't he have simply told her that his home had been broken into, why the evasiveness? "He didn't say anything to any of us about it."

"He may not know about it yet. His landlady," Alex consulted his notebook, "Sylvia Lenics, called 911 mid-morning after finding his room ransacked. She initially thought he moved out in a hurry—I guess that happens a lot at boarding houses—but the lock on his door was broken. She panicked and called the police."

Louise stepped aside to allow Alex access to the room. "Was anyone hurt? What did the police find? Did Sylvia or the other tenants hear anything? Bob told me that he had two housemates, and that Sylvia lived in an apartment attached to the main house." More violence in their small community. Louise shivered.

Alex removed his jacket and draped it over Louise's shoulders. "No one was hurt, because, thankfully, no one was home. The other tenants had gone to work prior to the break-in. We contacted them, and they both told us that Bob had left the house unusually early this morning. Ms. Lenics had been staying with family the past few days. When she arrived home this morning, she was inspecting the house to ensure there hadn't been any parties going on while she was away. It sounds like she runs a fairly strict boarding house. No smoking, no drinking, and no parties. The men share a kitchen, but they each have their own room with an ensuite. Ms. Lenics insists that their individual room doors are locked to prevent any accusations of stealing from each other."

Louise returned Alex's jacket to him. She was worried, not cold. "You think there may be a connection between that break-in and this one? Why?" Louise sprayed a little disinfectant on the counter, then retrieved a paper towel from the wall dispenser and wiped the counter dry. Although there was still a mess on the floor, she knew that Daphne and the staff had already cleaned the counters of the fingerprint dust. Still, her hands were restless.

Alex maneuvered his way through the boxes on the floor, heading towards the window. "Because the only room in the house that was disturbed was Bob's. The TV and audio equipment in the common living room was untouched, as well as other valuable household items that could have easily been sold at a pawn shop. I've put a rush on identification of the fingerprints taken here this morning—if the culprit's prints are in the system, we should have their names within an hour or two. The CSI team collected prints from everyone who works here earlier, except Bob and Eric, of course. Neither of them was here at the time, but we already had their prints on file anyway."

Louise halted her obsessive counter cleaning. "Did I hear you correctly? The police department has Bob's fingerprints on file? Why?"

"We have Bob's prints from that gum package Daphne retrieved for me yesterday. The CSI team recovered three good prints from it—a thumb and two fingers from the right hand. They compared those to the prints discovered on the clinic pen found at the warehouse. Not a match to Bob, but a fingerprint from a former convict by the name of Nat Bradley matched."

Louise flung the soiled paper towel into the nearby sink and yanked off a clean strip. "I'm not familiar with that name. He could be a client, but we didn't give those pens out to clients. How would this Bradley guy get a hold of one of our defective pens?"

Alex crept to the door and closed it quietly. "We suspect he got it from Bob. Bob's prints weren't on the pen, but they were found on other items that survived the warehouse fire. He'd been there, Louise. Possibly around the time of the fire."

Louise's heart raced. Bob wasn't merely a *possible* suspect anymore; there was now a real connection between him and a known criminal. She jerked her head around and stared at the wall that separated them from the staff room. Was there a master criminal—possibly a drug dealer or a murderer—in the room next to them? He'd been in her clinic, interacting with her staff and clients, for several weeks. Had they all been in danger?

When she inhaled deeply to calm her nerves, Louise's nostrils stung from the disinfectants that had been used to clean the room. She lowered her head and used the paper towel to squeeze the bridge of her nose, hoping to alleviate the discomfort. Was it the disinfectant or the stress that was bringing on a headache? She caught sight of the document she'd seen earlier. She bent down and, using the paper towel, retrieved it.

"Look at this. I found it before Officers Tomlin and Carter arrived this morning. They snapped a photo of it, but I don't know if it's been fingerprinted."

Alex produced a plastic evidence bag from his pocket and held it open so Louise could deposit the document into it. He perused the paper quickly. "It appears to be a shipping document. I imagine you have many of those, why is this one special?"

Louise snatched the bag from Alex's hand and tapped at the bottom right corner. "Look at this number. It says one thousand, but if you look closer, the last zero was typed over a period. The original amount was one hundred."

Alex shrugged. "Could be a simple typo."

Louise widened her eyes and tilted her head. Didn't he understand? "Or… someone is *falsifying* breeding documents. Eric hasn't been at the clinic for a month and no one else here would have a reason to do something like that, so maybe Bob is helping someone cheat the NKC guidelines. And I think we know who that is."

"Don't leave me hanging, Detective Miller. Who?"

"Ha ha. Funny. You know who. Nancy Wells. She and Bob were both acting strange today, the same day both the clinic and his apartment are broken into."

Alex gently slipped the plastic bag from Louise's grip. "I'll need to speak to both of them. Did you say Bob was here in the clinic?"

Louise lifted her hands. "As far as I know he's next door in the staff room writing up records. Other than a short appearance downstairs when Nancy Wells showed up over the lunch hour, no one has seen much of him today."

Louise led Alex down the hall to the staff room. She grasped the knob and shoved the door open a crack. "Hey, Bob, Alex would like to ask you a few questions about the NKC."

Alex glared at her. "Way to keep it casual."

Louise closed the door and turned to Alex. "Sorry. I'm not a *real* detective, remember?"

Alex shook his head then stepped between Louise and the door. "I wish *you'd* remember." He gently opened the door and peered into the room. "No harm done, he's not even in here."

Louise shoved Alex's back, propelling them both into the room. "Are you sure?" She scanned the small room. The donut box she'd robbed earlier was still in its place near the sink. On the other side of the sink sat the drying lunch dishes. Three chairs were neatly tucked under the table while a fourth lay toppled on the floor. One of the clinic laptops was sitting open on the table and beside it was a tiny pile of paper.

Louise shuffled through the papers. "These are Bob's notes, I think from patients he saw earlier in the week. This is maddening. He's not supposed to leave his records unwritten at the end of the day in case something happens and someone else needs to know what's going on with a patient."

"Really? That's what you are concerned about? Unwritten records?" Alex righted the overturned chair. "Someone got up in a hurry—you're missing associate, perhaps?"

Louise closed the laptop. "Records are important." She yanked a chair out and plopped into it. She tapped her fist on the table. "What is he up to? I think my brain may explode." She glanced at the clock on the microwave. "It's barely two o'clock and we've had a break in, I've driven around town looking for a crazy client, then Eric was at the bus depot but I couldn't get to him, and now you're confirming that our associate is definitely involved with a thug."

Alex sat facing Louise. "Eric was at the bus station? When was this?"

Louise shook her head. "It doesn't matter. He's not there now. It was earlier, when I was out running errands. He was at the bus station with a young woman, then I saw them again later near the bank in Georgetown. I was tempted to go and confront him, but…"

Alex smiled. "But common sense prevailed? I'm glad to hear it. Why didn't you call me? Or the police department?"

Louise sighed. "I did call you, but you didn't pick up. I honestly didn't think to call the police, but I don't know if I could have anyway. It's Eric. I still can't believe that he's up to no good. He's in trouble, I can feel it."

Alex furrowed his brow, squeezed Louise's shoulder, then rose to his feet. "We'll talk about this later. Right now my priority is to track down Bob Kurt and Nancy Wells. We have an APB out for Nat Bradley and his brother Brent. History tells us that when one of them is in trouble, the other isn't far away."

Louise rubbed her sweaty palms on her pants. "I don't suppose they drive a white van?"

Louise and Alex flew into the treatment room, startling Daphne and Heidi who were fitting Edwina, the dog Daphne had spayed that morning, with an Elizabethan collar. Their quick and noisy entry also startled the dog, and Louise stopped abruptly and shot her arm in front of Alex to force him to freeze. "Sorry."

Heidi massaged Edwina's ears until the dog relaxed, then Daphne secured the head collar in place. Daphne washed her hands while Heidi returned the patient to the kennel. Daphne nodded towards the dog. "She's doing great. I'm going to send her home, and Lincoln's already gone. I think it's best we don't have any patients in the building tonight."

Heidi joined Daphne at the sink. "Except Scarlet. We can't get a hold of Nancy Wells to let her know that we're closing early and she needs to pick Scarlet up."

Louise and Alex exchanged a look. Daphne frowned. "What's going on now?"

Alex tugged his notebook from his pocket and flipped it open. "Do either of you know where Bob's taken off to?"

They both shook their heads.

"Okay, I'll need Nancy Wells' contact information. Perhaps he's gone to her place. I'll need to interview her anyway."

Heidi's eyes widened. "Really? What did she do? Has being a mean and miserable person finally become illegal?"

Louise shot Heidi a look warning her that it wasn't time to joke.

Heidi mouthed, *sorry.*

Louise waved a hand in an *it's okay* gesture.

Daphne dried her hands then tossed the towel onto the exam table as she approached Louise. "What's going on?"

Louise stole a glance at Alex. How much was she allowed to tell Daphne and Heidi? Oh well, if she spoke out of turn, he was there to stop her. "It sounds like Bob has a connection with the people who burned down that warehouse a while back, and he may be forging breeding documents." Alex remained silent. "Nancy Wells may be involved too."

Alex sauntered over to the laptop on the technician's desk and tapped a couple of keys. "Any chance I might get Nancy Wells' address from you? She's a client, you must have it here in your records."

Louise joined Alex at the desk and closed the computer. "We can't give you Nancy's address without a warrant."

"Why? What's the big deal?"

"There are privacy laws that we have to respect. If I give you Nancy's personal information and you don't find a legal reason to justify it, or throw her in jail, she's the type of person to come after us with a bunch of lawyers."

Alex shot a pleading look at Daphne. "Daphne?"

Daphne shrugged. "Really, Alex? I'm the practical and sensible one, remember? You know Louise is right."

Alex blew out a breath. "I was hoping you might look the other way in an emergency. I should have known better." He shot her a wry grin as he returned his notebook to his pocket. "She's a member of the NKC. I suspect I can get her information through them—should be easy to obtain a warrant for that since their office is still an active crime scene."

He headed for the door. "Let me know right away if Bob returns."

Louise offered him a mock salute. "Got it, Chief." She regretted it as soon as she made the childish gesture. This was no time to be foolish.

Daphne glared at her. "Why do you treat him like that?"

Louise's cheeks warmed. Thankfully, Heidi had left the room after Alex. "Nerves, I guess. Inappropriate humor is my way of coping when there's a lot of craziness going on, and there is definitely a lot of craziness going on right now."

Daphne smiled, her eyes softening. "You're right, there is. I'm going to discharge Edwina then head out. Heidi and Rita are going too. I've already sent Shirley and Mary home."

Louise relaxed her shoulders. "Thanks. I need to grab a few things upstairs, then I'll be leaving as well. There's really no need for any of us to be here."

"No, there isn't. Scarlett has a comfy bed, food, and water, and our calls have been diverted to Cheryl's clinic in case there are any emergencies. Everything will be fine for the night."

Before returning to her office, Louise headed down the hall to the staff room. Her grumbling stomach reminded her that she hadn't eaten lunch—she couldn't remember when she'd missed so many meals. The past few days had been like nothing she'd ever experienced, not since the accident, anyway.

Louise directed her eyes heavenward. *God, please give me patience and understanding.* Along with forgiveness, they were two things she often struggled with. She needed patience more than ever to trust Alex and the police department to figure out what Bob and Nancy were up too. Before she left the clinic, she'd punch a security code in that Bob didn't know so that he wouldn't have access to the clinic should he choose to return later. *What could be so important, Bob, that you'd risk your career?*

The donut box sat on the counter with a single donut remaining. It disappeared quickly. When Louise opened the refrigerator to find a cold drink to wash it down, her heart skipped a beat. A jug of chocolate milk sat on a shelf. Louise lifted it out of the fridge and opened it. She poured the contents into the sink—it had expired two weeks ago. What a waste. *Whatever it is you're up too Eric, I hope you're not wasting your life.*

She took a glass out of the cabinet and filled it with cold water from the tap. After she'd sat down at the table, she caught sight of a phone sticking out from under an old cart they no longer used in the treatment area. Rita insisted that it might have some use, so it had sat in the same position near the door to the staff room, undisturbed, for two years.

Louise bent down and scooped up the device. It appeared to be the same type of phone Bob used. She turned it over and touched the screen—a text message popped up.

We have your partner. Bring the stuff or she'll pay the price.

The room spun around Louise. If this was Bob's phone, who was being threatened? It said *she*, so it wasn't Eric. Louise inhaled a deep breath of relief at that thought, but the relief didn't last long. Someone was in danger. Was this the emergency Bob had run out for earlier today? If so, why would he have returned so quickly? She read the message again and noted the time it had been sent—11:45. That was around the same time that Shirley and Mary saw the van following Nancy out of the parking lot. Had Nancy been kidnapped? *Was* that her car at the bank?

Bile burnt the back of Louise's throat. She tried to call

Alex, but the call went to voice mail. "Alex, I think Nancy Wells may be in danger. Call me."

She tucked her phone into her pocket, raced across the hall to her office, pulled up the veterinary software program on her computer, and typed Scarlet Wells into the patient ID field. After clicking on the appropriate buttons to print out a client information label, she grabbed her car keys in one hand and, still clutching Bob's phone in the other, ran downstairs, almost running into Daphne at the landing.

Daphne leapt out of the way to avoid the collision. "What are you doing now?"

Louise ripped the label from the pharmacy printer. "Nancy Wells is in danger. I think she may have been kidnapped." She showed the text on Bob's phone to Daphne. "I tried to call Alex, but he's not picking up. I'll head to Nancy's and meet him there so that I can give him this phone. Maybe they can use it to track the person who sent the message."

Daphne placed herself between Louise and the door to the parking lot. "We have no idea if Alex is going to Nancy's or, if he is, how long it'll take him to get there. We should call the police."

Louise pointed at the back door. "I agree. You should call the police, but in the meantime I have to get to Nancy's place to see if Alex is there."

Rita entered the hallway from the exam room. "Nancy's place? That's likely where Alex is headed."

Daphne shook her head. "No. He said that he had to get a warrant first then get the address from the NKC. That'll take a long time."

Rita grinned. "It will be much faster if someone left

the address on his windshield, unknown by her employers, of course."

Louise appreciated the initiative, but they were on thin ice ethically. She frowned.

Rita lifted her hands. "I didn't do it."

Louise smiled at Rita. "Okay, let's pretend none of knows anything about that, for now anyway. I suspect it's okay to break a few rules when someone's in danger."

"Do you think Bob and Nancy vandalized the AI room? Why would they do that?" Rita crossed her arms. "I still can't believe that Eric was involved."

Louise tried to squeeze around Daphne. "I don't think any of them are responsible for trashing the AI room. It would make no sense, and none of them had time to do it. Whoever broke in here overnight knew how to get in and out without a code, and without setting off the alarm. And they were looking for something specific. Probably the same people who ransacked Bob's room at the boarding house."

Daphne's jaw dropped. "What? When did that happen?"

"Sorry, I forgot to mention it. Alex told me after you left us to check on Edwina. It happened this morning after Bob left for work."

Rita chewed on her fingernails. "What could they be looking for in the AI room that might be at Bob's place? Why trash a bunch of semen containers?" She paced the hall. "They took one container and smashed everything else. The only semen vials they didn't touch were the ones in the hazardous waste container. I put them in there last Thursday after finding them in a cardboard box in a cupboard."

Louise cocked her head. "What were they doing in a cupboard? They're supposed to be kept cold."

Rita returned to Louise and Daphne's end of the hall. "Beats me. There were four of them in the box. Two had an unusual color. I assumed they were spoiled from sitting in the warm cupboard, so I disposed of them all. I thought someone must have tossed them in there and forgot about them. I was going to bring it up at the next staff meeting."

A thought raced through Louise's mind, too fast to capture the details. "Are the vials still in the container? Can you get them for me?"

Rita nodded. "Sure. The containers don't get picked up until next week." She hurried up the stairs.

Daphne stepped away from the door. "What are you thinking?"

Louise combed her fingers through her hair. "I can't quite put my finger on it, but I think they may be important. Listen, I promise I'll be careful. I'll drive to Nancy's with the phone and the vials. If Alex's car is there, I'll pass them on to him. If he's not there, I'll drive to his office. Fair?"

Daphne straightened her shirt. "I don't know. What if something happens along the way?"

Rita returned with the vials and handed them to Louise.

Louise grasped the vials tightly and lifted her hand in the air. "Don't worry. It's a short drive. What could happen?"

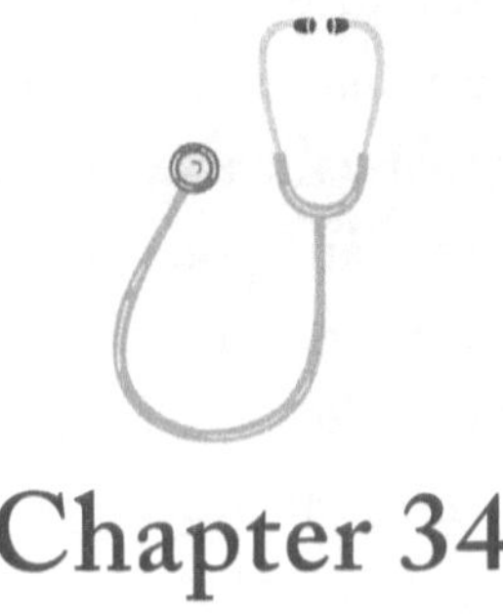

Chapter 34

FOR THE THIRD time in one day, Louise found herself driving east along the main street of Georgetown. The GPS told her to turn left at the intersection of Main Street and Rural Route 17, the street that Nancy Wells lived on. As she passed the bank she had visited earlier, she activated her left turn signal and eased into the turning lane. The townhouse she'd spotted Eric at earlier in the day was on the southeast corner, and across from there, the town's oldest building housed the public library.

When the light changed to green, Louise edged forward, but had to wait for a line of five cars to pass before she could proceed. "Come on, come on, come on." She resisted the impulse to honk at the seemingly slow drivers in hopes that they'd match her feelings of urgency.

In mere seconds, the traffic cleared and she was able to make her way onto RR 17. Not having driven this roadway in the past, Louise slowed her car when the GPS indicated that the destination was a quarter of a mile ahead on the left. As she passed a grove of pine trees, a small white bungalow with worn vinyl siding came into view. Number 35. No cars sat in the driveway. Louise maneuvered her car onto the uneven pavement, intending to use the unkempt lawn to turn around. Alex must have been here and gone already. *Drat! Now what?*

Assuming no cars meant that no one was home, Louise let up slightly on the brake and drifted to the back of the property. There was no harm in having a quick peek around as she redirected her car, was there? The end of the driveway was level with the back of the house. After that, a small sea of weeds and uneven dirt stretched in front of her.

At the back of the yard was a large wooden shed, complete with windows and a garage-style door at one end. Two pedestrian doors had been set into the side of the structure, each leading to a fenced-in run, most likely where Nancy housed her breeding and show dogs. A large ventilation fan sat on the roof, alongside a large A/C unit. The flooring of the kennels was made up of gravel, cement, and grass, with a perch and a bed in each. As nasty as Nancy was to other people, she appeared to take good care of her dogs. Louise wasn't sure how many dogs Nancy had, and she had no intention of entering that building to find out.

As she spun her car around, she noticed that the back door to the house was open. She shifted into park and tapped her fingers on the steering wheel. Should she investigate? Had Alex been there? If so, he wouldn't have left the door open. If he found the property like this, he would have posted an officer or closed the door. *I promised Daphne I'd leave if Alex wasn't here.* Louise's curiosity over-powered her sense of caution and she exited her vehicle.

Quietly creeping towards the house, she noticed that spiders had freely built their webs across the window frames. The thickness of the webs suggested that they had sat undisturbed for months, if not years. A cracked, brick walkway was barely discernable under the weeds, reminding Louise that she had better start paying closer attention to her own property.

The screen door, void of an actual screen, was closed, but the wooden door projected into the kitchen as though forgotten by the last visitor. Louise grasped the handle to the outer door and let herself in. Was it entering illegally if the door was open and she was concerned about the welfare of the occupant? Surely not! Convinced she had Nancy's best interests in mind, Louise welcomed herself into the sparsely furnished kitchen. An electric kettle and microwave sat on the counter top next to the refrigerator. A small poker table occupied the centre of the room, joined by a single chair.

Where do guests sit? Louise swallowed against the lump that formed in her throat. Louise lived alone, but she had plenty of seating available for guests. Was Nancy nasty because she was lonely? Or was she lonely because she was nasty? Maybe she preferred to be alone. Not everyone who was alone was lonely.

Remembering that Nancy may be in danger, Louise picked up the pace. Perhaps she could find something in the house to indicate where Nancy was. The living room, its walls painted gray, was as light on furnishings as the kitchen. A well-worn couch sat under the window that offered a view of the roadway. A small desk against the wall to Louise's right played host to a TV set that was probably older than she was.

In her peripheral vision, she caught sight of papers strewn on the floor of the room to her left. As Louise approached, she was reminded of the mess in the AI room. Had the same intruders been here? Drawers in a desk and a burrow hung open—the likely source of the documents on the floor. Louise scooped one up and gasped— it was a receipt for a semen shipment from Brazil, and the cost was only one hundred dollars. Bob had claimed that the product for Nancy's dogs came from England and was much costlier. Ten times costlier!

Louise yanked her phone out of her pocket and opened the album APP. There it was, the bloodied document she'd found at the NKC office. The word *razi* was actually part of the word *Brazil*. It was starting to make sense. Bob and Nancy were working together to falsify the documents that would identify the source of the semen Nancy used in her breeding dogs. Heat surged through Louise's body. Bob had been using her clinic, and her staff, to facilitate his unethical activities. She crumpled the paper up and shoved it into her pocket. When she found Alex, she'd have to show it to him.

Louise spun around and started to stomp out of the room when she caught sight of a few photos on the wall adjacent to the door. Surprised to see anything personal in a house that seemed so devoid of life, she found herself compelled to study them. Most of the photos were of Nancy and one of her dogs receiving a ribbon from a dog show official. Louise recognized one of those judges as Cliff Mariner. She also recognized Tim Gates in one of the photos, but a red X had been drawn on the glass over Tim's face. One photo stood out amongst the others—Nancy standing with her arm across the shoulder of a woman a few years younger.

Intrigued by the happy expression on Nancy's face, Louise

removed the photo from its hook and turned it over to see if there was any mention of who the other woman was. Instead, she found a newspaper clipping. Louise unfolded it and read the caption under the photo. She froze, then dropped the frame to the ground and raced to her car. Tears flooded Louise's face as the stress of the past week mixed with painful memories of her past.

The article on the back of the photo was about a car accident that had claimed the life of a young college student. Was that student the same young woman in the photo with Nancy? Who was she? Did Nancy lose someone close to her in that accident?

Louise felt a touch of sympathy for the woman who had been causing her and her staff so much grief for the past few weeks. She was reminded of her own past and how bitter and angry she was after the accident that claimed Zack. Louise lowered her head to the steering wheel. She had been driving that night, but their car was stopped at a traffic light. The other driver ran the red then hit the median, sending his vehicle airborne. It landed on Louise's car, killing her fiancé instantly. Louise had severe head injuries that affected her ability to learn and retain information. High school had been so easy, but college was a struggle. Many times she wanted to quit, but Zack's mother would convince her to carry on, in honor of him.

Louise raised her head, wiped her face with a tissue, and started the car. As she turned onto the road and headed back towards Georgetown, she thanked God for the people in her life who had helped her through the dark days, including her parents and her sister, Maryanne. She had met Daphne a few months later, and Daphne introduced Louise to Jesus. Placing all of her trust in Him helped her let go of the anger and grief and enabled her to forgive the man who had killed Zack. A couple of years later she met Alex, who'd made it clear over the past couple of years that he wanted more than a friendship. Louise did too, but could she bare the grief again if something happened to him?

Louise approached the library and pulled into the parking lot across the street. Would it be easier if Alex wasn't a police officer? If he had a safer job? She'd never know, because she would never ask him to give up his career. Her friendship with Alex had helped her forgive the police officer who'd had a chance to prevent the accident that night. The drunk driver had been pulled over an hour earlier by a young officer who chose to instruct the driver, who spoke with slurred speech, to go home, rather than arresting him.

Louise thought about her actions throughout the day and the past few weeks. Was she still having difficulties trusting law enforcement to protect the people she cared about?

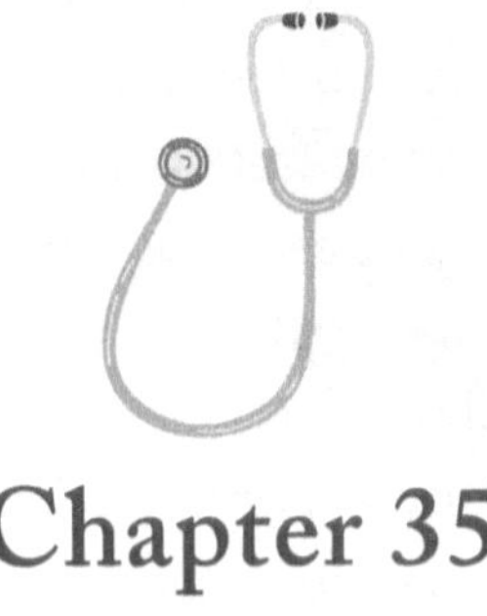

Chapter 35

LOUISE CLOSED HER eyes. *Father, give me the strength to trust others, and even more so, to trust You.* She sat quietly for a few minutes before opening her eyes. When she did, she spotted a white van exciting the library parking lot. It turned right, towards Main Street. Louise froze. What should she do? She had asked God for direction, and as soon as she opened her eyes, a suspiciously familiar-looking van had appeared.

Louise started her engine and followed the suspect vehicle south then west on Main Street. When the other driver was forced to decrease his speed by someone in a red sports car attempting to parallel park, Louise was able to see the license plate—ADST 289. *That's it!* She called Alex using the car's Bluetooth. He didn't answer.

The sports car was soon parked and the van continued on its way. Staying two car lengths behind to avoid detection, Louise followed. She prayed that they wouldn't turn onto Highway 15, a busy route that would take them north of town. Her prayer was answered—the van continued past the highway, not altering its route until they reached Rural Route 24 where it turned right.

RR 24, a two-lane country road, was familiar to Louise—she often used it when traveling from her home in north Coverdale to Georgetown. Massive fields of corn filled the landscape to the west. A row of rural homes to the east with large lawns and bountiful gardens reminded travelers of the benefits of country living. Louise would have turned left onto Concession 4 if she had been heading home, but the van continued north.

Before they reached the next public roadway, Concession 5, the van slowed then turned right into a laneway hidden by a grove of trees. Louise guided her car to the side of the road and shifted it into park. *Where are they going?* Her pulse quickened—did they know that she was trailing them? Following potential criminals onto a private roadway would be foolish and would no doubt ensure they'd notice her, so she remained in position and called Alex again. Again, her call went to voice mail.

"Alex, please call me back right away. I'll explain when you call." *Come on, Alex. Where are you? Why aren't you picking up?*

Confident that the hidden road couldn't be very long, Louise decided to search the area on foot. The grove of trees blocking the view of the laneway was situated on a small hill, separated from the road by a ditch.

Louise glanced at her footwear. "Hiking boots would be ideal, but at least I'm wearing running shoes. Too bad they're white… and new."

She exited the car, clicked the lock button out of habit, then headed for the ditch. The grass was damp, causing her feet to slide into the muddy water at the bottom, but she was able to brace herself against the side of the incline and prevent her behind from landing in the gutter. She shook her feet to get as much water off the shoes as possible, then used the tall fescue grass to aid her escape from the ditch. Reaching the other side, she used the trees and rocks to scale the hill.

The rich smell of pine, mixed with the earthy smell of the peat-moss, tickled her nose. A sneeze was building so she covered her nose and mouth with her hand—her muddy hand. *Oh great!* After wiping her face with the sleeve of her shirt, she grabbed a branch on the tree in front of her and yanked herself forward. A rock jutted out of the ground. She tried to use it as a foot rest, but her wet shoes slipped and her knee smashed against the jagged rock. The tear in her pants revealed a gash in her skin. Louise gritted her teeth to suppress the scream building within.

A strand of hair fell over her face. She used her muddy hand to push it away, leaving a cool streak of mud across her forehead. *A little camouflage can't hurt.*

When she arrived at the top of the hill, she could see the road and a clearing that housed a small red barn, as well as a metal garage. The buildings were old—a large portion of the barn's roof was missing, and there was more rust than metal on the garage. On the north side of the property sat a construction trailer in comparatively good condition. The trailer was parked on what appeared to be the remnants of an old farm house. Did the guys driving the van find an abandoned property and set up shop here? Set up to do what?

The now familiar van was parked in front of the trailer. Louise watched as the two men she'd seen both at the dog show and in her clinic's parking lot exited the van and marched into the mobile office. The windows were open, but she was too far away to hear what was being said. She tried to call Alex again, but hit the disconnect button when the recorded message started to play.

"I've come this far—I might as well find out what they're up to in there." Moving carefully from one tree to the next, she attempted to make her way down the hill. She only made it a short distance before the door to the trailer swung open and three men strode out, the two guys from the van, and… Louise sank low behind the tree. *It can't be.* She peered around the tree to convince herself she hadn't seen what she thought she'd seen, but there was no mistake. Tim Gates, the president of the NKC, was with the two guys who had been roughing up Bob at the dog show. The same two guys who had been loitering in the clinic parking lot, not once, but twice.

Did Tim find out that Bob was forging documents and send these guys to rough him up? *That's insane. It's a kennel club, not the mafia.* Louise rested her head in her hands. What were these guys up to?

Her attention was drawn back to the three men when they started shouting. Tim Gates appeared to be furious with the other two—his hands flew through the air as he pointed at them, at the van, at the barn. After his crazy arm motions ceased, the taller of the two ruffians headed to the barn while the shorter one returned to the van. The man who'd gone into the barn drove a large, black SUV out of the building and parked it next to the van. His partner stood by the sliding side door of the white vehicle. After popping open the back of the SUV, tall ruffian man joined his comrade at the van. He tugged open the door and reached in. Louise watched as they struggled with something, or was it someone, in the vehicle.

A woman, hands tied behind her back, was dragged out of

the van and towards the back of the SUV. Louise gasped then slapped a hand over her mouth, hoping they hadn't heard her. The person's mouth was covered with a gag, but Louise knew those fierce, piercing eyes. Even from this distance, they made her heart freeze.

I understand the mouth gag, but why tie her hands? Louise immediately regretted the unkind thought about Nancy. She was rude, but she was still a human being with feelings who needed compassion and understanding. *But seriously, why the hand ties, guys? She has a big personality, but she's less than half your size.*

The men loaded Nancy into the SUV and slammed the hatch closed before joining Tim Gates, who'd slid behind the wheel of the black vehicle. Clearly they were taking Nancy to a different location. Alex had commented, while watching a detective movie one night, that when a kidnap victim is moved to a second location, it is often the last location where they are ever seen alive. Louise's heart pounded on her chest wall so hard she felt as though it was trying to escape. Slipping and sliding through the muddy woods, she raced back to her car. She had to do whatever she could to help Nancy.

Thanking God for helping her to reach her vehicle before the SUV made it out to the road, Louise jumped in, threw the ignition into drive, and pulled a tight U-turn. Spotting a small grove of trees in the distance, she sped to it, turned into the driveway on the far side, then positioned her car so she could see which direction the SUV headed. She considered calling Alex again, but chose not too. He'd tell her to stay put, but that wasn't an option. Once she figured out where they were taking Nancy, she'd call him.

Chapter 36

THE CONSOLE ON Louise's dash flashed to life, indicating an incoming phone message. It was Alex. She stabbed the map button—the incoming call message vanished. "Nice to know you're alive." Wisdom dictated she answer and let Alex know what she was doing, but the less rational part of her brain told her to let it ring through to the answering service. She'd stick to the plan—find out where Tim Gates and the other men were taking Nancy, then inform Alex of their whereabouts. When the vehicle she was following stopped at a red light while traveling south on RR 24, Louise got close enough to see that the SUV was a Ford Escape.

The traffic light flicked to green and the Escape continued

on its way, past Main Street towards Highway 401. Louise's heart sank when the driver eased the vehicle onto the on-ramp that would take it to the east bound lanes of the busiest highway in Canada. She watched as the SUV easily merged into the speeding traffic, but when her turn came, she was blocked by a black and white truck hauling a transport trailer. She slowed and watched a fifty-foot long advertisement for chocolate chip cookies roar by while checking her mirrors for an opening behind the semi. Seeing that there was room for her car behind the truck, Louise shot onto the highway as soon as it passed.

She wanted to move over to the middle lane and pass the black and white beast, but a yellow half-ton delivery truck drove in that lane, confining her to the right lane. The car behind her was still a safe distance away—she depressed the brake to allow the smaller truck to pass, then flew into the middle lane. Quick glances over her shoulder and in the mirrors told her that the left lane was free of vehicles as far as she could see. She inhaled deeply, applied pressure to the gas pedal, and maneuvered into the fast lane, finally able to speed past the yellow truck.

It was now late afternoon and the start of rush hour, which usually lasted at least three hours in this area of southern Ontario. The traffic ahead was heavy with cars and trucks of various colors and sizes. Two sedans motored along the highway in front of the delivery truck—after passing them, Louise returned to the middle lane and continued her search for the vehicle carrying Nancy and her captors.

The overhead sign advertised that the next exit—to Hilton Street and the Georgetown Marina—was two miles ahead. Louise buzzed by the black and white semi, now to her right, to find a rusty red dump truck ambling along in front of it. Debris was flying out of the open back of the slow truck—she squinted and ducked when a piece of Styrofoam cooler hit her windshield. Augh. She waved her fist at the driver, but forced herself to calm down so she could focus on the chase. Thankfully—no damage had been done to her vehicle. She glanced into the rear-view mirror in time to see the same piece of garbage smack into the grill of the car behind her. Louise shook her head at the irresponsibility of driving on the highway with such an insecure load. *Sure, Louise, judge others while you're speeding around trucks and driving like a maniac.*

As she approached the front end of the dump truck she spotted Tim's Escape two cars ahead of it. The right signal was flashing—he was getting off the highway at the Hilton Street exit. Louise sighed and smacked her steering wheel. Now what? She didn't have enough time to get in front of the dump truck. She'd have to slow down and let both the dump truck and the semi pass. Applying pressure to the brake, she peeked into the rear-view mirror. The green compact that had been traveling behind her almost made impact with her bumper, but the driver was able to swerve into the left lane with only inches to spare while applying pressure to his horn.

Louise winced. *Sorry.*

The two trucks sped by on her right, then Louise signaled a change to the right lane before cutting off a speeding purple Mazda. Another horn reminded her of her bad behavior. *Sorry. You shouldn't be speeding, but it's not your fault Nancy went and got herself kidnapped.*

At the end of the off-ramp, a driver could turn left or right onto Hilton Street. Louise spotted the suspect vehicle in the left turn lane. This would take them south to the Georgetown

Marina. Where were they going? Why would they transport Nancy to the Marina?

A parade of cars sat waiting to turn towards the marina—unusual for this intersection at this time of day. *Thank you, God, for a traffic jam.* Without the back up of vehicles, Louise wouldn't have known which way Tim had turned, but now she had a clear view of the SUV carrying him and his thugs. Louise turned left when it was her turn, then proceeded south.

Hilton Street curved east and led past a row of low-rise condominiums built along the shoreline. Louise had been looking into purchasing one of these fairly new condos as an investment that her sister could rent while finishing college. Not wanting to lose sight of the Escape, she brushed off the urge to peer over at the building of interest. The public roadway ended at a private drive that took travelers to the marina parking lot.

Louise stopped her car on the side of the drive and watched Tim Gates as he backed his SUV into a spot beside a restaurant. He exited his vehicle, slammed the door, then marched along a cement pathway that led to the front door. He was followed by the taller of the two ruffians. Louise scratched her head—it was an odd time to stop for a snack. Were they meeting someone in there?

From her vantage point, she studied the geography of the marina. It was situated on a small plot of land—the only structure the one-story, brick bungalow that Tim Gates and his companion had entered. The marina and its boat slips were situated north of the peninsula and the lake. A wooden dock ran parallel to the land adjacent to the restaurant's deck. A public picnic area, complete with swings and slides, separated the parking lot from the lake. Sailors found their way to the slips via a narrow channel on the eastern border—guided in or out by a red and white, mechanical lighthouse that sat proudly at the end of a mile-long cement pier. The pier was dotted with black cormorants and seagulls, eagerly awaiting their next meal from the sea or passing humans.

Louise guided her car farther into the lot and stopped behind a large garbage bin, so that she was now hidden from the men who had been leading her on the chase. Not seeing anyone who might be able to spot her, she exited the car and quietly closed the door. She crept to the bin, suppressed a gag reflex at the overwhelming odors of rotting food, and peeked around it to see if Tim and his friend had come back out. A familiar figure ran from the building, but it wasn't Tim or the other man... it was Eric! What was he doing in there, and why was he fleeing the premises?

Chapter 37

THE LUSH GREEN grass tickled Pansy's feet as she strolled across the field with Indigo. The afternoon sun was a pleasant change from the gloomy, gray skies of yesterday. She'd spent most of the previous day in the barn pretending to muck the horse stalls. Li'l sis had taken to the horses immediately when they arrived on the Wick farm three years earlier, but Pansy, though she initially enjoyed other aspects of farm life, hadn't. She was embarrassed when her first attempt at tacking up a horse ended with the animal running off right after she started tightening the girth. It frustrated her that she was still expected to share in caring for the smelly beasts, especially when she would have preferred to spend her time with Indigo, or her boyfriend Rex.

Pansy had grabbed the pitchfork from the dusty corner of the barn and stabbed at the dirty straw, then shuffled the urine-soaked clump from one part of the stall to another. That would do for now. After slamming the stall door closed, she tossed the pointed tool where she'd found it and dusted off her hands. The forecast for tomorrow, and the rest of the week, was sunny and dry. The horses would be turned out to pasture in the nice weather—they'd be fine another night. In the meantime, she'd have time to convince her sister to do the nasty job of cleaning up after them.

Earlier today, Pansy had smiled as she disembarked from the school bus. She had been correct—the horses were outside, frolicking in their paddock. Now all she had to do was once again convince her young shadow to do barn chores for her.

The laneway to the house was a quarter mile long. Pansy used this time to make up an excuse as to why she couldn't do her own work. Too much homework? Sore back? Headache? Allergies? Sore stomach? No, she'd used all of those excuses in the past couple of weeks—she'd need something new.

Indigo was waiting in his usual spot on the porch as she approached. The vet had explained to them that the reason the old guy wasn't running to meet her at the bus anymore was arthritis, which afflicted old dogs the same way it attacked older humans. Indigo's joints were swollen and sore, especially on damp days. The medication the vet had prescribed for him helped, but he was still not the same dog she'd fallen in love with that day Ms. Jane deposited them in their new foster home.

When Pansy was home, Indigo followed her from house to barn, room to room, and field to field. His company was welcomed by the weary teenager—Pansy finally had some- one she felt safe to confide in without risk of being ridiculed or scolded. Both she and Li'l sis loved being with Olive and Hugh Wick, who treated them no differently then they likely would have treated their own children, but Pansy wasn't able to completely shake off her mistrust of adults. Her own parents were wonderful for the first six years—she'd only known the Wicks for three.

Indigo rose to his feet when Pansy patted his head. "Come on boy, let's go for a walk before dinner."

They sauntered towards her favorite spot by the creek that ran through the western field that housed the heifers. Indigo would normally race ahead, but after the dampness from the previous day, he was content to stay by Pansy's side. An electric fence bordered the paddock, and Pansy grasped the wire and raised it far enough to allow her and Indigo to pass under. Mr. Wick had told her early in her days on the farm that there was no need to activate the fence as long as the cows thought it was active. Initially she was hesitant to touch it, but after discovering that it was not even connected to the electrical panel, her fear of death by electrocution subsided.

"Hey boy, my birthday is in a few days. Mrs. Wick will probably want to throw a party, but I'd rather hang out with Rex." She frowned. "They don't like Rex. I don't know why."

A gentle wind blew across the creek, rippling the water that rushed around the rocks reaching up through the sparkling surface like icebergs. It was peaceful to watch nature flow freely around obstacles; if only life could be so simple. Pansy chose a stone from the embankment and cast it onto the water. It skipped three times before joining previous skipping rocks at the bottom of the stream. She sat on a rock by the water's edge—one with a natural depression that provided an excellent seat for a tired teenager. She tossed another stone towards the water, but instead of skimming gracefully along the water's surface, this one flew across the width of the creek and smashed into a tree on the other side. The sound startled Indigo who stared at her, his head at a tilt.

"Sorry, bud. I'm a bit frustrated. I don't want to have a party if I can't invite Rex, and I know Olive and Hugh won't let me go out with him. So what if he dropped out of school? Lots of kids do. It's no big deal. I still go to school." She flung another pebble across the water. A chipmunk ran for cover.

Pansy gazed into Indigo's eyes. "I miss my mom. Why did she have to die? What did I do so bad that she died on my birthday? I thought she loved me." Pansy lowered her head to her hands and let the tears flow. Indigo licked her forehead, then started to bark.

A squirrel in a tree sent the old dog back into puppyhood. Seeming to forget the pain of the arthritis, he leapt at the tree repeatedly.

"Silly old dog. You can't catch a squirrel. When will you learn?" Pansy laughed at her furry companion. Indigo always seemed to know when she needed a distraction. His tongue flopped out of his mouth. She laughed harder, then gave him a bear hug. "You're the best dog ever."

Dinner was eaten with no family drama, but with dessert came the conversation Pansy was dreading.

Olive laid a plate of shortbread cookies in the center of the table before serving a bowl of chocolate mint ice cream to Pansy, Li'l sis, and Hugh. Once the others were served, Olive took her seat with her own bowl of the icy treat. "Pansy, you're turning sixteen this year. We'd like to have a party, you know… a sweet sixteen, but your school grades have been very poor lately."

Pansy furrowed her brow and glared at Olive, then Hugh. It was one thing for her to decline a party, but what was Olive saying? They weren't offering to throw her a party because of school grades?

Pansy straightened in her chair. "I don't follow."

Hugh filled his lungs with air as he set his spoon on the table. He leaned in and held Pansy's gaze. "You were a good student until you started spending time with Rex. I've expressed my concerns about that boy, yet you continue to see him."

Pansy had met Rex the previous summer at a beach party hosted by a mutual friend. She quickly fell for the seventeen-year-old, handsome boy with the athletic body. Despite his physique, he wasn't on any of the school sports teams because he had dropped out after being arrested for marijuana possession.

Hugh shoved his bowl away. "We've tried to give you everything you need. Not just a place to live but a real family. I don't understand why you need to see that boy. There are a lot of boys at your school who we'd be happy to have sit right here at this table and join us for a meal."

Olive scooped up Li'l sis's empty bowl, and the three untouched bowls, and deposited them in the sink. "We got a call from the school today. You've been skipping classes. We're at a loss as to how to reach you, Pansy. You have such a promising future. You're a smart girl, but if you let Rex lead you down the wrong road, that will all be lost."

Pansy fought back the tears. Why were they being so mean? She stood so abruptly that her chair toppled backwards with a crash. She eyed the three people at the table. Li'l sis sat quietly, tears in her eyes. Pansy righted the chair, then ran to her room.

She grabbed her backpack and emptied the contents onto her bed. "No party? No problem." She sat in her room for an hour and waited. Her foster parents had a Bible study to attend—she'd wait until they were gone, then she'd go to the one place she knew she'd be wanted.

The car's motor started, and Pansy listened as the sound of the engine gradually decreased. When she couldn't hear it anymore, she flung the bag over her shoulder and stomped downstairs.

Li'l sis sat on the couch watching TV. She tapped the button to silence the volume. "Where are you going? I think you're probably grounded."

Pansy sneered at her and headed for the door. "I'm going where I'm wanted."

Li'l sis rose from the couch and followed Pansy. "No, really. Where are you going?"

"Don't worry about it, kid. They won't miss me a bit, I'm sure."

"What are you talking about? You're leaving? Really leaving?" Li'l sis tugged on Pansy's backpack. "What about me?"

Pansy replaced the backpack over her shoulder and shrugged. "What about you? You'll stay here and you'll be just fine without me around."

"You're scaring me, Pansy. What do you mean 'without you around'? Where are you going?"

Pansy cupped the knob and yanked the door open. "Don't say anything okay? I'll call you when I'm settled."

Li'l sis' face reddened as tears dampened her cheeks. "Settled where? Where you going?"

Pansy gave her little sister a hug before bolting out the

door. She didn't want to cry in front of Li'l sis, but the tears wouldn't stop when she heard Li'l sis call after her.

"You're no different than Mom and Dad. Remember them? They left us and now you're leaving me." A door slammed. Silence.

Pansy hopped onto her bike and rode to Rex's house. His parents were cool—they didn't care whether or not he went to school. They didn't care who he hung out with, or if the police had to bring him home. They let him have all the parties he wanted, and sometimes they partied with him and his friends. That's where she wanted to live—a place where she'd have the freedom to do what she wanted. And best of all she'd be with the love of her life.

Rex's car sat idle in the driveway. Good. She wouldn't have to go looking for him. He wasn't always available when she'd phone or text—sometimes it would be a few days before he would respond, but that was okay. He was seventeen and probably busy. Some of her friends suspected that he was cheating on her, seeing other girls. Pansy deleted those people from her contacts list.

Her knock on Rex's door went unanswered, so she let herself in as she'd done many other times. The door was never locked. Voices emanated from the family room in the back of the house. She skipped down the hall, certain Rex would be excited to have her move in with his family. She heard his voice first, then someone else's—a woman's. Pansy gasped when she saw who was on the couch with Rex. The TV was shouting out dialogue, and Rex had his arm around a girl from school.

Pansy stiffened. "What's going on?"

Rex's chin jerked up. He caught Pansy's eye, then stumbled to free himself from his companion and stand. "Pansy. What are you doing here?"

Pansy crossed her arms. "Does it matter, Rex? Does it? I thought you cared about me."

Rex laughed. "I do." He nodded towards to the girl still sitting on the couch. "But I have other friends too. Betty and I are just watching a movie."

Betty grasped Rex's hand and pulled herself up. She ran an imaginary line down his cheek with her finger. "That's right, Rex." She winked at Pansy. "We're watching a movie… for a school project." Betty laughed and flopped back on the couch.

Rex waved his hand at her. "Shush. You're not helping."

Betty leapt to her feet, without help this time. "Shush? No one shushes me. I'm out of here." She brushed past Pansy. "He's all yours."

Pansy glared at Rex. Her friends were right. Olive and Hugh were right. How could she have been so stupid? Rex was almost an adult, another adult who couldn't be trusted.

She spun around and stormed out of the lying cheat's house. Tears clouded her vision as she pedaled her way back to the Wicks' farm. The whole school was probably laughing at her. She'd almost run away from home for that loser. She had told Li'l sis she was leaving, but now she had nowhere to go.

She found herself riding up the lane to the house she'd called home for the past three years. A happy home. Her shoulders relaxed when she saw that the car was still gone—Olive and Hugh weren't home yet.

The door was locked and Pansy didn't have a key. They never locked the door when someone was home—but she'd left her kid sister all alone. Pansy lowered her chin. How could she have done that? The one person in the world she could truly count on, and she'd not only been willing to leave her for some loser guy, but she had left her alone in the house.

Pansy knocked and waited a few minutes. Finally, the door flew open. Li'l sis stood frozen for a few seconds before crossing her arms and glaring at Pansy. "So. You're back. I guess that off-the-farm world ain't as glamorous as you thought. Or did you forget something? Like your mind. I've been looking for it since you left, but you lost it real good this time."

Pansy smiled and fist tapped her sister's shoulder. "Nice grammar. Obviously I can't go anywhere with you talking like that. Someone needs to watch out for you."

"I can do just fine, thank you."

Pansy pulled Li'l sis into a bear hug. "How about we keep this between us?"

Li'l sis pulled back and grinned. "Sure, but it'll cost ya."

Pansy waved her hand in the air as she headed to the kitchen. "Whatever." Li'l sis had made that threat many times in response to Pansy's requests to keep a confidence, but Li'l sis never collected on it. Pansy had been wrong to think that no one cared about her. They had the Wicks, and she and Li'l sis would always have each other. She was sure of it.

Chapter 38

LOUISE WATCHED AS Eric ran along the cement path, then crossed the damp lawn. He glanced over his left shoulder, lost his footing, and hit the ground hard. Louise gasped, then retreated behind the garbage bin. He'd hit his head. She wanted to run to him, but who was he running from? She couldn't leave him lying there, but if she rushed to him, she would draw attention to both of them.

Louise pressed her back against the dirty bin, then crept to the other end and made her way around it. From this vantage point she could see that Eric had sat up. He was waving his hand as though telling someone to get down. Louise followed the direction of the gesture—his car was parked parallel to a dry-docked yacht, and the woman from the bus station stood beside it. Louise returned her gaze to Eric as he rolled onto his knees and pulled himself up. Then she turned her head towards the car in time to see the woman climb into the passenger seat and duck down. *They're hiding from someone.*

Eric glanced over his shoulder again, then started towards his car. Louise stepped out from her hiding spot, far enough that he could see her, and waved at him. "Eric. Over here."

Eric snapped his head in Louise's direction. His eyes widened. He rotated his torso right, then left, then right again. He seemed uncertain of what to do or where to go. His attention shot from the restaurant to Louise to the car and back to the restaurant.

Louise motioned for him to join her. "Eric. Over here."

Eric inhaled deeply, then trotted towards Louise. As soon as he was close enough, she grabbed his jacket and pulled him behind the bin.

"What are you doing here? Where have you been?" Her heart was racing, emotions battling for dominance within her. Happiness to see him, relief he wasn't injured, anger that he'd disappeared, worry that he seemed to be in trouble.

Eric stared at Louise—he appeared to be suffering from his own internal conflict. His pupils were dilated, and a tear ran down his cheek. Was that fear? Guilt? Shame?

Louise gave him a hug. Danger surrounded them, but she couldn't help herself. "I've been so worried about you. The police are looking for you. They think you've been involved in multiple robberies."

Eric lowered his chin. "I'm so sorry. I promise you I didn't do anything illegal. I've been..." He glanced at the car where his companion was still hidden. "I've been helping a friend." His breaths came in short gasps.

Louise squeezed his hand. "Take it easy. I take it the friend is the woman hiding in your car over there?" She tilted her head towards Eric's vehicle.

"You saw her? That's not good. I told her to stay hidden until I let her know it was safe." Eric's face turned red. "Her ex-husband, I saw him in the restaurant. And Bob was in there too. We've been avoiding them. He's a really nasty guy. Sally, that's her name, needed help to hide from him until we could get enough money for her to leave town."

"Your friend was married to Bob?"

Eric shook his head. "What? No! Bob's friend is Sally's ex. His name is Nat, and calling him nasty is being nice. He used to hit her, a lot. She asked me for help and I said okay. Then one night when Bob and I went out for wings after work, Nat sat at our table and started talking to Bob. It freaked me out. Bob introduced us, but I already knew who he was because Sally had shown me a photo."

"Why did you take off? Why didn't you simply tell me or Daphne what was going on? We could have helped you."

"I'm sorry. I should have, I know, but Daphne had her baby, and, well… I assumed you would call Alex."

"Alex could have helped Sally."

Eric wiped his eyes. "Maybe, but you always hear stories about abused women who end up dead after getting a restraining order. If I told Alex, he would want to arrest Nat."

Louise nodded. "That's all true. There are no guarantees, but disappearing wasn't smart. You're a suspect now in a burglary and a murder."

Eric stiffened. "Murder?"

"A judge with the National Kennel Club was murdered around the same time you stopped showing up for work. The police have a video of you and one of your old buddies, Keith Giles, in front of the NKC building in Amherst the same night Cliff Mariner was killed. You were handing a package to Keith."

Eric peeked around the bin, then turned back to Louise. "I don't know any Cliff Mariner. I *was* in Amherst one night with Keith because Sally needed money for a bus ticket." Eric kicked a rock with the toe of his shoe. "I sold the baseball card you gave me. I'm so sorry. I didn't want to part with it, it really meant a lot to me, but Sally was desperate."

Louise let out a huge breath. "That explains the card being in Keith's possession. I saw you at the bus station earlier today, but obviously Sally didn't get on a bus—she's still with you."

Eric peered around the bin again. "We can't stay here. If Nat sees me, he'll know that Sally is nearby. I can't believe he's here. His boat is usually docked in Amherst; that's why we arranged to meet Sally's parents here."

"Her parents are on the way? Why didn't she go home to them long ago?"

"Her parents are members of the Amherst boat club. That's how she met Nat. They disapproved of the relationship, so she ran away and married him. She hasn't spoken to her folks in a long time. At the bus station earlier, I had a ticket for her to go out west, but she decided to call them. They were out sailing this morning and said it would be quicker to meet her here. I have to warn Sally that her ex is here."

Eric started towards his car, but Louise pulled him back when she saw Tim Gates and his companion exit the restaurant.

"Stay out of sight. That man in the suit over there kidnapped one of our clients earlier. I've been following them."

Eric's jaw dropped. "What? Murder? Kidnapping? Where's Alex?"

Louise reached into her pocket and retrieved her phone. "I was about to call him when I spotted you."

Eric grabbed Louise's arm. She dropped the phone as he retreated farther behind the bin, pulling her with him. "That guy beside the suit, that's Nat Bradley! Sally's ex. I'm not surprised he's involved in a kidnapping. I went down to the docks to talk to him one day, thought I could convince him to leave Sally alone, but when I saw him smacking his younger brother Brent around, I changed my mind."

Nat and Brent Bradley—why did those names sound familiar?

Louise tilted her head. "That explains why you were seen at the docks."

"I was?"

"Yes, Jenny's boyfriend, Roger, spotted you down there the other night. Alex is concerned that you've gotten mixed up with your old gang again. I have to admit, the evidence against you seemed to be mounting."

Eric pressed his hands together. "I promise you, Louise, I've just been helping Sally. That's all."

Louise clasped his shoulder. "I want to believe you, but why were you meeting with Bob in there?" She pointed towards the restaurant. "He's been up to... well, I'm not sure exactly what yet, but something."

"I wasn't meeting Bob. I went in to use the men's room, and when I was leaving I spotted Bob at a table. I hid behind a wall in case Nat was with him, then suddenly Nat and that other guy come in, march over to Bob, and sit with him. Bob was obviously nervous. Kept adjusting his tie."

"He does do that a lot."

"Anyway, once I was sure none of them were looking in my direction, I bolted."

The ring tone on Louise's phone started up. She snatched the phone off the ground and accepted the incoming call to silence it. It was Alex.

Pressing the device to her ear, she whispered, "I can't talk now. I'm at the Georgetown Marina with Eric. Tim Gates and his thugs are here. He and one of them went into the restaurant and met up with Bob."

"What is Eric doing there?"

"Long story, but he isn't mixed up with anything illegal."

"I'm sure he told you that, but… Anyway, both of you stay put, and stay out of sight—I'm on my way." The call ended.

Eric directed his attention to his car. "Oh no. I need to warn her."

Louise glanced up from her phone. Sally had climbed out of the car and was waving at Eric. From Sally's position, she couldn't see Nat. *Hopefully he can't see her.*

Eric started towards Sally. Louise grabbed his sleeve. "Stay here. If they see you…"

He spun out of the coat, leaving it dangling in Louise's hand. "I have to warn her that Nat is here." He bolted across the parking lot.

Louise gritted her teeth, then peered around the corner of the bin. Did they see him? Nat was pointing at the yacht parked along the dock and talking to Tim. They hadn't seen Eric, or Sally. Louise released the breath she'd been holding, and watched Eric as he encouraged Sally to return to her hiding spot. Once she was in the car, he joined her, and they both ducked out of sight.

Louise rested her hand against the bin, then wiped it on her pants. *Ick.* Eric was safe for now—from what she observed Nat hadn't seen Eric or Sally. But how long would any of them be safe here? Her young technician and his friend were waiting for Sally's parents to arrive. Louise was waiting for Alex.

Loud voices drew her attention to the SUV. Tim and Nat were situated beside the rear of the vehicle, and Nat was yelling at the man who had remained behind. He called the guy Brent, then slapped the back of his head. *Eric was right, that guy is way past nasty.*

Brent started the engine and backed up until his hatch was only a few feet from the yacht's gangway. Eric had said that the Bradleys had a yacht. Louise's heart raced—if they took Nancy onto the boat, they could dispose of her body easily. Louise punched Alex's number into her phone.

He picked up immediately. "What's going on? I'm almost there and I've called for back-up."

Louise crouched down and cupped her hand around the phone so he could hear her better as she whispered. "It looks like they might be taking a ride on a yacht."

"That's not good. What does it look like?"

Louise shrugged. "I don't know, it's a boat." She stole another peek at the water vessel. "There's a name on it. Finding Freedom. Ha. Kind of ironic."

"Louise."

Louise heard the seriousness in Alex's voice. He was right. This was no time for lame jokes. "Sorry. There's a number on it too." She opened the camera app on her phone. Zooming in, she was able to get a photo of the seven-digit number. She sent it to Alex via text.

"I think that's a license, similar to the plates on a car. I'll contact the coast guard and get them to look into it."

Louise heard more commotion by the SUV. She held the phone up with the camera app still open so that she could see what was happening without having to stick her head out. Tim Gates opened the hatch, then Nat Bradley yanked Nancy out by the collar of her jacket. Still holding her, he tossed Nancy into his brother, then Nat returned to the restaurant.

Alex asked a question, but Louise hadn't been listening. "Sorry, Alex, what was that?"

"Do you think Nancy is working with Tim and the other guys?"

Louise focused on Nancy—her hands and legs were trembling, and she was still bound and gagged. "I'm pretty sure she isn't."

Brent Bradley hoisted a long board from the deck and propped it against the boat's siderail, then Tim, with his hand pressed against Nancy's back, forced her on board. Louise cringed when Nancy fell off the board onto the deck. Tim jumped into the vessel and, grasping the collar to her flimsy coat, yanked her to her feet. Nat and Bob—who had remained in the restaurant while the others dragged Nancy out of the SUV—joined Brent at the boat ramp. Louise frowned. It didn't appear as though Bob was there voluntarily either. Like Nancy, Bob was forced up the make-shift ramp, as Nat walked behind him, pressing what looked to be a concealed gun into his back.

Louise dropped her hand to her side. There was more going on here than forged breeding documents, but what?

Alex voice rose from the device clutched in her fingers. "Louise?"

Louise moved to the other side of the bin, then dashed towards the restaurant and hid behind a sign advertising events that the marina was hosting that weekend. She was close enough to touch Tim's SUV, but out of sight of the occupants of the yacht.

"What's going on?"

Louise pressed the phone to her ear, but kept her voice to a whisper. "Can't talk, they'll hear me. They're getting on the boat."

"What was that? You're getting on a boat? Bad idea. Stay put. We're on our way."

Louise shoved the phone into her pocket. "Get on board? I hadn't thought of that. Good idea."

Chapter 39

FINDING FREEDOM WAS a three-level watercraft similar to the yacht owned by Louise's colleague, Dr. Josh Jackson. Louise and Alex had joined Josh and his wife on several trips along the shore of Lake Ontario the previous summer. Louise enjoyed the outings and was looking forward to another, but now she focused her mind on the structure of the vessel before her.

She was certain that the lower deck housed the living area, complete with a kitchen—or galley as Josh had pointed out—a three-piece bathroom, and two small bedrooms. In addition to the rooms, there was likely a multitude of storage compartments—all of which would be ideal for concealment. Louise had teased Josh and his wife about smuggling items into Canada from the US if they exceeded their spending limits when shopping south of the border. *I doubt these guys are worried about getting good deals at the big box stores. But what if...*

The engine started. Louise had to the think fast. Shortly after boarding, the four men and Nancy had disappeared into the main cabin on the middle level. The glass panels were covered with the same one-way window film that Daphne had been wanting to install at the clinic—it was impossible to see what was going on inside. At the back of the same deck was a double seat that faced forward, and behind that there was a small space occupied by only a storage bin. A gangplank sat in the closed position alongside the bin. Why hadn't the shorter thug, Brent, used that instead of the wooden board? Could Louise use it to get onboard? No. There wouldn't be time to open it then close it again, or for her to figure out how to operate it.

The door to the cabin opened and Brent stepped out. He glanced in Louise's direction and she ducked behind the sign. Had he seen her? He wouldn't know who she was, but no doubt he'd want to know why someone was spying on them from behind the advertisement board. Louise dared to peek at the thug. She wiped her brow—he had turned his attention to the rope that tethered the yacht to the dock. When he released it, Louise's pulse quickened.

She watched as Brent went inside, then she raced to the rear corner of the yacht. She grasped the railing with both hands and threw her body over the side, landing by the wooden bin in the space along the stern. Lying on her left side, legs crumpled against the fiberglass hull, she caressed her left shoulder. *Ouch!* It didn't feel broken, but she'd have a nasty bruise the next day. She lay still. As long as she stayed low, they wouldn't be able to see her. But what now? They were pulling away from the dock and she was trapped between the seat, a storage compartment, and the water—on a boat with a group of criminals, and what appeared to be at least two guns.

Should have listened to Alex. Alex! Louise tugged the phone from her pocket. Her shoulder muscles relaxed when she saw they were still connected. She propped herself up on her elbow but a bolt of pain reminded her of her injured shoulder and she leaned against the seat, keeping her head low. "How close are you?"

"What have you done?"

"Why would you immediately assume I've *done* something?"

"Please tell me you're not on the boat!"

"I wish I could, but…"

"Louise!"

"I know. Stupid. You have permission to yell at me later, but please tell me you're close. They've pulled away from the dock, but we haven't left the marina yet."

"I'm almost there, but I don't have a boat. I'll have to wait for the coast guard to pick me up. Just stay out of sight. And Louise…"

"Yes?"

"No heroics."

"No kidding! I think they have guns." She raised herself enough to peek over the seat. The door to the cabin remained closed. "They forced Nancy and Bob onboard. Nancy fell. She may be hurt."

"The coast guard has one unit heading to the marina to meet me. A second unit will be on the lookout for you. What does the yacht look like?"

"Its very similar to Josh's, but the lower half is blue. The top half is white. There's a plain yellow flag flying from the mast."

"They may be meeting another boat, and the flag will make them easier to spot. That'll work to our advantage."

The door creaked open. Louise hit the end button on the phone, then opened the text app and clicked on Alex's name. "Had to hang up. Someone came out on deck."

A seagull flew over and deposited a white, gooey clump onto the storage bin. *Nice. Almost got me.* Alongside the bird feces, she spotted red lettering.

Life jackets. The door opened again. She raised her phone enough that the camera gave her a view of the deck. Whoever had come out must have gone back in—she was alone.

"Phew."

Louise lifted the storage lid, retrieved a yellow vest, and popped it over her head. *Perfect fit. Thank goodness, because you could never be too careful on the water.*

She reached in and snagged a second jacket, then looked into the bin. It was empty. *I guess a bunch of thugs with guns aren't too worried about water safety.* She hugged the extra vest against her chest in case Nancy needed it. It was a foolish thought—Nancy was tied up inside, surrounded by thugs and guns, and Louise was hiding outside with no safe way of getting to her. She'd need to find a way into the cabin if Alex or the coast guard didn't arrive soon.

The distance between Louise and the dock was increasing much faster than she would have liked. She soon had a close up view of the cement pier and the birds who called it home. They seemed to be staring at her with pity as she passed. What did they know that she didn't? Had they previously witnessed humans going out to the depths never to return from a watery grave? *Don't be foolish, Louise, they're merely birds waiting for a snack.*

Louise placed the spare life jacket to her side, then crouched lower against the seat, pulling her knees close to her chin. If the boat was the same as Josh's, someone could access the upper deck from the cabin, and that was the most practical place from which to pilot the yacht through the narrow channel to the lake. Would she be visible from that vantage point? *God, please keep me hidden until help arrives.*

As they cruised past the lighthouse, Louise's limbs numbed. The wind was increasing, and with every foot they advanced on their journey, the temperature seemed to fall. Was it the cold in the air or the coldness of the people in the cabin that caused Louise's skin to chill? What were they planning to do with Nancy and Bob? What would they do with her if she was discovered?

She focused on the shoreline and the shrinking structures at the marina. Eric was safe, and she had no doubt that what he had told her about helping Sally was the truth. She'd convince Alex of that later… but would there be a later? She had to trust that God was in control of this situation, but that didn't answer the question about whether or not she'd see Alex again. And what about Maryanne, or Daphne, or the other people that meant so much to her? Who would feed Oscar? She would trust God, and she'd stay hidden until He provided a way for her to get free.

Flashing blue and red lights appeared at the marina. Warmth returned to her aching limbs—it had to be Alex and the police. She resisted the urge to leap to her feet and wave her hands at her potential rescuers. They wouldn't hear her, but the men who held Nancy and Bob captive would. Still, help was on the way.

Louise's heart sank when she felt the surge of the boat accelerating. Tim and the Bradleys had likely also seen the activity at the marina, and now they were going faster—much faster—towards the center of the lake and the international border.

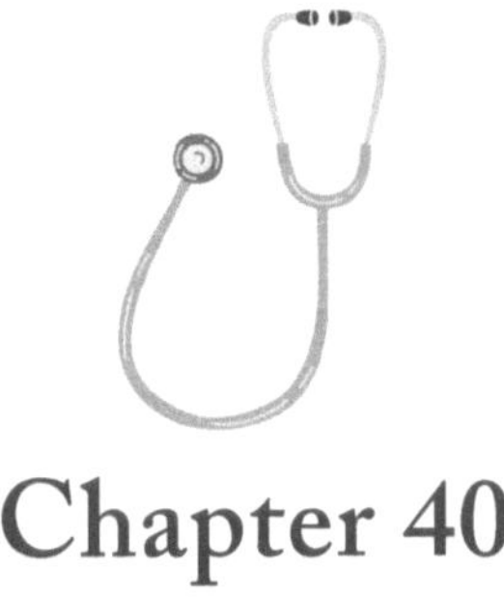

Chapter 40

WAVES CRACKED AGAINST the side of the hull, casting unfiltered lake water onto the deck and Louise. She shivered against the ice-like droplets as they stabbed at her bare leg, reminding her of her fall into the ditch and the tear in her scrub pants. The light jacket she wore over her scrub top provided little protection against the cold of the wind and water. Why hadn't she brought a warmer jacket? Who followed after criminals in surgical scrubs? She made a mental note to wear more appropriate clothing the next time she found herself chasing kidnappers.

Her phone was still imprisoned by her fingers, so tightly that her joints were aching. She wanted to send Alex a text, but there were only two bars and the battery was low. How far was the US-Canada border? Would she still have cell coverage once they crossed it? She glanced at the screen.

Alex had replied to her earlier text: Keep your phone on. Call my number and leave the line open so that I can hear what's going on.

Louise opened the phone app and clicked on Alex's name, but when the Call Failed message appeared her eyes glazed over with tears. She had two bars. The phone should work! She tried a text.

"Battery dying. Can't dial through. Staying hidden. Check my trunk. Hurry!"

Louise squeezed her knees tighter to her chest when the cabin door creaked. Despite her best efforts, she couldn't make herself any smaller, so she closed her eyes and held her breath. The next sound she heard was familiar—it reminded her of Oscar's midnight hairball depositing missions. One of his favorite locations was the doorway to the bathroom, the perfect location to ensure she couldn't miss stepping in the gooey mess during one of her own late-night missions.

Someone was seasick. It couldn't be Nat or Brent because, from what Eric had told her, they were experienced sailors. Could it be Tim Gates? He seemed to be the leader of the group, why would he make use of a water vessel if he couldn't hold his lunch when it was wavy? Louise relaxed the grip on her knees. Nancy was tied up, which left Bob. It had to be him, but could she trust him? He hadn't come onto the yacht voluntarily, but he might be willing to turn on her if it meant saving himself. Her only choices were to trust Bob and get into the cabin on her own terms or risk being discovered by the others.

Certain that the nausea victim was her soon-to-be-former

associate, Louise rotated her body enough to sneak a peek over the top of the seats. It was him. He was still wearing the khaki pants and white shirt he'd worn to the clinic earlier that day. Bent over and grasping the railing with both hands, his abdomen lurched repeatedly. The tie he'd been tightening all day was now flapped over his shoulder, protecting it from the contents of his stomach.

Louise had to get his attention without drawing the scrutiny of the others. She watched as he drew a handkerchief from his pocket and wiped his face. *Who uses a handkerchief these days? Focus, Louise.* She willed him to turn left so she could wave him over, but he turned to his right and headed towards the cabin. Louise scanned her miniature environment for something to throw at him. A pebble, a nail, anything large enough for him to feel but too small to be visible or to make a loud noise when it hit the deck. The only thing behind the seat with her was the extra life jacket and that was too big.

He reached for the door handle. Desperate, Louise made her best attempt at imitating a seagull. He didn't react. She did it again, this time sounding like an angry seagull. The strange noise worked—Bob glanced over his shoulder and scanned the horizon. Louise ducked down but waved her fingers above the seat, motioning for him to sit. Would he understand her hand signals? She prayed that he would. If the attention of the others was drawn by the sounds of a tortured seabird, any hope she had of making contact with Bob would be lost.

Pressure on the seat back told her that someone had sat down. "Bob."

He spun in his seat and glanced down at her. "Louise! What are you doing here?"

She made a counter-clockwise motion with her index finger. "Turn around. Keep your eyes straight ahead."

Bob redirected his focus to the bow then leaned back so that he could hear Louise over the roar of the motor. "What are you doing here?"

"Keep your voice down. If those friends of yours find me…"

"They can't hear us. The cabin is sound proofed. The owner doesn't like the sound of the waves. And they're no friends of mine. Anyway, you shouldn't be here. Did you follow me?"

"No. I followed Nancy and the others. I found your phone at the clinic, and Mary saw that mysterious white van follow Nancy out of the parking lot. The message on the phone led me to believe that Nancy was in danger. I was looking for Alex when I saw the van in Georgetown and followed it. They made a pit stop at an abandoned property and transferred Nancy into a SUV."

Bob swallowed loudly then gagged. "Sorry. I need some water. Did you find Alex? Does he know where you are?"

"He knows I'm on this boat, and he knows that you are too. The police know that you're involved with those Bradley brothers. They have your fingerprints at the warehouse those thugs used for, well, I don't know what they used it for. All I know is that they burned it down."

Bob cleared his throat. Was he yanking on his tie? "Listen, Louise, this isn't what you think. They are bad news, all of them. Nat, Brent… and Tim."

Louise harumphed. "What I think is that you brought danger to our clinic. I'm glad Eric wasn't involved with whatever it is you and your thug buddies are up too, but you put him in danger too. You're the reason he disappeared for a month."

"I am? How?"

"Never mind that right now. What are you and Nancy mixed up in? And more importantly, how are we going to get out of this mess?"

"I don't know. I'd been hiding from the Bradleys all day; that's why I took off this morning after seeing that the AI room was ransacked. I was sure it was them. I waited across the street until the police left, then planned to hide in the clinic until I could come up with another plan."

Heat rose in Louise's chest. "And put the rest of us in danger? How thoughtful of you."

"I'm really sorry about that."

"So sorry that when I found you cowering in the staff room earlier, you cast doubt on Eric's character to save yourself. I'm having a hard time feeling pity for you. I'm wet, my knees ache, and I think I cracked my humeral head."

"I was trying to help Nancy out. She doesn't have anyone in her life, no friends or family. She asked for help to, well…"

"Get out of town? Was that you who searched for flights on Daphne's computer?"

"It was, but the flights were for me, not Nancy. I thought that if I took off, they'd leave her alone. I was wrong."

Louise noted the ebbing of the waves—the yacht was slowing down. Was that a good sign or a bad one? It would be easier for Alex and his colleagues to reach them, but it also might mean they were closer to their destination. Louise's blood cooled at the thought. Was their destination the middle of the lake to dispose of Nancy and Bob… and Louise, once they found her? Or was Alex correct that they were meeting another boat? Neither of those prospects was reassuring. Louise inhaled deeply to calm her nerves—it didn't work.

She wanted to scream, but this was not the time to holler at Bob. "It seems you *were* wrong. What are you mixed up in?"

"Like I said, I intended to help Nancy out. It was innocent enough. No one was supposed to get hurt, but then Tim, well… he found out what we were up too and—"

The cabin door crashed open. The owner of the faintly familiar voice was obviously frustrated. "Bob! What are you doing out here? Can't take that long to barf. Get back in here so we can keep an eye on you." The door slammed closed.

Louise held her breath. Did they have company on deck? Was she about to be discovered? Her limbs relaxed when she heard Bob say, "That was Tim. He's gone back in."

Louise shifted her weight to relieve the pressure on her backside. Sitting crunched up in the small pace was causing her muscles to tighten. She was reminded of the many assaults that her body had endured since she'd started following the van from Georgetown. The worst injury was sustained when she leapt onboard after Brent untied the rope anchor. "I have an idea. Do you see the rope?"

"Sure. There's the rope for when the boat is docked and a shorter one, about the length of a dog leash, looped around the end of it."

Louise resisted the urge to jump up and grab for the rope herself. "If you can get the smaller one free, we can use it."

Bob got up. Louise heard him grunting as he worked. "What are we going to do with this?"

Louise shook her head at her own plan. Would it work? "You're going to use it to take me captive. I can't stay out here. I'll either freeze to death, or they'll find me. Either way, it won't end in my favor. I'm hoping that if you can convince them you found me out here, they'll make me the third hostage rather than the first drowning victim."

Bob leaned over the back of the seat with the rope in hand. "What do I do with this?"

Louise touched her wrists together then lifted her arms to Bob. "Do you know how to make a quick release knot?"

He nodded.

"Good. Loop the rope around my wrists using a quick release, but make sure that the release end is the short end. You hold onto the tightening end and pretend to drag me into the cabin."

Bob squinted. "I don't know. I'm not much of an actor."

Louise rolled her eyes. "I've noticed, but we have no choice." She thrust her hands towards Bob and he tied the rope as instructed. Once it was secured, Louise held the short, release-end in her hand as Bob helped her climb over the seat.

The occupants of the cabin looked confused when Louise followed Bob through the narrow doorway. Bob yanked on the long end of the rope as Louise had instructed him to do, and she feigned being thrown slightly off balance by his action. *Give them a good show, Louise.*

Tim Gates rose and approached Louise, but the Bradleys remained seated, their mouths agape. Nancy, hands tied and mouth still covered with tape, sat in the far corner of the room with her head down.

The cabin was decorated with white-vinyl seats along the starboard and port. Towards the bow a curved stairway led to the flybridge similar to Josh's yacht, as Louise had suspected earlier. A table, cluttered with maps, small cardboard boxes, and several beer cans, ran the length of the cabin between the seats. The floor was muddy, and the smell was similar to the one that emanated from the men's locker room after one of Alex and Joe's hockey games.

Tim's gaze swept over Louise. "What do we have here, Bob?"

Bob adjusted his tie. Louise wanted to slug him. "I found her hiding in the back, behind the seat." He directed his thumb to the stern. "Back there."

Tim slapped his forehead. "You really aren't very good at this, are you, Bob? I know where the back of the boat is." He shook his head. "Moron."

Bob lifted the rope. "I tied her up… for you. So she'd be, um, secure."

Tim stared into Louise's eyes. She resisted the urge to look away. His eyes were cold and dark, his black irises encircling the void of his pupils. Was he wearing colored contact lenses, or was that a reflection of his soul? He grasped Louise's chin. "You look familiar. Have we met before?"

Louise swallowed hard. "No, we've never met. I did see you at the dog show a few weeks ago." She tried to control the anger rising in her. "You were yelling at poor Cliff Mariner while he was giving me and my friend a tour."

Tim produced a laugh reminiscent of a Saturday morning cartoon villain. Louise pressed her lips together to suppress a nervous giggle. All that was missing from Tim's reaction was the wringing of his hands. He was still gripping her jaw and she attempted to pull away from his slimy fingers. He acquiesced by loosening his grip, but not until after giving her a quick shove. Her neck snapped, but having anticipated his cruel action, she was able to keep herself from falling backwards.

Tim spun around and stomped towards the bow, then

made another rapid turn and resumed his soul penetrating stare. "Yes, *poor* Cliff. The fool he was, he found himself in the wrong place at the wrong time."

Louise's face flushed. Did this guy kill Cliff? Why? Cliff had been at the NKC offices that night to find the certificates for the next day's show winners. That couldn't possibly be a motive to kill him. But Tim said he was in the wrong place at the wrong time. Had Cliff stumbled upon something? Would they have killed him because he caught them forging breeding documents?

Louise was unable to hold back her curiosity. "Cliff caught you all forging documents, didn't he?" She held her breath. Would they throw her overboard now?

Tim laughed again, and this time he did wring his hands. Louise choked on the fishy stale air she sucked in then held her breath. Laughing at Tim Gates would be a mistake. Possibly a fatal one.

Chapter 41

LOUISE MAINTAINED HER lock on Tim's eyes. She'd played this staring game with Oscar many times and hadn't lost yet—he always averted his gaze first. On the other hand, Oscar was a cat who relied on Louise for food and shelter. Tim Gates was a cold-hearted criminal who smirked at the death of an innocent man. Louise shifted her attention to Nancy who remained seated at the far end of the bench on the starboard side of the cabin. She was unusually quiet and, despite the mention of Cliff, murder, and forging breeding documents, never raised her head. *Poor Nancy. What have they done to you?*

The voice of evil drew Louise's focus back to Tim.

Tim waved his hand in the air. "Brent! Get up top and see if our colleagues are in sight yet."

Brent grabbed the binoculars from the bench beside him and hurried to the flybridge.

Tim made his way to Bob and Louise. Her body froze. Was this it? Was he going to throw her overboard? She tightened her grip on the loosening end of the rope and closed her eyes. *Thank you, God, for the life jacket.*

Tim enclosed his hand around Bob's tie and yanked on it, throwing Bob off balance. Using the tie, Tim swung Bob towards the bench on the port side of the cabin, then struck Bob's chest with a force so strong it threw Bob onto the seat. Tim held his index finger inches from Bob's nose. "Don't move."

Bob's jaw dropped as he moved his head slowly from side to side. He looked at Louise and mouthed, *Sorry.*

Louise furrowed her brow as she focused on the young veterinarian-turned-criminal. Tim snatched the tightening end of the rope from Bob's hands and yanked on it. Louise grimaced at the pain but remained silent. She watched Tim's hand, closed around the natural fiber binding that held her wrists together, slide closer to the knot. Her heart raced—did he know his knots? Would he untie this one and apply one she couldn't escape from?

Tim reached the knot then raised Louise's arms. He forced her backwards to the opposite end of the bench from Nancy. "I don't know how you ended up on this yacht, but no matter. We have business to take care of, and then we'll take care of the dead weight."

Louise's knees buckled and she fell onto the seat. Dead weight. Herself, Bob, and Nancy. Over Tim's shoulder, she could see the sun peeking out from the clouds, shooting sun-rays to the water's surface. Louise suppressed a smile. They weren't dead yet, and Alex and the coast guard were on the way. More importantly, God was in control, not Tim Gates.

Footsteps on the ladder drew Tim's attention away from Louise. He rubbed the palm of his right hand as he turned. Had he given himself rope burn? Louise smiled at the thought.

Brent leapt into the cabin, skipping the last two steps. "No sign of Mr. Jones's boat."

Tim shot a look at Louise. "Quiet, fool. We don't use names, remember?"

Brent shrugged. "What's the big deal? Who're they gonna tell?"

Tim slapped his forehead. "That's not the point. You need to be careful." He turned to Nat. "Get your idiot brother under control."

Brent raised his shoulders and stepped closer to Tim. "Hey man, no one calls me an idiot."

Tim pulled a pistol from under his jacket and matched Brent's step, then rested the gun on the young thug's chin. "I'll call you whatever I want."

Nat, who had been seated between Nancy and Louise, jumped up and hopped over the table. He pulled the two men apart. "Settle down, guys. We have a job to do, and Tim, if you want to use this boat in the future, you won't threaten my family."

Tim returned the gun to its holster. "He burned down our warehouse!"

Brent shrugged again. "It was an accident, man."

Tim shook his head. "Throwing a lit cigarette onto an oil-soaked floor is *not* an accident. It's stupid! You can't even count. If you'd taken more care to make sure Bob here was delivering the correct number of vials, we wouldn't have all these extra passengers today."

Brent flopped down beside Bob. "Whatever!"

Tim returned his attention to Louise. "What *are* you doing here?"

Louise's eyes darted around the cabin. "Good question." She swallowed hard. Not the time to be witty. Tim didn't react outwardly to her comment, but she reminded herself to choose her words carefully. "I saw the text you sent Bob, and after seeing Nancy's car abandoned at the bank earlier, I went looking for…" *Don't tell them about Alex.* "For Nancy. I was worried about her."

Brent slapped his hands together. "Ha!" He pointed at Nancy. "Worried about *her*? Man."

Tim waved at Brent. "Quiet! Go on… what's your name?"

Louise's chest tightened. She didn't want this man to know her name, but then she remembered Who was in charge. "Louise. Dr. Louise Miller."

Tim head seemed to spin as he shifted his gaze from Louise to Bob and back again. Louise narrowed her eyes and shook her head. *No, his head didn't go 360 degrees. Just my imagination.* She covered her mouth with her wrist to obscure her reaction.

"So, you're one of the owners of the clinic Bob has been working out of. You take concern for your clients a bit far, don't you think?"

It was Louise's turn to shrug. "Couldn't help myself. Some of us are descent people who care about others. After I left Nancy's house, I saw your van at the library and I followed you."

Tim's nostrils flared and he glared at Brent. "She saw Nancy's car? You left the car at the bank? I told you to get rid of it."

Brent shrugged. "I did. I dropped the crazy lady at the barn then after I ate my lunch I went back for the car."

Tim's face flushed. Louise wondered if his nostrils could get any larger. "After lunch? *After lunch*? You left our hostage's vehicle sitting there while you filled your face? You'd better hope this nosy vet is the only one who made the connection between the car and the missing breeder."

Brent waved toward Nancy. "Calm down, man, no one's missing her. Dog show's over and, well... the mouth gag's for a reason, dude."

Louise wanted to move closer to Nancy—to pat her on the arm and comfort her. No one deserved to be spoken of that way, or to be treated the way she'd been treated today. Louise remembered the lonely atmosphere of Nancy's house and the newspaper clipping. The article about a car accident and the death of a young woman. Who was this Brent guy to judge Nancy? She was not a pleasant person to be around, but as far as Louise knew, Nancy didn't make a habit of kidnapping and murdering people.

Tim rubbed his head. "This changes things. We can't sit here waiting for the others, we're too exposed."

Nat, who had returned to his seat, grabbed a phone from the table and clicked on the screen. "We could head west to the Toronto Islands. Wouldn't take long at full speed to get there. We can send a message to Mr...." He paused. "... To our colleagues about the change in location."

Tim shook his head. "No. Too many people around there. Contact the others. We'll head east, past Pictou County, towards Kingston. There are loads of islands and inlets that can provide a place to hide out if needed. Brent, change course. You do know which way east is, don't you?"

Brent lumbered to the starboard control panel. Tim slapped him on the back of the head. "No. Upstairs. Pilot from up there so that you can keep an eye out for the coast guard." The long end of the rope lay by Tim's foot. He kicked at it. "I doubt our visitor joined us without telling anyone where she was."

Brent disappeared upstairs while Nat frantically typed into his phone. Nat's phone worked! He seemed to have access to a navigation map, and now it appeared that he was texting. Louise wanted to access her own phone to check the bars, but she'd have to be patient. If she released her ties too soon, she'd find herself engulfed by icy cold waves before Alex reached her. She scanned the horizon for any signs of a rescue boat, but as far as she could see, she, Bob, and Nancy were alone with their captors. *Where are you, Alex?*

The sudden acceleration and quick turn of the yacht threw Nat to his left. Instinct brought Louise to her feet to avoid being crushed by the large man, but her balance was off and she fell to the floor. Nat's head and shoulder crashed into the bench. Louise used her elbow to prop herself up and found herself staring directly into Nat's face. His eyes were vacant, but his reddened face and furrowed eyes made her wince. Was he going to take his fury out on her?

Nat shot to his feet. "Brent! You fool, you're going to get us all killed." Nat sped up to the flybridge.

Louise's mind was spinning. They were momentarily free of two of their captors, but one remained in the cabin. Tim, the leader of their little group of evil bandits. Before Brent made the sharp turn, Tim had been standing in the corner opposite her. Now he was behind her, but why was he so quiet? Her stomach twisted and turned—could she make it to the railing before the bile churning deep within her made an appearance? Instinct made her rotate her head toward the door to the deck. A jolt of adrenaline raced through Louise's body and her stomach settled. Tim, the menacing villain, was now crumpled in the small space between Bob's bench and the wall. He was so still Louise focused on his chest to see if he was breathing.

A gurgling noise drew Louise's attention to Nancy, who was rubbing her chin on her shoulder. Tim appeared to be unconscious, or dead, and the Bradleys were on the flybridge. Nancy must have seen this as a chance to remove the gag. With one last tug at the gag, Nancy freed her mouth.

She attempted to stand, but her feet and hands remained tied. "Is he dead?"

Louise shook her head. "I don't know. If he's breathing, it's pretty shallow." Her own hands were still tied, and while she could free herself, she was reluctant to let that fact be known until she had a plan. Could they make an escape? Could the three of them overpower Brent and Nat?

Nancy rolled her eyes. "I'm not speaking to you. I asked Bob. He's the doctor here." She glared at Bob. "Bob? Is he dead?"

Bob stared straight ahead, his face pasty gray, his fingers wrapped around the base of his tie.

Nancy tried to rise again. "Bob?"

Louise shot her a look. "Shh. If the thugs upstairs hear you, they'll come down."

Nancy's nostrils flared. "Don't you shush me. Nobody shushes me."

Louise wanted to rub her temple to ease the growing discomfort in her head. Any attempt to overtake Nat and Brent had a faint chance of success with Bob and Nancy working with her, but without them, she was on her own. She scrambled to her knees and examined the water—still no sign of rescue.

She sat on her heels. "Bob. Bob!"

Bob's head rolled to the side. "Huh?"

Heat rose in Louise's cheeks. "Huh? That's all you have to say? We need to figure out a way to get out of this situation. The coast guard should be here by now. It's a big lake though, maybe they can't find us. Still, we haven't been gone that long…"

Bob remained still. "Huh?"

Louise sighed. They were stuck on a boat with murderers and needed to find a way to escape. For the moment they were free of scrutiny and Louise's curiosity at the root cause of her current situation overcame her common sense. She addressed Nancy. "What have you two been up too?"

Nancy shook her head. "You'll have to ask Bob. All I wanted was a few extra bucks to move out west. I wasn't hurting anyone."

"What were you doing that wasn't…"—Louise made air quotes in her mind—"hurting anyone?"

A quivering, squeaky voice came from Bob's direction. "We forged a few documents. That's all. Nancy wanted to get the semen for her dogs from Brazil because it's a lot cheaper, but the NKC wouldn't allow it. If she wanted to maintain registration of her breeding dogs, she had to use semen from other registered dogs."

Louise thought back to the slip of paper she'd found in Tim's office and the document she'd found in the AI room after it had been ransacked. Her suspicions were confirmed—Bob was importing semen from Brazil and altering the documents to give the appearance that it came from England. Not only were they cheating the NKC, but where was the money from the clinic going? Louise had a new reason to be furious with Bob, but the monetary cost to the clinic paled in contrast to the human cost. The paper from the NKC office had Cliff's blood on it. Had Cliff found it the night he was murdered? Is that why they killed him?

Nancy sneered. "We didn't hurt anyone."

Louise's blood pressure rose to a dangerous level. "You didn't hurt anyone? You are most likely responsible for Cliff's death!"

Nancy rolled her eyes. "That's not possible. Why would anyone kill someone because of dog pedigree?"

Nancy had a point. It was a question that had been plaguing Louise all afternoon. Why would someone kill another person over forged breeding documents?

A shaky voice from behind told Louise that Tim was no longer unconscious. "Don't move."

Instinct overpowered Louise's caution, and she whirled around to face him.

Tim sighed then aimed his gun at Louise. "I told you not to move. Do none of you people know how to listen?"

Despite the pain building in her knees, Louise remained frozen in position as Tim rose to his feet. He positioned the open end of the barrel against Louise's pounding temple. "Get up."

Using the table, Louise pushed herself up with her right elbow. She was now face to face with the man who could end her life in a flash. Heart pounding, she refused to divert her gaze.

Tim moved the barrel of the gun to Louise's jaw then jerked his head towards the bench. "Sit down!"

She sat.

"You ask a lot of questions. You want to know why Cliff got whacked?" Tim's eyes darted around the cabin. "You won't be able to repeat anything to anyone, so let me set your curiosity at ease."

Tim pointed the gun at Bob. "Your employee here…"

Louise glared at Bob. "*Ex*-employee."

Tim raised his free hand to his chest. "My apologies. Your *ex*-employee here provided us with an opportunity we couldn't pass on. When Ms. Wells made a scene at a dog show a while back it got me thinking. Why would she go ballistic over a client bringing a puppy to a dog show? With a little trip through the filing cabinet, I discovered that Nancy's past few litters hadn't been DNA tested. The NKC rules insist that litters be tested randomly to show that none of the members are using unregistered dogs in their breeding program. I did some more searching and found a document that gave me the information I needed."

Nancy tried to rise again. "What do you mean? Where could you have found something like that?"

Tim laughed. "In your filing cabinet. Nat and Brent are masters at breaking and entering without leaving a trace."

Was it Louise's imagination? Could she feel the heat emanating from Nancy's glowering eyes? "You broke into my house? How dare you!"

Louise examined the ceiling. She herself was guilty of entering Nancy's home without an invitation.

Tim mockingly slapped his own forehead. "My apologies for that little *faux pas*. Anyway, it didn't take long to find out that Dr. Kurt here was responsible for altering the forms. A little digging into his background was all we needed to do to find his connection to a couple of forging experts." Tim bobbled his head like a pendulum on a clock. "It got a little dicey when he got fired from that job, but then he got a job with you." He waved the gun towards Louise.

She instinctively tilted away from the line of fire. "You used my clinic to cheat the NKC and dog owners?"

Tim laughed again. "No. We had more precious cargo than a bunch of dog semen. Once I knew that Bob was importing Nancy's stuff from Brazil, it made sense to make use of his unsavory behaviour. And what could he say? He either cooperated with us or faced a malpractice hearing."

Bob lowered his head. "I'm so sorry, Louise. They were going to ruin my career. I didn't see any harm in changing a few documents for Nancy, but when Tim blackmailed me, I... I had no choice but to cooperate. No one was supposed to get hurt."

Louise squeezed her eyes closed to ease the pain in her head. "What did you do, Bob?"

Tim slapped his thigh. "What did he do? He did something really stupid. He tried to cheat us. And he almost got away with it too. That idiot Brent can't count, Bob, but I can. Did you really think that you could withhold a few vials for yourself?" Tim shoved the gun into Bob's jaw and pushed his head up. "Are you one of those people with a death wish? Like to live dangerously? You'd have to be to try something so foolish."

Bob wiped his hands on his pants, leaving a wet mark on his lap. "I'll do better next time. The first time I put the vials in the wrong fridge, but I found them. I don't know where the last two went. I was surprised by the nosy clinic manager when I was unpacking them—she seems to be around every corner, lurking. I tossed them into a cardboard box, but when I went back for them, they were gone. Give me another chance. I'll look for them again. They have to be in the clinic somewhere. Please let the ladies go."

"Ha. Too late for that. Once we meet up with our colleagues, we'll pass the product we do have onto them, along with you."

Bob, his shirt wet under the arms, adjusted his tie. He gulped.

Tim pushed the gun into Bob's jaw. "That's right, Bobby boy. You can explain to our buyers why the shipment is short. After that, you'll be their problem. You see, we don't need you anymore, and I can't simply let you go. Using AI shipments to bring cocaine in from Brazil is not cost effective. The vials are too small, and we can only change a couple of vials per container. Nope. We've already come up with a better plan."

Louise clamped her teeth together as heat rushed through her body. They'd been using her clinic to smuggle cocaine into the country? Alex had told her about a new source of cocaine in town… in liquid form. It was all fitting together now. Kidnapping and murder over a falsified dog lineage didn't add up, but doing so over drugs... It wasn't surprising that drug smugglers would have little regard for human life. Anyone willing to supply life-destroying drugs to other human beings for a profit would have no concern for others.

Heidi had noticed early on, when the breeding program started, that the number of vials in the shipping containers didn't match up with the paperwork. Bob had snuck two of them into his pocket on one occasion, unconcerned about ruining the semen meant for the Bagley dog, Molly. He wasn't worried about temperature, because cocaine didn't need to be kept cold. Bob had told Louise out on deck that the Bradleys were the ones who trashed the AI room—they must have been looking for the vials that Bob hid in the cardboard box. He was wrong about them still being in the clinic. Louise knew where they were, they were in the truck of her car. One thing still didn't make sense.

Louise shivered. "Why did you kill Cliff? He wasn't involved in any of this. I'm sure of it. He was such a kind and gentle soul."

Tim flopped down beside Bob and patted Bob's leg. "Cliff.

Another fool. Like I said earlier, wrong place, wrong time. When Nat and Brent saw Bob at the dog show last month, Bob tried to get out of our little deal. The boys roughed him up a bit then headed to my office later that day to get the proof we had against him." Tim jumped up. "I don't know what they were thinking. We didn't need it, but off they went anyway. They found the paperwork, and they found Cliff holding the very document that proved that Nancy and Bob were importing from Brazil, not England. Nat had no choice but to do what he did. Cliff would have turned Nancy and Bob in and we would have lost our supply route." Tim chuckled. "Ironic. We're going another route now anyway because, like I said, the volumes were too small. Live and learn."

Nat returned to the cabin. "We located a small, uninhabited island with lots of trees. It should keep us out of view long enough to meet up with our colleagues. I radioed our new coordinates. Turns out they were coming from the east, so they'll be here soon."

Tim returned his gun to its holster. "Splendid. Once they get here, we'll take care of the passengers. Bob is going to accompany the package. What happens to him after that is not my concern. Ms. Wells here, well… I'm sure we can find a nice place for her to have a rest. A very long rest." Tim grinned at Nancy. Nancy spit at him.

Nat nodded towards Louise. "And that one?"

Tim rubbed his chin. "I don't want the bodies washing up on shore too close together." He pointed at Louise with the gun. "We'll take this one out to deeper waters once the deal is complete."

Chapter 42

LOUISE FINGERED THE rope in her hand and scanned the cabin for something she could use as a weapon. The only thing visible was an unopened six-pack. Could she jump up, untie her hands, grab the case of beer, and whack both Tim and Nat hard enough to knock them out? The answer was an easy *no*.

Louise shifted her attention to what was happening outside. Land grew closer as the boat slowed, circled around the south end of the island, and then came to a stop about five hundred yards from the shoreline. The heavy forest on the island obstructed the westward view, meaning that Nat had been correct. Anyone coming from the west, including Alex and the coast guard, would not be able to see them. There were thousands of small islands in this area of Lake Ontario. It could take hours for the authorities to search all of them. Louise said a quiet prayer for a helicopter.

Tim grasped Louise's arm and yanked her to her feet. With his free hand, he retrieved his gun from its holster and waved it at Bob. "Get up." Bob stood.

Tim aimed the gun at Nancy. "You too."

Nancy remained seated. "I'm not going to cooperate with you. Why should I?"

Louise groaned as Tim's nails dug into her skin. "How about I pop a few bullets into the vet here?"

Louise stared at Nancy, her eyes pleading the breeder to rise to her feet. Nancy didn't move. "Go ahead. She's nothing to me."

Was Nancy bluffing? Trying to buy time? Louise's eyes darted around the cabin. Was it getting smaller? Were the walls moving towards them? Louise gagged at the putrid air mixed with the cold hearts that surrounded her. She was in this mess because she wanted to help Nancy, now this same person was daring a murderer to kill again. To kill Louise.

Tim dragged Louise closer to the door to the deck, then stopped and turned towards the bow. "Brent! Get down here and get that woman under control. Bring her out on deck. Nat, bring Bob along. Before we turn him over to our buyers, he can watch what happens to people who try to cross us."

Louise squeezed her eyes closed. *God, please please please help*! She strained to listen. Were those copter blades she heard?

The sound of shoes stomping on the stairs filled the air and she opened her eyes. Brent was scurrying down to the cabin. "There's a helicopter approaching from the north. White body with a blue tail."

Energy burst through Louise. White and blue—the colours of the Bathurst Region Police Department. They were close.

Tim flung Louise onto the bench. "Brent, get back up on deck and keep an eye on that chopper. And get us out of here. We'll meet up with the others in deeper water." Tim glared at Louise. "Looks like you and Nancy will be sharing a gravesite after all."

Soon after Brent returned to the flybridge, the motor sounded and the boat sped towards open water. Louise lowered her head. Did the helicopter pilot see them? Was he even looking for them? And if so, would he know which boat they were on?

The glare of the sun reflected off the port windows, telling Louise that it was setting behind her. How much daylight remained? She still had her life jacket on, but it wouldn't do her much good in the dark. No one would see her floating in the vastness of Lake Ontario. If she didn't drown first, she could be run over by a steamship. Louise shook her head to force the unpleasant thoughts out. She had to believe that the helicopter had spotted them.

The yacht came to a stop miles from land. Tim, still holding his gun, motioned for Louise and Bob to get up. They did. Nat latched onto Bob's arm and Tim grabbed the long end of the rope that encircled Louise's wrists. She tightened the grip she had on her end of the rope. Brent rushed into the cabin and lifted Nancy from her seat by the collar of her shirt. Nancy struggled, but the ties around her wrists and ankles prevented her from making contact with her captor.

The three men forced their prisoners onto the deck. The

cold penetrated Louise's skin and chilled her bones, but she stood tall, refusing to show weakness. She glanced over at the seat where Bob had sat to chat with her. There was no way she'd be able to retrieve the second life jacket. She hoped that they would at least untie Nancy before throwing her overboard.

Brent motioned to Tim. "Over there. The other boat. It's got the yellow flag. Must be them."

"Perfect." Tim shoved Louise onto the seat. "Don't move." He grabbed the binoculars from Brent. "That's them. Okay guys, get rid of the women. Bob will go with the package as planned."

The younger of the Bradleys lifted Nancy onto the guard-rail, her back towards the water. He steadied her for a moment, mocking her, then untied her feet.

Tim frowned. "What are you doing? Just get it over with then toss the other one. And when you're done, return to the bridge." Tim grabbed Bob by the tie and dragged him into the cabin.

Louise stared at Brent and gulped. Would he do it? She bolted up. "Wait…"

Nancy disappeared. A splash. Brent leaned over the side and waved at her. "Goodbye loud, cranky lady."

Without thinking, Louise shot forward, pulling on her end of the rope and shaking it off. The force of her impact on Brent sent them both over the side of the boat and into the icy water.

Adrenaline shot through Louise as she forced her aching arms into motion. She wanted to take in air, but she was under water. Flapping her freezing limbs, she made her way to the surface, gasping before her mouth was out of the water. She choked when the water hit her throat, but was able to take in a breath. Grateful for the life jacket that kept her head up, she pushed on the water to spin around. She had to find Nancy.

Brent was clinging to the ladder at the back of the boat. "Help. Help. I can't swim. Nat!"

Splashing sounds could be heard to Louise's left. She rotated her body—Nancy was thrashing in the water. Louise doggy-paddled to the frantic woman and slid an arm around her waist. "Nancy, I've got you. Calm down. If you keep struggling, we'll both drown."

Nancy tore free, the motion causing Louise's head to go under water, serving her another mouthful of foul-tasting liquid. She spit it out then managed to grip onto Nancy's waist again.

Nancy continued to struggle. "Help! They're trying to kill me. You're one of them. Let me go. You're all killers."

"Nancy. Calm down. I'm not one of them. I'm Dr. Louise Miller. From the vet clinic."

"Then what are you doing out here? You're one of them. I knew it. You stupid vets are all the same."

Nerve-tingling pain assaulted every one of Louise's muscles. How much longer could she hold on to this flailing woman who was verbally abusing her? Louise scanned the surface of the water, searching from one end of the horizon to the other for any visible signs of help. There were none. When Nancy stopped thrashing, Louise lifted her chin heavenward and mouthed, *Thank you!*

Voices and scuffling noises drifted to them from the back of the boat. It wouldn't take Tim and Nat long to drag Brent back onto the yacht, so Louise started kicking her legs to get away from the vessel. The life jacket was keeping them afloat, but for how long? Louise couldn't let go of Nancy to attempt to swim to shore, and she wasn't convinced that she'd make it anyway. Her legs and arms were too fatigued. If rescue didn't come soon, they'd both drown.

Nancy stopped fighting Louise physically, but she was still screaming, allowing water to enter her mouth and cause her to cough. Louise tried to reason with her. "Nancy, keep your mouth closed. You're swallowing too much water."

Something hit the water beside Nancy then it happened again. A pop sounded in the distance, followed by a splash. An object whistled past Louise's ear. "They're shooting at us. Kick your feet, Nancy. We have to get away from the boat."

"Don't tell me what to do. Do you know who you are talking too?"

"Yes, I'm talking to the person whose life I'm trying to save. How about a little help?"

Nancy sighed then started kicking her legs. Working together, the two women were able to put a little distance between themselves and the yacht. They were fortunate that Tim and the Bradleys were poor marksmen.

Nancy screamed. "I've been hit. I'm going to die." She began to thrash around again.

"Were you hit?" What would she do if Nancy started to go into shock? Or passed out?

"I've been shot. Look at all the blood."

A small amount of blood floated in the water beside Nancy's arm. Louise examined as much of Nancy's head, neck, and shoulders as she could see, but failed to find a wound. Had Nancy been shot below the surface of the water?

"Where does it hurt?"

"Oh, this is so unfair. All I wanted to do was go out west."

A couple of white feathers floated past Louise's shoulder. Straining her neck to scan the water behind Nancy, Louise spotted a seagull lying on the surface—bleeding.

"Calm down, Nancy. Are you feeling any pain?"

Nancy hollered, "What kind of question is that? I've been shot. Look at the blood."

Floating in icy water, in the open waters of Lake Ontario, with murderers shooting at them, Louise grinned. "I see the blood, but I don't think it's yours."

"Then where did it come from?"

"From that dead seagull behind you."

Nancy turned her head. When she saw the seagull floating beside her, the volume of her screams doubled. "Get it away from me. They're such dirty birds."

Louise shook her head as she increased the force of her kicks, trying to get them away from the shooters. Relief that Nancy hadn't been shot was short lived as she realized that the bullet that had killed the seagull could have easily hit one of them.

A second engine roared from behind them. Louise stopped kicking. Was that the boat that Tim was expecting? The shooting had stopped, but why? Were they going to leave Louise and Nancy's fate up to their business colleagues?

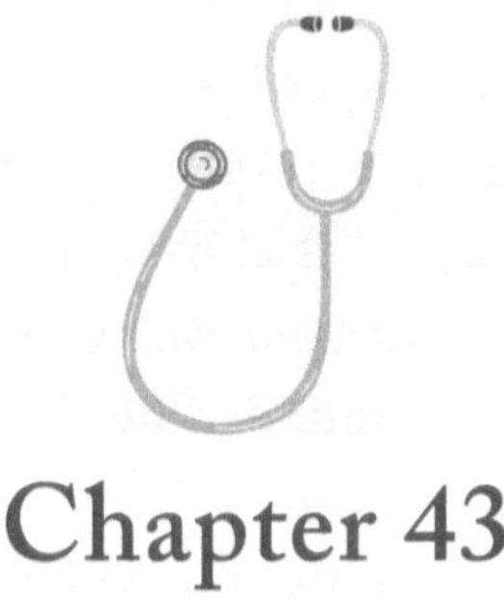

Chapter 43

A LIGHT DRIZZLE SPRAYED Louise and Nancy as the turbulent waves tossed them about. The wind had picked up and the setting sun glowed a brilliant red and orange behind the advancing clouds. The gray sky to the south west warned Louise that a storm was approaching, and that if rescue didn't arrive soon, they would be lost to the waters of Lake Ontario.

Her muscles ached against the fatigue of paddling, holding Nancy—whose hands were still tied—above the water, and the abuse that had been inflicted upon them since her wayward adventure began earlier in the day. Why hadn't she listened to Alex and stayed out of things? She'd be home now, cuddled by the electric fireplace with Oscar, watching a reality baking show on TV.

Nancy groaned. Louise shook off her negative thoughts. If she hadn't followed the SUV to the marina and snuck onto the yacht, Nancy would be dead now. They weren't out of danger, but they were still alive, and as long as they had breath in their lungs, there was hope. Louise raised her eyes to the sky. *God, you've brought me this far, I trust that you have a plan.*

The second engine was getting closer and the waves higher. Louise kicked her legs to the right to spin the two women to the left. As the unknown vessel came into view, a loud voice thundered overhead. "Put your weapons down and throw in your anchor. You are surrounded by the BRPD marine unit and the Canadian Coast Guard."

What sweet words. Louise waved her free arm in the air. "Over here. Help us. Over here."

A surge of icy water slapped against her back then raced over her head, forcing her underwater. Louise swallowed some of the putrid liquid, but was able to get herself and Nancy back to the surface. The yacht carrying Tim, the Bradley brothers, and Bob was accelerating towards the US border. A BRPD water cruiser, identifiable by its logo and standard blue and white colours, pursued them.

An overwhelming sense of dread overtook Louise. They hadn't seen her, and now they were leaving her behind while they pursued Tim and the others. She didn't have the energy to stay afloat much longer, and it would soon be dark. "Wait! Come back. Please."

A familiar voice called out. "Are you okay?"

Despite the pain and fatigue, Louise found the energy to spin around. A third boat, about a hundred yards from them, was approaching. Louise rubbed the rain drops from her eyelashes to clear her view. It was a red and white Coast Guard patrol vessel with what appeared to be four people in uniform on board.

Nancy started flailing. "Over here. I'm over here. Help me."

Nancy's movements splashed more water into Louise's mouth, and she choked when the fishy water hit her throat. It was becoming more difficult to stay afloat, hold onto Nancy, and breathe. The increasing height and volume of the waves created by the advancing rescuers and her companion's motion pushed Louise under the surface again. She held her breath and closed her eyes. Was this it? Was she going to perish when rescue was so close?

Something seemed to be pulling her down. The weight of her legs was immense and she was losing her grip on the crazy breeder lady. Louise couldn't hold on anymore. Her arm slipped away from the person she'd risked her life for. As she reached for Nancy's leg, her arms were assaulted with purposeful kicks. She was sinking into the depths…

The life jacket jerked upwards, pressing into her armpits and forcing her head back. She was floating through the water, then the sky. *Is this what death feels like?* Instinct told her lungs to suck in air once her head breached the water's surface. She was being dragged towards a boat. Her limbs too weak to protest, she could only hope that the good guys had her. Multiple hands grabbed at her jacket and arms—they yanked her up and she flopped onto the deck and lay there motionless, eyes closed.

"Louise? Are you okay?"

Louise opened her eyes. Alex was kneeling over her, his face close to her, his mouth forming the same goofy grin he'd worn the first time they'd met. She coughed up a little of the rancid water she'd swallowed.

Alex wiped his brow then helped Louise sit up. He handed her a towel. "You had us all worried."

She eyed him. "You don't look worried." Her throat burned from the assault of the icy lake water. The rain had stayed south of them, but the winds were still bitterly cold on her wet skin.

"I was." Alex wiped his eyes. "Believe me, I was. But then…" His grin widened. "Then I saw you out there, kicking away and well… I don't know… I was impressed that you weren't panicking."

Louise's numb fingers struggled to remove the life jacket. "Really?"

Alex dabbed Louise's face with a second towel before helping her take off the sodden jacket. "Really. Trust me, the last few seconds were a bit dicey. Billy, the coast guard officer there," Alex pointed to one of the men wearing a blue shirt under an orange PFD, "was trying to pull Nancy on board when you slipped under. Thankfully, I was able to grab the back of your life jacket. I'm surprised it worked as well as it did." He cupped his hand around the discarded jacket and raised it in the air. "It's pretty poor quality."

Louise caressed Alex's cheek. "I had Someone watching over me, and I knew he'd send you along eventually."

Nancy stomped her foot. Louise snapped her head in the direction of the sound—she had forgotten that she and Alex weren't alone. Nancy glared at Louise before rolling her eyes. "Oh brother." She rose to her feet and thrust her hands towards one of the crewmen. "Get me out of these things. My hands are killing me."

The Coast Guard member cut the rope that had bound Nancy for several hours. Her wrists were raw, the rough material having torn mercilessly through her skin. "What a mess."

She grabbed the wet cloth offered to her and wrapped it around the wounds. After flopping onto the bench, she lowered her head and commenced to rock back and forth like a baby.

The radio Alex had attached to his belt beeped. He clicked on the talk button. "Did you get them?"

A staticky voice responded. "We did. All four suspects apprehended without incident. The US coast guard has been alerted and will be on the lookout for the other vessel. We'll rendezvous with the RCMP at the marina to turn over the suspects. It's a federal matter now."

Louise struggled to her feet then sat on the bench opposite Nancy. "They were meeting another boat out here. They were smuggling drugs from Brazil, through *our clinic*."

Alex returned the radio to its holster. "I know. We *real* detectives figured it out."

Thinking about the events of the past few hours and weeks, Louise started to shiver. "Bob was using the AI program to supply cocaine. He put us all in danger. Why would he do that?"

Alex sat beside Louise and put his arm around her. "I don't know why, but we do know how. Daphne gave the CSI team access to the clinic after I spoke to you. They found traces of cocaine in the shipping containers, in a cardboard box in the AI room, and in one of the exam room refrigerators. We retrieved the vials that were in your car. Two tested positive for cocaine. They haven't identified the contents of the others yet."

Familiar landmarks came into view as they sailed west. They had to be drawing closer to the Georgetown marina. "Did you tell your people what it was?"

Alex laughed. "Nah. I thought I'd let them have the fun of figuring that out for themselves, since it's not dangerous."

The patrol vessel carrying Louise and Alex drew alongside the dock behind the marina restaurant. The same slip that Finding Freedom had been docked in when Louise stowed away after seeing Nancy and Bob forced onboard. Aching from head to toe, Louise accepted Alex's hand as she disembarked the smaller boat. The sun was now almost completely below the horizon. The marina was lit up by parking lot lights and the headlights of multiple BRPD police cruisers. Finding Freedom, with its interior lights on, entered the marina inlet, followed by a BRPD vessel. In the parking lot, adjacent to the garbage bin that had shielded Louise and Eric from Tim and the Bradley brothers' view, sat two RCMP cruisers and four officers.

Louise started to laugh uncontrollably, followed by a torrent of tears. Alex led her to a picnic table a few yards from the RCMP cruisers. "Sit for a bit. You've had a taxing day." He eyed her torn scrub pants and bruised face. "Are you sure you're not seriously injured? I think we need to get you checked out at the hospital."

Louise sniffled. "I'm fine. No physical injuries that time won't heal. No broken bones or concussion. I was thinking about Cliff Mariner. Poor Cliff. He was killed for money. Greed. He didn't deserve that."

Alex rubbed Louise's back. "No. He didn't. Sadly, he's not their only victim. These drugs are killing a lot of people. And messing up the lives of so many others."

Louise rested her head on Alex's shoulder. "I don't get it. How can people be so selfish and greedy? No matter what life has dealt you, there's always the option to be a good person." Movement on the coast guard vessel caught her eye, and she watched Nancy push away the seaman who tried to help her disembark.

Alex nodded. "I agree. We have to decide for ourselves if we want to make a positive influence in our world or a negative one. Sadly, so many make the decision based on greed. We live in a sin-filled world, but we can't let that stop us from looking for the good in people."

Louise straightened. "That's so true. Eric is a perfect example of that. Here we, well, you, thought that he was involved in criminal activity again, but all along he was helping a friend. Even at the risk of losing his job. I'm so proud of him, although I am annoyed that he didn't tell us what he was up too. He simply disappeared without asking for help."

Alex gave Louise's shoulder a squeeze. She tried not to react to the resulting discomfort. "Frustrating, isn't it, when someone you care about goes running off trying to play a hero."

The irony wasn't lost on Louise. They walked quietly towards Alex's car before he spoke again. "I was mad that you did something so stupid."

Louise tapped him on the back of the head. "Hey!" This time the jolt of pain was too intense to hide. She grasped her left shoulder and turned her head away so Alex wouldn't see her wince.

Alex didn't seem to notice her reaction. "But…"

Louise plastered on a smile and returned her attention to him. As a veterinarian, she had a lot of practice smiling for a client with a new puppy whilst still grieving the long-time patient she'd just euthanized.

Alex raised his index finger. "I'm also impressed that you

not only survived without major injury but also managed to save Nancy's life. I can't believe you jumped into the lake. You never want to go swimming."

"That's because I can't swim."

"You can't swim? You jumped into the lake and you can't swim?"

"What choice was there? Nancy's hands were bound. Mine weren't. Anyway, I had a life jacket on."

"A lousy life jacket. You both could have drowned."

"But we didn't."

Alex stopped walking, turned to Louise, and clasped her shoulders. "But you could have."

Louise pushed his arms away. "But we didn't." Her tone ended the could have-didn't debate.

Alex retrieved the notebook from his pocket and flipped it open. "We did a background search on the lady you just saved. Her full name is actually Pansy Nancy Wells."

Lousie frowned. "Pancy Nancy?"

"Not Pancy. Pansy. It's a flower. I think."

"Okay, people name their kids after flowers. No big deal. But Pancy Nancy? Who does that to their child?"

"Pansy! Anyhow, her name is the least of her worries; she had it hard from a young age. Her mother died on her ninth birthday. Drug overdose." He shook his head in a sympathetic motion. "Suicide by prescription drugs. It's sad that anyone would get that desperate. The poor girl—by that time her father was drinking heavily, and after his wife died he took off. With her mother dying the way she did, I'm surprised Nancy was mixed up with Tim Gates and the Bradleys."

Louise tilted her head as she gazed at Nancy who was standing by the RCMP cruiser speaking with an officer. "I don't think she had any idea what Tim was up to. Bob said as much, and Nancy genuinely seemed surprised when Tim revealed everything about the drug trafficking to me. She was unusually quiet onboard. Maybe that's why. Maybe she was thinking about her mother."

Alex stared at Louise. "Tim told you everything? We'll need you to make a statement and relay all he told you to an officer."

Louise continued to watch Nancy, a woman who lost both parents as a child, then… the newspaper clipping. Who was the other woman? She glanced up at Alex. "Did she have any other family?"

Alex frowned. "The only adult social services could track down was an aunt who refused to care for the girls, so they ended up in foster care."

Louise's pulse quickened. "Girls? As in more than one?"

Alex nodded. "She had a younger sister."

Louise closed her eyes. Alex didn't say *has* a sister, he said *had* a sister. The woman in the photo she'd seen at Nancy's house was obviously younger than Nancy. They both looked so happy in the picture, but there had been an accident and a young college student was killed. Was that Nancy's sister? Her younger sister?

"What do you mean 'had'? Is she the one who was in the photo at Nancy's?"

Alex eyed Louise. "What photo? Should I even ask how you know about photos in Nancy's house?"

Louise averted her gaze. Alex already had enough reason to be upset with her, and Nancy had a less than pleasant reaction to the news of people entering her home when Tim revealed that Nat and Brent had been there. "It would be better for everyone if you didn't."

Alex paused then clasped Louise's hand. "Nancy's sister was killed by a drunk driver on her way to college after having visited Nancy for Christmas vacation."

Louise drew in a large breath and held it. She was relieved that Alex didn't press her on her on her knowledge of the photo, but her heart ached as she remembered her own loss due to the actions of a careless driver who had spent the night drinking, then chose to drive. Louise was reminded of her struggle to forgive the man who'd caused her so much pain. Would she have turned bitter and angry like Nancy had she not chosen to forgive?

"Do you think that's what happened to Nancy? Why she's so mean-spirited?" Louise watched as Nancy tried to get closer to the BRPD boat as Bob and the others disembarked. The RCMP officer she had been speaking with was doing his best to hold Nancy back.

"I don't know. I'm not surprised she'd have had difficulty letting go of the bitterness and anger. The people in her life who should have been looking out for her failed to do so. Sometimes people hold on to the bad in life and lose perspective. The foster parents were kind people, but losing her sister was probably more than she could bear."

Louise wanted to feel sympathy for Nancy—they shared a similar loss—but the physical aches she was currently battling reminded her of the reality of their present situation. "I'm sad for her that bad things happened in her life, but her actions led to Bob's actions, and that led to danger to people I care about."

Alex popped the hatch and motioned for Louise to sit. "Having a hard time feeling sympathy?"

Louise watched as Bob, who was now handcuffed, was led

to one of the police cruisers. "Maybe later, when I'm not so wet. I guess we'll need a new associate at the clinic. Bob will have an uphill battle once he gets out of prison. If he goes to prison. Either way, I don't think I'll offer him his job back."

Alex sat beside Louise. "I'd say that prison for Bob is a certainty. Not sure how long he'll get. It may depend on evidence he can provide against Gates and the Bradleys, but there's already a lot of evidence against them, so anything Bob has to add may not be very helpful."

"The more evidence to put these guys away the better."

Alex clasped Louise's hand again. "You'll need to forgive Bob, you know?"

Louise sighed. Alex was right, but at the moment she was very angry with Bob. "I suppose I can do that; he *was* trying to help Nancy, however misguided it was. I'll even buy him a new tie, but I'm still mad at him."

"The anger is understandable, but I'm glad you can find forgiveness towards him. What about Nancy? Can you forgive her for her behavior?"

A sense of relief flooded Louise when she spotted Tim Gates in handcuffs, along with Nat and Brent. "Lots of people have tragedy in their lives. It's no excuse for treating others badly."

Alex hopped to his feet and faced Louise. "No. But forgiveness isn't accepting the bad behavior. It's letting go of the negative thoughts and feelings towards the other person."

Louise frowned. "Self-healing?"

"No. Not self-healing. When you forgave the person who killed Zack, you didn't do it on your own. You did it with God's help."

Louise gingerly lowered her feet to the ground and tried to put her arms around Alex's waist. Her arms were too painful to lift, so she settled on leaning against him. "True. And with your help." She straightened and walked towards the cruisers that held her captors.

Alex followed her. "Forgiveness prevents bitterness. I see it all the time. A lot of crime happens because someone is holding a grudge."

Louise stopped and faced Alex. "No worries. I'm not going to commit a crime."

Alex sighed. "I'm sure you're not, but like Nancy, people who don't forgive end up hurting themselves more than anyone else."

Louise tapped Alex on the shoulder. "I hate it when you're right. Fine! I can forgive Nancy, and I'll definitely pray for her, but I'll need to fire her as a client."

Alex stopped walking and turned to Louise. "Why?"

Before Louise could respond, Nancy approached them. When she reached them, she stared into Louise's eyes for an uncomfortable few seconds, then pointed her shaky index finger at Louise's face. "This is going to be very inconvenient for me, Bob being in jail. That cop over there told me that he'd be going to prison. What am I going to do now?"

Louise stood in silence, staring back at the woman who would have been dead if Louise hadn't jump into frigid waters to save her.

Alex spoke to the back of Nancy's head. "Ms. Wells, you may want to call a lawyer. From what I've been told, you weren't involved in the drug smuggling, but you were falsifying records and selling pups under false pretenses."

Nancy spun around. Louise could only imagine the fury on her face. "Who are you? What do you know about it? I've done nothing wrong. And the only competent vet I know is going to jail. Who can I trust to take care of my dogs now?"

Louise stood in stunned silence as Nancy marched to the other side of the parking lot and yelled at the seaman who'd dragged her out of the water.

Alex nodded. "Yes. Firing her seems appropriate."

Louise and Alex stepped aside as three police cars edged by them. The first two each carried one of the Bradley brothers. In the back of the third cruiser sat Tim Gates, a scowl on his face. As the vehicle passed Louise, her eyes locked onto those of the man who had tried to end her life. His lowered eyelids struck Louise as odd—was he questioning how this lady veterinarian had triumphed over him? Louise held her hands out, palms up. She shrugged as she raised her chin—she knew how—One far more powerful than Tim Gates was in charge.

After the back end of the cruiser cleared them, Alex curled his fingers around Louise's. "Nancy is definitely a good example of what we were talking about. No doubt holding onto the pain of her past has led to the bitterness she's spewing at everyone today." He paused, briefly." "Now, what about Rita?"

Louise freed her hand from Alex's grip. "What about Rita? I can't think of anything she would need forgiveness for."

Alex waved his hand. "She threw illegal drugs into the garbage."

Louise raised her index finger. "But not just any garbage. She put them in the biohazardous waste container."

Alex moved closer to Louise—his eyes narrowed. "True, but if she hadn't done that, Nancy may not have been kidnapped."

Louise held her position. "True, but if she hadn't done that you may not have caught your smugglers."

Alex backed up slightly and combed his fingers through his hair. "We would have eventually."

Louise squeezed his shoulder. "I'm sure you would have, but

as for Rita, she kept dangerous drugs off the street. I think she deserves a raise."

Alex grinned. "Yes, she was simply doing her job, so I suppose that that too seems appropriate."

A thrill shot through Louise when she spotted Daphne and Eric exiting the restaurant and hurrying in her direction. Daphne gave Louise a hug then slapped her on the left shoulder.

Searing pain shot through Louise's back and her knees nearly buckled. "Ow. That hurts!"

Daphne crossed her arms. "I'm glad it hurts. It means you're not dead. Are you crazy? I was in shock when Alex told us you were on a boat with Cliff's murderers."

Massaging her arm, Louise gazed at her shoes. "Sorry. I didn't mean to worry you. It was a spur of the moment decision. I admit I regretted it later… a little."

Daphne clapped her palms together. "Thank God it ended well." She nodded towards Eric. "Eric called and filled me in on what he'd been up to. I came down to the marina to pick him up because when his friend Sally left with her parents, she still had his car keys. I figured we could wait here together and pray for your safety."

Louise hugged Eric with her uninjured arm. "Thanks."

"Come on, Eric. I'll drive you home." Daphne motioned for him to follow her. "I need to get home too. Joe has probably paced a hole into our kitchen floor by now. I'll call him from the van to let him know you're okay." Daphne hugged Alex. "Take care of her, and don't let her out of your sight."

Daphne and Eric loaded into Daphne's van and disappeared down the road.

Louise pawed her pockets for her keys as she limped towards her own car.

Alex matched her step. "Back to what we were talking about. What about you?"

Louise narrowed her eyes. What had they been talking about? Forgiveness, Bob going to jail, and Rita deserving a raise. "I'd like a raise too, but my boss is pretty cheap."

Alex stopped, grasped Louise's right arm, and turned her to face him. "You *know* what I mean. This business of running around town following criminals."

What Louise had done was foolish and dangerous, but the adrenaline rush was unlike any she'd felt before. Her actions had led to a positive outcome for both Nancy and Bob. They'd have legal trouble, but they were alive. Three criminals were off the street—more if their US counterparts were caught.

Louise grinned. "Oh, that. It was kinda fun."

Alex's face flushed. "Fun?"

"Yes. Fun!" Louise yanked her arm free and reinitiated the journey to her car. Her whole body was protesting every move-ment she made, forcing her to take each step with care but, too proud to show weakness, she moved faster than was wise. She was now certain that her left shoulder was fractured—she'd go to a walk-in clinic tomorrow. Ice, rest, and acetaminophen would be the prescription, and she could do that on her own tonight. The pain in her body paled in comparison to the havoc the events of the past few hours were playing on her nerves and emotions. She was struggling to control the contrast of tears and giddiness that welled up inside her. Louise used the tactic she was most com-fortable with in a tough situation—humor. "I'm wondering what adventures the next murder mystery will bring."

She could only imagine the frown on Alex's face as his voice bellowed across the parking lot. "Not appropriate, Louise." She ignored him. He called out again, "Louise!"

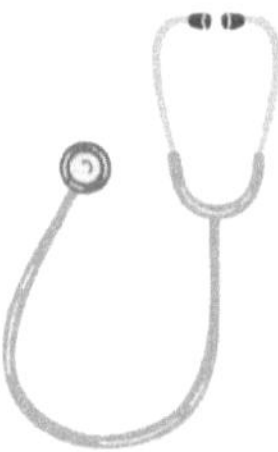

About the Author

After graduating from the Atlantic Veterinary College at the University of Prince Edward Island, Dr. Karen Cullen moved back home to southern Ontario where she has since worked with companion animals in traditional veterinary hospitals, cat-only clinics, and emergency clinics. She currently offers a mobile ultrasound service to many veterinary hospitals east of Toronto. Along with caring for our furry friends, Karen has always had a passion for storytelling. This manuscript is a result of her challenge to herself to write a clean, fictional murder mystery based on the veterinary profession. Afterall, veterinary medicine is not unlike detective work — the patients cannot verbalize what is ailing them so the clues (physical exams, lab work, etc.) and witness statements (client observations), amongst other diagnostic aids, help veterinarians solve the mystery (determine a diagnosis and formulate a treatment plan).